First published in Great Britain in 2024

Copyright © Nigel G Howard 2024

Published by Victor Publishing - victorpublishing.co.uk

Nigel G Howard has asserted his right under the Copyright, Designs and Patents Act 1988 to be identified as the author of this work.

ISBN: 9798326234667

PUBLISHING
victorpublishing.co.uk

Over the Boundary and Under the Covers

By
Nigel G Howard

Over the Boundary and Under the Covers

Contents

Over the Boundary and Under the Covers

Thanks

I thought it only appropriate and right that before the book starts, I say a big thank you to in particular two people who believed I had a novel "in" me. These being Roy and Sue Parkinson. I'll be honest I doubted whether I had the energy to see such a project through, but they had such belief in me I couldn't resist the challenge and almost felt obliged to deliver. The beginning was difficult but as the story and characters developed it sometimes became a kind of therapy and release from the Parkinson's Disease I have suffered from for 15 years plus. I actually became Reg Birtles for those periods of writing. Blessed release! Thanks Roy and Sue. Long may we meet around the boundary and discuss what's happening between the covers! Only you the readers have the right to make a judgement as to whether it's been a worthwhile effort.

About The Book

I'd like to make something crystal clear. Reg Birtles and all the associated characters and events in this book are pure fiction. I won't deny that some of the characters and names are loosely linked to actual people, places, and events I have known and experienced. But that's as far as it goes. If anybody "thinks" they are in the story and takes offence, then I offer my apologies in advance. My intention is to make you smile…sometimes at yourself. I hope I succeed.

Thank You
Nigel G Howard. May 2024

—

1

A Sorry State and Reg's Master Plan

It was a cold windy evening in the winter of 1978 as Reg drove his Austin Cambridge through the gates of his beloved cricket club. As always, he took his time to drive up the road which followed the curve of the boundary, and when taking this journey, he would search in his memory for long hot summer afternoons in years gone by when Reg was quite literally in his pomp. Birtles, a ferociously fast opening bowler who terrorised batters with his namesake deliveries known as *Reg's Rocket* and the *Birtles' Bouncer*. Striking fear into batters with aggressive and hostile bowling. Reg had been, without doubt, an outstanding amateur bowler in his time.

However, Reg's search into the memory bank today stopped short as he looked across the ground that he graced for many seasons. Broken benches, overgrown bushes, discarded drink cans, overflowing rubbish bins and motorbike tyre marks on the cricket square presented an ugly, unattended, unedifying landscape.

This was in contrast to those halcyon days that Reg's memory usually tapped into as he drove round to the clubhouse past the sightscreen at the end of the ground. The sightscreen was in a sorry state, laying flat on the ground due to recent high winds and having suffered impact damage to the wooden slats on its inglorious descent one windy November night.

Reg sat in the car outside the clubhouse. The sightscreen summed up everything about the club's present state. After years of glorious triumphs, it was at an all-time low. Finishing bottom of the league the season before had been on the cards after several years of steady decline. Again, Reg surveyed the landscape and delved into his mental archives but his search once again reaped no reward. It was indeed a depressing thought. Much work was needed both on and off the field if the club was to return to the glory days of years gone by - which now only resided in Reg's head. If only he was thirty...no even twenty years younger, then he'd show them how to do it. Especially on the field.

But he was now planning a return to the glory days by doing whatever it took to put the club at the top of the tree again.

Reg was attending the first committee meeting of the new year, one which he had decided was going to be the year the club was going to bounce back. He knew it would be hard work but if everyone, players and members alike, pulled in the same direction it could be achievable. But such a simple strategy needed strong leadership. After years of what Reg described as 'wishy-washy management' by the committee where everything went to a "bloody vote" it was time for a change. In Reg's mind there was only one person who had the courage, drive, passion, and ideas to get things done. That was him. He had already made it clear during the winter months that things were going to change, whether people liked it or not. Reg's ideology and philosophy had already had a few airings to several members during Sunday afternoon drinks in the clubhouse. It wasn't challenged in public, but then again anyone who knew Reg would think twice about challenging his views - especially after several pints of Lion Bitter on a Sunday afternoon. Reg Birtles.... Club Chairman and mastermind of the club's Great Leap Forward. To those who had witnessed Reg's Sunday afternoon rantings it was clear democracy at committee level wasn't going to be a priority

Reg was a simple, straightforward bloke. At 55, he had been a club player and member for nearly fifty years. For almost all his senior years he had served on the club committee and despite his shortcomings was indeed a well-respected and hard-working member of the club. An engineer by trade, he deployed his skills making various pieces of military equipment at the local Royal Ordnance factory. As a player Reg had proved to be a ferocious fast bowler who had accumulated many victims as he charged in from his relatively short run up, which went in tandem with his even shorter temper. Several times Reg had finished top of the bowling averages as the club basked in the sunshine of several title triumphs and a number of cup wins. Although possibly not as tall as he was in his pomp, Reg presented and exuded a dominant presence both physically and personally. His hair was now receding, displaying tiny red spots on his head which he said was the result of uncontrolled welding sparks landing on it down at the Royal Ordnance factory. Reg was a one-man powder keg whose complexion when angered would suddenly transform from a pale pink to an almost psychedelic shade of puce mixed with purple.

Reg's attempted walk down memory lane was interrupted as he spotted a grey Volkswagen Beetle coming through the gates. Reg knew the driver well. It was groundsman Harry Flatley who had been invited by Reg to tonight's committee meeting as a one-off. The objective being to get an up-to-date report on the state of the ground equipment.

Reg decided to wait until Harry had parked up next to him. He thought that it would show a measure of respect to Harry, a man who historically he didn't like and very rarely saw eye to eye with. However, if Reg's master plan was to succeed, he would need Harry firmly on his side. Much to Reg's disappointment - but not surprise - Harry parked behind the groundsman's hut...he couldn't have parked any further away.

"Awkward git," mumbled Reg as he climbed out of his Austin Cambridge and, without taking breath, demonstrated a totally insincere smile and offered a loud, vociferous, disingenuous, "Evening' Harry". Harry closed the door on the Beetle and started walking towards Reg.

"Evenin' Reg... I see the motor bikes have been back. Little bastards...Where's the plod when you need 'em?" Without giving Reg a chance to reply and in a split-second, Harry not only answered his own question but added his own theory.

"That PC Bob Gordon. Calls himself a local crime buster. Too busy playing snooker down St Greg's and chasing motorists. Whatever happened to the bobby on the beat, eh? Now they give 'em a panda car and you never see 'em." Harry then used a method of conversation he frequently employed by switching the topic to something German.

"Wouldn't happen in Germany you know…no discipline. Makes you wonder who won the war…. bring back National Service. That's what I say."

Harry Flatley had been groundsman at the club for over ten years. His knowledge of what was required to do the job was unchallenged. Although Reg wouldn't dare question his abilities in maintaining the ground, he was frequently at odds with Harry's methods. Like Reg, Harry was a former player. A right arm offspin bowler who could certainly give it a tweak. He possessed within his repertoire a wide range of different deliveries which he christened himself. This included *The Flopper*, *The Skidder*, *The Tosser*, *The Tempter* and *The Squirter*. The fact that each of these deliveries were actually basically the same ball mattered not at all to Harry as he waxed lyrical on how he bamboozled batters with this unplayable range of deliveries.

Modesty and the ability to keep his opinions to himself were not two of Harry's character strengths. If the subject of conversation was about cricket, inevitably he would engineer the conversation to a match where he had single-handedly turned certain defeat into unexpected victory with his bowling. Harry's ability to put his own spin on the truth was as legendary as his ability (in his own opinion) to spin the ball. Although very few of the older people around the league who witnessed these epic efforts would challenge Harry for verification of the actual facts. It just wasn't worth it. One of his nicknames being *Harry the Bull*….the bull being a reference to bullshit. It wasn't just his cricket heroics that Harry loved to wax lyrical about though.

One of his other and most frequently used nicknames for Harry was *World at War* which was an award-winning TV series from a couple of years back. The reason being Harry's preference to push the direction of travel for any conversation to the topic of his World War Two heroics or anything remotely German. He had been (in his words) a "tank driver" during the war and indeed served under Montgomery during the African Campaign. Unlike his epic tales of cricket heroics which could be questioned by those present, Harry's tales from the African campaign had to be taken at face value. Harry wasn't just any old tank driver though. According to him, he was almost Montgomery's right-hand man. If Harry hadn't been around in those days, then the Hun would have steamrollered across North Africa without batting an eyelid. His advice on everything from the colour of the tanks to the right time to move the tanks in formation for battle was (allegedly) taken on board by Monty as they drove Rommel and his cronies retreating towards Tripoli.

Harry and Reg walked side by side towards the venue for the meeting, the old changing rooms being the location. Harry looked at Reg and stopped him just before he entered the door.

"Listen Reg," said Harry, "I know we haven't seen eye to eye over the years but I just want to let you know that I understand what your tryin' to do and you'll get my support for what it's worth. I know what it's like when your back's against the wall. We all need to pull in the same direction. Just like El Alamein in '42…. I remember saying to Monty…"

Reg quickly realised that Harry had reverted to type and instead of being at the club talking to him, he had suddenly drifted continents and time into North Africa in 1942 and was in discussion with Montgomery.

Cutting in on Harry before he (in his imagination) started his tank, got into full flow and was just about to salute, Reg grabbed his arm. "Thanks Harry…it means a lot to me. But you know it won't be easy getting things through the committee. Everything has to go to a bloody vote. Well, in my opinion, democracy has to end somewhere and common sense must prevail. I mean, for a start there's too many women. Don't get me wrong, I've nowt against women but they should only be involved on bloody womanly matters such as deciding what type of lettuce we use for the teas. No Harry, when it comes to the important matters such as cricket professionals and finances, they should leave the room and brew up".

"Yes, I agree" said Harry "Too many bloody women. By the way, is that Verity still a single woman?"

"Yes" said Reg." But she's very fragile after what happened to her husband... Don't you go getting any ideas about burying your bone with her. We need her on board. She might be a woman, but she is treasurer and I need to be opening her purse, not you opening her legs, so keep your distance, Harry. Keep your Old Spice in the bathroom cabinet. I know you're in the market for a new bit of fluff, but Verity's off your radar. Anyway, I'm proposing a singles night soon in the big room. There should be a bit of desperate middle-aged crumpet around to pick from to entice back to your gaff".

The two men then followed each other through the doors.

A critical meeting was about to begin...

2

The Committee

Like the rest of the ground, the venue for the meeting was in a depressing state. The paint peeling off the timber exterior of the building emphasising the sorry decline. There was a smell of what could be best described as a combination of well-used winter green ointment and stale male body odour.

In the middle of the room sat a large table where a full-size canvas cricket kit bag sat. It probably hadn't been moved since the last home game of the previous season and still had various pieces of equipment inside. These items being a cricket shirt, a pair of batting pads, a scorebook, an empty tube of *Head and Shoulders* shampoo and an odd batting glove. The whole feeling of the building was an atmosphere of decaying, sweaty decline.

Reg took his place at the top of the table and surveyed his fellow committee members as one by one they took their places.

The ever immaculately dressed Richard "Dicky" Hampton was first. The club president for many years, Dicky had also been Reg's opening bowling partner in the glory days. An absolute gentleman who, despite his advancing years, was never backward at coming forward when there was the merest scent of a woman. Wearing one of his trademark silver-buttoned blazers and smoking his trademark pipe, Dicky was debonair personified. His impeccable manners and carefully chosen words were the product of being a World War Two pilot in the RAF. Unlike Harry, whose tales from North Africa were dubious in truth at best, Dicky had the medals to prove it. Remembrance Day would see Dicky's blazer sagging through the weight of medals whereas Harry's reaction would be a stand-off if anybody so much as praised Dicky's substantial collection.

"Bloody Biggles showing off! I've no need for gongs on my vest to prove my part in tanning the Hun. Just bloody showing off if you ask me…bloody gong wobbling I call it".

Reg liked Dicky. Although they were culturally miles apart, Reg was sure he could rely on Dicky's support when it came to the big decisions. The fact that Reg also knew that Dicky was having a dalliance with the club cleaner Edna Pilling and was prepared to keep it quiet reinforced Reg's position of strength and grip on Dicky.

With the club President (Dicky) and club Chairman (Reg) the power triumvirate was almost complete. The only person missing from the senior officials was club secretary Charlie Mather.

"Where's Charlie?" questioned Reg. "We can't start without him as we need a full quorum for tonight's meeting. I've got a lot of proposals that need discussion and decision, and we can't do it without the club secretary".

What Reg actually meant was he had some ideas that needed railroading through committee and he for sure needed Charlie's support.

Within a minute of Reg researching Charlie's whereabouts the club secretary walked in and took his place to the right of Reg at the top of the table.

The axis of power was now complete. Reg, Dicky and Charlie, like icons of the Roman Empire. The future fate of the club firmly in their hands. Except it wasn't. As much power and influence as these three possessed there were of course several other committee members who needed to be convinced of Reg's master plan for the revival of his beloved club.

It was indeed a full committee meeting that night with nobody absent. The rest of the committee consisting of treasurer Ms Verity Tinkle, the Reverend Adrian Gawsworth, Jim Burrell, Norman Harris, Queenie Hodgkiss and husband and wife Brian and Eunice Braithwaite.

From his position of power, Reg briefly analysed each member judging whether they would be pro or anti his proposals.

The Reverend could be a problem. Reg saw him as a God botherer who knew nothing about cricket. The Reverend's only interest being financial after the scandal of the junior section funds being "lost" prior to the men's annual weekend away in Blackpool a couple of years ago. He was proposed and elected along with the recently widowed treasurer Verity Tinkle during what became known as the "summer of financial discontent". Reg knew that the Reverend and Verity would have no truck with any large financial outgoings that Reg had in his master plan.

Jim Burrell was a decent guy. However, he was known to sit on the fence when it came to the big matters, and he could be possible trouble. Someone else who fell into that category as far as Reg was concerned was Queenie Hodgkiss. Another one who knew nothing about cricket and was only interested in bingo on Monday nights.

Charlie Mather was secretary-elect. A man who never watched cricket. His main role as secretary was to answer the post, deal with the brewery and manage the resident darts, snooker, and dominoes teams. Charlie was a boozer who Reg regularly described as "First engineer on the Red Nose Express". Here was a man who would frequently proudly announce that, if he were to appear on the TV programme *Mastermind*, his specialist subject would be 'drinking Lion Bitter'. Indeed, Charlie was deadly serious when he described himself as the perfect "indoor athlete".

Due to Charlie's avaricious boozing, his financial outgoings frequently exceeded his incoming revenue. This would inevitably lead to a request for a "fiver till Friday" to Reg who happily funded this borrow, safe in the knowledge that he had Charlie right in the very same place where that fiver came from: Reg's pocket. In Reg's opinion, Charlie presented no problem.

Husband and wife team Roger and Eunice Braithwaite were recent additions to the committee. Unlike the vast majority of members, they were not indigenous locals, having recently moved north from the suburbs of London due to Roger being promoted. Eunice didn't work and spent her spare time at the swimming baths and gym keeping her figure in trim. Although in her early 50s, Eunice looked and had the body of someone 20 years younger. Reg's mind wandered as he mulled over the voting intentions of the Braithwaites. Not only did his mind wander, but so did his eyes as she shuffled past Reg in her ever-so-tight cheesecloth shirt and loon pants. Reg was sure in previous conversations that she was giving him the eye, and was convinced he was in with a chance. As Eunice sat down, he refocused on the meeting and the voting intentions of the Braithwaites.

Reg pondered...They were cricket lovers and never missed a first team game home or away and would surely want a stronger more competitive team. Reg reckoned he could count on them.

This was the meeting that would change the direction of the club and Reg Birtles was determined to be the man to guide it back to its former glories.

Reg was ready.

But was everybody else ready for what could be a tricky meeting?

3

The Meeting

Inside the changing room, the ten committee members, plus Harry Flatley, all sat in anticipation as Reg stood up and read the minutes of the last meeting. It didn't take long.

"Now," Reg said as he stood, statesmen like, "We have an agenda for tonight's meeting but due to time constraints we might not cover all items. Therefore, I have prioritised the agenda as I see fit".

However, even at this early stage in the meeting a challenge came from the floor. It was no surprise to Reg when the Reverend Adrian Gawsworth, wagging his finger stopped Reg in full flow. "You've prioritised the agenda have you Reg? And on who's authority might I ask have you done your prioritising? I'm guessing that's a daft question though?"

Reg wasn't surprised at the Reverend challenging him, but was surprised it came so early in the meeting and the issue being challenged. However, Reg was ready with a counter statement.

"Look, Reverend, we've got to start somewhere. What do you suggest? We all drop to our knees and send a prayer asking for advice on the meeting agenda up to your big mate in the sky?"

This statement had a different response around the table. A deep frown and shake of the head from The Reverend and a giggle from Eunice that didn't go unnoticed by Reg.

Reg then turned his frustration into an almost blasphemous statement with total disregard to the Reverend's presence.

"For Christ's sake, we're five minutes into the meeting and we're havin' a bloody vote. How in God's name are we supposed to get anything done?"

A calming influence then presented itself in the shape of Richard "Dicky" Hampton. In between puffs on his pipe, he said, "Let's leave God out of it…we really need to press on. We've been here ten minutes and discussed nothing except the agenda. I propose we accept Reg's agenda.... any objections or do we need a vote?"

After a silence that seemed to last for minutes but in reality, was no more than ten seconds, the silence was broken by Reg who confidently continued: "Right then. Let's move on." In Reg's mind he'd already won the first battle of the evening. Control of the agenda was important.

As with most meetings of this type there was a structure which had to be observed prior to getting to the current and topical agenda. Charlie Mather did a roll call of all the committee members.

He then turned to treasurer Verity Tinkle for a report on the state of the club finances. Verity responded with articulate precision: "Cash in the bank £13,234. This month anticipated outgoings £2300. All looking healthy Mr Chairman".

This was music to Reg's ears. Despite the dilapidated state of the ground the club was indeed fiscally thriving. To make this financial jigsaw even more appealing this report reflected a period of the year that was usually quiet. This was the financial platform that Reg needed for the first step of his master plan.

Reg wasted no time in moving to his agenda. "Right. Item one on the agenda: The professional for next year". The professional or "Pro" was a player who each club in the league had to have. In short, a player who had the qualifications to have played at a professional level. The selection for this player could make or break any club's season.

Reg continued his pitch, "We need a top-class professional. Someone who's going to put us back on the map. I think we are all agreed last year's pro was a flop along with the last five professionals. But I've got just the bloke, and if you hear me out, I think you'll agree with me".

Reg felt like he was gaining momentum. His head was beginning to sweat, and the 'welding spots' seemed to be growing with the stress of this speech.

"I've spoken to Harold Haltz and sounded him out as to how much he's after and I think it's well within our budget".

Dicky Hampton interjected "But he's staying at Minton after a great season last year and….".

Reg interrupted Dicky… "Excuse me Dicky. I've sounded him out and he's open to offers. There's been a falling out with Minton. The scorer got knocked up and there's a suspicion that Harold's the father. He is denying it of course and he's willing to take a blood test. It's caused ructions over at Minton. Anyway, I've had a chat with him he's interested. And there's a bonus. He wants to bring over his younger brother as overseas amateur. He's a really good prospect and is as keen as mustard. We could be on to something good here if we get a wiggle on".

The professional Reg had in mind was an Australian called Harold Haltz. Known as Harold H throughout the league, he had spent his first season in the league at Minton Cricket Club where he scored over 1000 runs and took 70 wickets as Minton won their first league championship in their history. A genuine all-rounder who really mixed in well with the social life around the club. Especially according to local gossip, with the young lady who was the Minton scorer. Although nothing could be proved (yet) it was clear that Harold was persona non grata at Minton.

Reg felt he had the advantage and was keen to push it home. "It's a no-brainer, and he's not asking for a fortune".

Verity Tinkle wasted no time and asked the question. "Just how much will these Australians cost? You've got to remember he'll want his air fares and his accommodation paying and if there's two of them that's two lots of airfares".

It was now that Reg played what he considered his trump card. "No need to worry about air fares. I've spoken to Terry Fiddler from Battersby's Travel and in return for a sponsorship board and advert on this year's cricket shirts he's willing to use some money from their slush fund to pay for their flights. And all Harold H wants is £2000 plus bonuses".

Reg then received some unexpected support in the shape of Eunice Braithwaite. "I think it's a great idea. Think of it…. two new faces around the club. That'll stimulate the place all round and certainly create some interest for the junior section".

Dicky Hampton added support to Reg's proposal. "You've certainly done your homework here Reg. I've no doubt about Harold H's ability but what type of player is his brother? What skills and performance can he bring to the team. What's his age and background?"

Reg replied. "He's an all-rounder like his brother. From what I have researched he is one of the fastest white pace bowlers in local and provincial cricket."

Dicky further questioned Reg. "Have you got any performance statistics from last season Reg?"

Reg decided to give them the truth. It was pointless trying to hide it. If his master plan was to work, word would soon get out about Harold H's brother Trevor. "There's no statistics for last season. He spent 18 months in jail for pinching a motor. Reckons it was a fit-up though".

Verity Tinkle was visibly shocked. "So, we're on the verge of offering employment to a car thief and his brother who can't keep his trousers on. The reputation of the club will be in the gutter, not to mention the local press who will no doubt have a field day should this misdemeanour become public. I despair!".

The Reverend Adrian Gawsworth predictably backed up Verity's sentiments. "I'm not sure this is setting a good example Reg. The kids need role models. These two sound like direct descendants of the original Australians from years ago. In short, convicts!".

Reg felt he was being challenged and went on the offensive. "I propose a motion that I offer Harold H a contract for next season, and he brings his kid brother with him…is anybody going to second it?"

Dicky Hampton gave Reg the boost he was looking for: "I'll second it." Reg gave Dicky a sideways smile of approval and quickly put it to the vote.

"All in favour raise your hand" ….Reg scanned the room. Those in favour were himself, Dicky Hampton, Charlie Mather, both of the Braithwaites and Harry Flagg. John Burrell raised his hand in a tentative manner to push the vote firmly in the direction Reg required. Reg did the maths and realised he'd got part one of his master plan in motion. It was indeed moving, but this was only the beginning.

Charlie Mather took control of the meeting and asked Reg what was still on the agenda. Reg was buoyant and read out the remaining items, adding his own opinion to each one.

"Well, we've sorted the big one out, that being the professional. Reg, can you call him in Australia and make him an offer? The other issues we can take a quick look at and spend more time on them at next month's meeting."

"Starting with, and in no particular order of importance, the Miss Bolton competition. This will be an entirely new concept never seen at the club before. A chance for the local female talent to compete for the title of *Miss Bolton 1978*. At the moment the position is this: As far as sponsorship goes I've spoken to Arthur Butterfield from Butterfield's Bakery. As long as he gets to be on the voting panel that decides the eventual winner, I think he'll sponsor it. He wants to call the winner 'Miss Butterfield's Bakery Crumpet 1978'.

This prompted a sharp response from the Reverend Gawsworth.

"Another debaucherous step for the club on the road to Sodom and Gomorrah! Don't expect me to sell any tickets or indeed be associated in any shape or form with this lecherous lewd demonstration of neo-pornography".

Reg regained control of the meeting by quickly shifting the subject.

"Quiz Nights are back on every week starting next Thursday. We don't make a fortune, but it brings a few in and we've got a new quiz master. He goes by the name of *Barry the Scientist*. He used to be host at the Pilot Arms but got the bullet when his brother-in-law won the jackpot bonus question prize three weeks on the bounce".

Reg pushed on very swiftly as he knew the next item would receive a thorny response. "Now I know the next topic is going to cause some ructions, but we've got to explore every avenue possible to keep the finances flourishing".

He paused and drew breath and almost whispered the next sentence. "Singles night…it's something they do down the

Legion and it's really took off. I think we should give it some consideration for the next meeting".

The normally easy-going John Burrell looked over his glasses with a disapproving look. "Crikey Reg, don't you think we're serving the sins of the flesh enough? I mean Miss Bolton with all the ladies in their swimsuits followed by what basically should be titled 'I'm available night'…. you'll have people thinking Paul Raymond's moved his Revue Bar from Soho to our club!"

The Reverend Gawsworth weighed in: "Goodness me. Singles Night. It might be suitable for a rabble of skirt-chasing men and loose women down at the Legion, but we would do well to remember we are a cricket club and as I said before, we have the juniors to think about. What sort of example are we setting?"

Harry Flatley had been quiet but chimed in, laughing. "I've heard about the Singles Night at the Legion…A lot of the folks who go are anything but single. No, a lot of them are married and just after a bit on the side. The women who go there are looser than a bag of bolts. Not that I've been of course. Wouldn't lower me standards."

Reg shifted topic very quickly. In his opinion he'd given the committee something to think about fundraising-wise. He was anxious to get this meeting over as he feared there could be a "re-vote" on the approach to Harold H as professional for the upcoming year.

"Right, I think it's time we called this meeting to a close. We'll have another meeting to look at the other topics in depth in the near future. Not that they aren't important, they are, but we're running short on time. The only other thing I'd like to do is give our much-respected groundsman the opportunity to update us on the state of his equipment…if you'll pardon my choice of phrase."

This was a poor attempt by Reg to humour the committee which fell flat with only Eunice Braithwaite offering a smile and a giggle which once again didn't go unnoticed by Reg.

Harry Flatley stood up and reached for the peak of his cap and then proceeded to straighten it. This was a habit he repeated almost every 30 seconds. Even though it wasn't in need of any straightening. For some reason Harry had gone from being an occasional outdoor cap wearer to a full time indoors and outdoors cap wearer for reasons that would become apparent in the coming weeks.

Harry elaborated. "Well, for the most part, everything is in good condition. Thanks largely to my strict maintenance programme. I remember Monty saying to me back in '41 that the way we maintained our tanks would be a key factor in tanning the Hun. Listened to me did Monty, and look what happened."

Reg, mindful of another epic Harry Flatley tale from the North African desert, stopped him in his tank tracks. "That's good news then Harry, although I thought there was a problem with the heavy roller?"

Harry held the silence and took a sharp intake of breath. He shook his head and said, "That heavy roller should only be used by nominated people. Too many people think they can just turn it on and roll up and down. That's where the problem is. Why, last week I had to tell the under 13s manageress to get off the bloody thing. There is a slight problem with the gearstick which keeps sticking in. But I know how to position it. Now if it had a Volkswagen gearbox it wouldn't wobble about so much. That's why Rommel failed in '41... they had the wrong gear boxes in the Panzers...instead of Volkswagen they 'ad Mercedes. Big mistake."

Harry was back in the desert in 1941 but this time instead of re-living every manoeuvre and chat with Monty he raised his eyebrows, adjusted his cap again and sat down quietly.

Reg realised there was one more topic that needed a mention that wouldn't be such a hot potato as some of the previous items. "By the way, before we adjourn, I'm pleased to let the committee know that it's our turn this year to host the final of the Brunton Cup. It's a chance for us to rake in some cash as its usually well attended. Especially if two of the better supported clubs make the final".

"That is good news, Reg." said the Reverend Adrian Gawsworth and added, with a hint of sarcasm, "At last, a chance to make some money without resorting to the depths of, dare I say it, sexual depravity. I'm sure, if you got your way Reg, during the winter you'd open up as a brothel…or maybe one of those dubious clubs where all sorts of nefarious activities take place."

These allegations were like water off a duck's back to Reg who announced: "There being no other business of urgency, the meeting is now closed."

Following that announcement everyone made their way to the much more comfortable surroundings of the clubhouse.

The meeting was over, and Reg had achieved his main objective. His master plan was on a roll. Plus, he was pleasantly surprised with the support he'd received from the lovely Eunice Braithwaite. She was indeed a more than welcome addition to the committee.

4
Aftermath...The Clubhouse

The members of the committee all made their way back to the clubhouse and mingled into their respective groups of friends who were all keen to know the outcome of the evening's meeting.

The clubhouse wasn't an expansive building. Unlike the changing rooms it was a brick and block building built some twenty years ago with a grant from the council. Despite the emphasis on indoor sports in the shape of a snooker table, a dartboard and several domino and card playing tables, it was both comfortable and cosy. At a recent committee meeting Reg had proposed the installation of a pin ball machine which had proved to be a popular addition. As the members chatted, a constant, blue-tinged hazy waft of cigarette smoke floated throughout the room.

As soon as the meeting finished Reg was on the phone to Australia. He knew that other clubs would be interested in Harold H and he wanted to seal the deal as soon as possible. The phone call went well with both Harold and his brother committing themselves for the upcoming season.

Reg entered the club. He was in buoyant mood and clutching a pint of bitter sat on a stool at the end of the bar. Such was his happiness he decided he was going to have a cigar. He was happy and wanted everyone to know. He summoned the attention of the steward: "Ay up Brian, chuck us a mini-Castella will you?"

He then changed his mind very quickly "I tell you what, make it a large Castella...I feel good tonight and while you're at it, have a drink on me Brian."

Brian was the club steward. Although everyone knew him by his nickname *Brains* on account of his resemblance to the *Thunderbirds* TV programme character. This was mainly due to his huge glasses. "Are you sure you want a king-sized

Castella Reg? You know how they play havoc with your chest".

"Since when have you become the club doctor Brains? I know me own body and I'm in the mood for a king size. Now pass it over 'ere and let me enjoy the moment. This is a big day for the club and 'specially for me.. Reg Birtles."

Brains was another long-term member who had become steward a few years earlier. He was a good bloke who would do anything for the club. In fact, he soon realised that the job of steward involved more than just changing barrels of beer and serving the members. He was indeed the go-to man in the club. Apart from organising the staff rota, Brains was more of a club manager. However, he felt his weekly wage didn't reflect the hours that he put in. In short, he was fed up with being the dogsbody. He looked at Reg and decided to strike while the iron was hot. Brains wanted a rise. He wasn't in a great position both financially and personally as his wife had recently decided that she preferred women to men and left Brains and their two children for the captain of The Golden Lion's ladies darts team.

Brains went for the jugular and posed his position to Reg. "Ere Reg…. I've been thinking. The council have jacked me rent up, the twins are both starting secondary school and need new uniforms. Plus, my Hillman Imp's on the blink, and no wonder with all the gear it keeps bringing from the cash and carry. It's a bloody Hillman Imp for God's sake. Not one of Pickford's low loaders. Last week a big plastic bottle of blackcurrant cordial broke and went all over me leopardskin racing seat covers. So come on Reg, what's the chances of the committee granting me a rise?"

Reg took another puff on his Castella and paused before speaking: "I don't see any problem, Brains. It's the rest of the committee that's the issue."

This was the response that Brains expected. He felt undervalued and taken for granted.

His train of thought was soon diverted though as following another huge intake of the king sized cigar, Reg began to wheeze into his own smog. This very quickly developed into a coughing fit with Reg's face turning from pale pink to pale purple. "Ere Reg, you feeling all right?" said Brains. Reg was too busy spluttering to answer and carried on coughing. His elevated position on the stool had now been involuntarily vacated as he leaned on the bar with his head resting between his hands. Such was the noise generated by Reg's coughing fit that all the members in the clubhouse were expressing varying degrees of concern.

As Reg continued his spluttering and coughing, assistance manifested itself in the form of fellow committee member Eunice Braithwaite. Eunice told Reg to stand up straight and try and breathe normally. As he did this Eunice administered several hefty slaps to Reg's upper back area. After about thirty seconds Reg's convulsions began to subside and his face returned to its usual colour.

Reg quickly felt better and he was more than pleasantly surprised at the fuss Eunice was affording him. She was indeed a good-looking woman.

Reg's face broke into a smile as she rubbed her hands up and down his chest.

"Do you want to have a lie down in the medical room Reg?" asked Eunice. Reg's mind began to wander into the extremes of fantasy. He imagined he was in the medical room. Alone with the lovely Eunice dressed in full nurses' outfit…. a full-length medical bed awaiting…the door locked from the inside…the smell of fresh Dettol punctuating the air…

However, Regs fantasy was soon cut short as groundsman Harry Flatley interjected: "He needs to be on his feet. I remember rescuing one of my pals from a fit like that as we approached Tripoli. Had the sand of the desert storm in his chest as well. I wasn't in it for the gongs though. Leading tank ours was…".

Nobody was listening to Harry. His words were wasted. They'd heard it all before.

Over the Boundary and Under the Covers

5

Start of Season Disco and The Brothers Arrive

Reg looked in the bedroom mirror and was comfortable with what he saw. The fruits of his trip to the local boutiques known as Stolen from Ivor and Paul Adams Menswear were indeed the height of fashion in 1978 and (in his opinion) made him look rather suave.

He wanted to look his best for the club's disco. This annual event was the precursor to the start of the cricket season. It was the first event where Reg could officially appear as a single man following his divorce from Hillary. It was also the night that Reg was going to introduce the new professional and his brother. Although nobody knew that Reg had in fact asked Harry the groundsman to pick them up from the airport.

A new grey jacket with red check and flared lapels covered a white crimplene polo neck. Accompanied by a black pair of flared hipster trousers and black wet look slip on shoes.

Yes. Reg liked what he saw.

As he turned and posed in front of the mirror, he took a large intake of breath in order to retract his stomach which was protruding slightly over his belt. He took a few seconds to debate whether to fasten his jacket or leave it open. He opted for the open look thinking the jacket buttons and stomach/beer belly maybe couldn't hold that sort of pressure. Especially if Reg got into the groove with the music on offer and began throwing some shapes on the dance floor. The hit film Grease was all the rage and although he might not be John Travolta, he considered himself to be quite a nifty mover. He went to the bathroom cupboard which, since Hillary's departure, was sparsely populated. There was, however, a small tube of *Ambre Solaire Instant Suntan* and a tub of *Bylcreem* hair oil.

Not wishing to look out of place, Reg had used the sun cream whilst on holiday in Spain as his skin wasn't too receptive to the hot rays of Majorca. He pondered and thought about the pros and cons of putting the cream on or leaving it off.

Putting it on would make Reg feel much more attractive to any potential females. Also, it would boost his personal confidence. The downside would be if the room temperature was anything above cool the suntan cream would become streaky and run down his face causing embarrassment. He decided to leave the suntan cream in the bathroom cupboard.

Before going downstairs and ordering a taxi, Reg had one final fashion addition. He reached for his medallion. Another item along with his suntan cream that had its origins in happier married days in Majorca. Sadly, for Reg he couldn't strut his medallion on his bare chest as a previous attempt at this look brought Reg out in a never-to-be-medically-diagnosed itchy blue rash which conflicted with his suncream addition in Majorca.

The white crimplene polo neck gave Reg the perfect platform for his medallion as he adjusted the chain to position it just above his slightly bulging midriff.

Reg was now officially divorced from his ex-wife Hillary after twenty years plus of eventful marriage. This ended after Reg discovered she was playing away with Barry the bin man.

Reg was indeed, in his own words, 'Out on the prowl'. His target range for females wasn't restricted. He decided that as he'd had the dirty done on him any female was fair game, it mattered not that they were married. Nobody gave Reg any sympathy when Barry the bin man was hopping off the back of the bin wagon and going missing whilst the rest of the bin men finished off the estate. No, any female was now a target. As groundsman Harry Flatley observed, "If it looks remotely female, between the ages of 18 and 65 and has all its own limbs then it's on Reg's radar."

Reg decided to get a taxi to the club. After all, if he did get lucky he now had an empty house to go back to instead of having a grope in the Austin Cambridge. In a previous semi drunken dalliance in the vehicle, Reg managed to get the trouser leg of his flared Falmer jeans trapped over the handbrake thus releasing it which led to the car making a short unscheduled trip down a small hill at Crommy Lodges Nature Park, where, fortunately, it came to a stop resting against a tree. He was lucky that night as he'd had well over the legal limit and could have been breathalysed.

The taxi turned up on time and, leaving it to the last-minute, Reg applied a more than generous coating of his favourite after shave, Hai Karate.

Reg knew and was surprised at who the driver was. It was Jock Tuck. Jock worked at the local battery factory and was shop steward. Originally from Glasgow he was well known in the local community. "Still on strike Jock?" said Reg. "Aye, we are Reg," replied Jock "Tight fisted bastards are no for movin' . We've asked for a reasonable 20 percent and they no havin' it."

"So, you're doing a bit of moonlighting driving the taxi?" Said Reg, "What'll happen if you get found out?" Jock delayed his reply as he hadn't given it much thought. "I'll cross that bridge when I get to it. In the meantime, I've got tay put food on the table for me and the bairns. Anyway, what's happening in your club tonight? Ya dressed tay kill man… Anybody female on ya radar?"

Reg spoke confidently to Jock. "I've still got it Jock. The chat and the charm gets a bird on the arm. Many a good tune been played on an old piano or whatever the saying is. Maybe for you Jocks it's many a good tune played on an old pair of bagpipes!"

Reg chuckled at his own statement as Jock looked in the rear view mirror and saw, for the first time, Reg's medallion… "Fay Christ's sake Reg, what's that hanging round ya neck? I did nay see yee at the last Olympics? Or is it one of them kids Duke ay Edinburgh awards?"

Reg responded "Look Jock. Your mob have no room to talk when it comes to clothing fashion. Don't tell me men wearing a skirt and lobbing tree trunks for the national sport is normal. You may mock my medallion, but I'll tell you what. It's a real fanny magnet if you ask me."

Jock soon changed the topic of conversation. "Hey, Reg, I believe your havin' a Miss Bolton Competition. What's the chances of me being one of the judges. I could do with a bit of excitement these days. All I seem to do is drive this taxi and stand round the brazier outside work. Being off work's no fun at home with the missus giving me grief."

Reg thought cautiously before delivering a reply. He liked Jock a lot but knew that after a few pints he could get a bit rowdy and leery. In short, he wasn't ideal judge material. A previous function a couple of years back had seen Jock involved in fisticuffs. "We've not decided on the format yet never mind who's doing the judging. I'll let you know when its decided."

The taxi pulled up outside the club. Reg paid the £1.20 fare, supplemented with a 30p tip.

"Thanks fa' that Reg, and dinnae forget the judge's job when it comes up."

Reg made a swift exit from the taxi and headed for the club. He headed for the games room first for a pre-disco pint. This was a routine that almost every single male member undertook before heading to the disco.

After one pint and about twenty minutes of chat Reg headed for the function lounge. As ever, Brains was behind the bar. "No Castellas tonight Reg? You never know, one more fit and you could have Eunice in the recovery position in the medical room!" Brains chuckled to himself.

"Just stick to serving Brains. Any more sarcastic or flippant remarks and any support from me for your pay rise will go right down the Khazi. You understand?"

"OK Reg. I understand," said Brains, rolling his eyes.

Reg surveyed the almost full function room. The DJ for the evening, Jimmy "Spangles" Spanner was well known on the local music circuit and was much in demand for his disc spinning and ability to (in DJ talk) "fill the floor". He was resident DJ for the *Sunday Afternoon Soothing Soul Sessions* nights at nearby Throbbers Night Club. Reg reckoned he could get Spangles to do his proposed singles night as this didn't impinge on Spangles' other vinyl and strobe light commitments.

Over in the corner, sat with their mum Joyce, were the Blower sisters Susie and Shirley. These two young ladies were the daughters of Ronnie Blower who had been a member of the club for many years. He was 95 percent deaf and, in order to help him understand the conversation going on around him, wore a very obvious pink plastic battery-driven earpiece. This worked well most of the time although when the club purchased a new all singing all dancing TV for the games room it transpired that any time the volume was turned up with the remote control, Ronnie's earpiece omitted a wailing sound which meant he had to turn it off, such was the pain he suffered.

Ronnie's girls were both blessed with good looks and were not backward at coming forward when it came to attracting male attention. Both of them worked at the local garment manufacturers where they were employed as sewing machinists with their mum Joyce. She was much younger in her outlook on life than Ronnie and, with the desired effort and enough make-up, could almost pass as the twins' elder sister.

They lived within walking distance of the club in a semi-detached property next to the house that had been selected as accommodation for the season for the professional and his brother. The fully furnished accommodation had become available, and Reg had sealed the deal very quickly.

Reg turned his attention to the Braithwaites and, in particular, his very own Florence Nightingale in the shape of Eunice. She looked great in a tight-fitting blue one-piece low-cut dress and high heels. It was a close-run thing over what would likely pop out first. Either Reg's eyes or Eunice's boobs as she vigorously danced away to *Disco Inferno*.

Although on the face of it she was happily married, there was indeed something about Eunice that gave Reg signals that he was in with a chance. However, tonight wasn't going to be that night. Reg had other things on his mind.

The dance floor was quite full with Eunice being the centre of attention even though it was also blessed with many other females of varying ages, size, and availability. This included

Maureen Pollitt who was unfortunately known as *the club bike*. Maureen wasn't as bad as everybody liked to paint her. Now in her mid-30s, she had, for many years, been single but was well versed in the art of the one night stand. Very often her flat close to the ground was deemed as a more than cosy end to the night for errant males looking for a little late-night solace.

Reg looked around and spotted the captain Iain Redwood with a number of first team players. He made his way over and began chatting to him, addressing him by his nickname. "Hi Reddy, how's it going?" said Reg, straining to make himself heard over the sound of *Boogie Wonderland*. Reddy replied. "Not bad thanks Reg. Hey…when's the pro and his brother arriving? You know we need a players meeting before the start of the season."

 Reg took a drink of his beer and began to smile "Sooner than you think Reddy…sooner than you think!" Reddy wasn't in on the plan to introduce the pro. The only other person who knew was Harry Flatley the groundsman.

In the meantime, Reg's co-plotter and one time nemesis Harry Flatley had made his way to Manchester Airport and picked up Harold and his brother Trevor. Once in the car and after the formal introductions, they began to chat. Harry led the conversation directing his question at the younger of the two brothers: "Reg tells me you're a pretty nippy right arm medium fast bowler Trevor?"

Trevor replied in a typical confident Australian manner: "Medium fast….Jeez…I'd describe myself as fast/red hot. I can't wait to send a few of my screamers down the track. I'll have them jumping round the crease like baby kangaroos!" Harry stopped at the traffic lights and took a long look at Trevor who was almost hyperventilating as he excitedly dispatched his vision of bowling at full speed. "Sounds like you'll need plenty of hard tracks to deliver that sort of bowling. Don't forget most of the wickets in this league are like puddings on account of the rain we get." Trevor was having none of it though and quizzed Harry further. "Well Harry let's wait and see. What's the track like at our place then?"

This gave Harry the platform to wax lyrical about his work. Modesty not being one of Harry's characteristics, he wasn't going to pass up an opportunity given to him on a plate. "Even though I say so myself, it's a great batting track. Best in the league by a country mile. You'll have to put a shift in if your gonna challenge the bowling averages."

Harold then took over the conversation, taking it in a different direction: "What's happening tonight Harry? Me and our Trev have had a long flight you know and could do with a stretch of shuteye." Harry responded: "Reg has decided to introduce you both tonight at the annual start of season disco. There's a room full of members who are all keen to meet and get to know you!"

Trevor reacted quickly to this, "So there's a few pints of the old amber nectar on offer then Harry? Sounds good. Any Sheilas on the disco dance floor?"

Harry replied, "Something like that. It's usually a good night."

The VW Beetle pulled up at the red telephone box close to the club. The smell inside was dreadful. Obviously, it had been used on a regular basis as a stopgap men's urinal.

Harry dialled the club and as soon as the pips began, he pressed his 2p coin in the slot. Brains answered, "Cricket club. Brian your underpaid and overworked steward at your service!"

"Cut the crap and put the violin away Brains. Tell Reg Operation Oz is 99% complete," said Harry. Brains wasn't in the plot and attempted to question Harry further, but Harry was having none of it. "Just tell him what I said Brains!"

Brains put the phone down and made a waving gesture to beckon Reg over. Reg approached the bar looking puzzled. "What's up Brains?"

Brains relayed the message to Reg. "I don't know what's happening, but Harry's been on the blower and says to tell you Operation Oz is 99% complete, whatever that means?"

With that information Reg headed straight across the dance floor which was full and swaying to the sounds of Rose Royce. Reg whispered something in DJ Spangles' ear. As the last few bars of *Car Wash* filtered through the speakers, Reg took the microphone off DJ Spangles and began to speak.

"Ladies and Gentlemen. Can I have a bit of order please? First of all I'd like to thank you all for making the effort tonight. I'm sure you're having a good time. I'm sorry the pasties are a bit late, but Butterfield's Bakery has suffered a rat infestation, so we had to change supplier for the night to Pearsons Pies. I'd be interested in your comments on the quality as we may be looking at Pearsons for upcoming functions. Anyway, the reason I've taken the microphone off Spangles our DJ is to give you all a surprise."

At this moment Reg's speech was interrupted by howling electrical feedback which brought groans of pain from the members. Reg tried to stop this by tapping the microphone vigorously on the table. Not only did this fail to stop the feedback but the sound of the tapping came straight through the speakers. Spangles the DJ wasn't amused either. "Ere Reg, that microphone cost me six quid….and it's a microphone not a hammer. It's that bloody gong round yer neck and yer crimplene sweater that's causing the feedback. Take the bloody gong thing off!"

In a moment of acute embarrassment, Reg conceded and like some disgraced Olympian, removed his medallion.

The feedback stopped, Reg tapped the microphone in true compere style and re-started.

"As you know our beloved club has been in the cricketing doldrums for a few years. Well, it's time for a change and in order to achieve that we've got not only a top professional for the season, but also a top overseas amateur in the shape of his brother. Would you all join me in welcoming, all the way from Australia, our professional for this season: Harold Haltz and his brother Trevor."

With that prompt Harry and the two Australians entered the room to a round of applause. Harry rather milking it more than he should have, leading the entourage to the disco desk where Reg was furiously clapping his hands.

The next part of Reg's master plan was firmly in place. The Aussies were here.

6
Net Practice and Cricket Meeting

The first net of the season was arranged towards the end of the very successful start of season disco. As usual net practice was always on a Tuesday evening, weather permitting of course, and served as not just a practice but also a chance to have a drink and wait for the selection committee's picks for the weekend.

Sadly, over the last few years, the net practice usually lost its appeal around the same time the club tumbled out of the Brunton Knock-out Cup and the performances were heading in a one-way direction to the bottom end of the table. The ignominy of last season's bottom placing was the final straw for Reg, thus the implementation of his master plan.

However, Reg and captain Iain Redwood hadn't been idle during the winter. A number of players had been approached and some recruited. Most had been attracted by the opportunity to play with Harold H as a professional and his brother who, according to 'sources down under', was a raw talent.

Reg had finished early. There was nobody else around on the ground apart from Harry Flatley who was busy sat on his mower cutting the outfield. It was a freakish warm April night, and the ground was looking much better than it did during the bleak winter months.

Thanks to a couple of well-attended work parties, the sightscreens had been re-erected and painted. The benches had been repaired and painted and the score box had been given a coat of white masonry paint.

Reg took this opportunity to shout Harry over and asked him to switch off the mower. Harry climbed down taking care to ensure his cap stayed firmly on his head.

"Harry. Any chance of helping me put up the nets ready for the lads when they get here?" Harry broke into a sarcastic smile and responded quickly.

"Not a chance Reg. Why should I? You're not here every Tuesday night when the nets are left out for me, Charlie Muggins to take down and cart over to my garage. They think just because they play cricket, they've a divine right not to put the nets away."

Reg knew that Harry was absolutely right but decided to see if a combination of social charm and outright bribery would work. "Tell you what Harry, help me put the nets up and I'll buy you a couple of pints later in the club. What do you think?"

With that offer Harry stopped his ascent to the mower, turned round and tipped his cap. "I'm not a man who can be bought Reg but, in this case, I'll do it. Just for you." Reg smiled. "So, you'll do it without the ale then?" Harry's reply was fast and firm. "Will I bollocks! Two pints it is."

Reg and Harry spent the best part of half an hour erecting the practice net. The nets were old and had seen better days, but were better than nothing.

Once erected, Harry morphed into World at War mode. "These nets remind me of the camouflage we used to cover the tanks in the desert. I gave Monty the idea of covering them up with thicker palm leaves. It kept the snakes at bay during the evening. Nasty rascals them desert snakes. Always went to bite your feet. Slept with me boots on for six months I did."

Reg wasn't listening. His attention had been diverted by a gleaming brand-new red Hillman Avenger pulling up on the car park. He was well aware that the driver was the lovely Eunice Braithwaite. She had recently started a *Bums and Tums* keep fit class on a Tuesday night.

He quickly made his way across to the car park and towards Eunice who was taking some workout equipment from the boot of the Avenger. Reg peered inquisitively. "Good evening, Eunice. How are you? Have you many for the bums and tums night? I was talking to Charlie, and he says you've got a growing class." Eunice shut the boot down away from Reg's prying eyes and replied. "Yes Reg. We're doing very well. There's more and more every week. Although there's a growing number of young girls from the estate attending. I really should call it *bums, tums and single mums night*. I'm sure you know what I mean!" she chuckled.

Reg replied, "They're no trouble are they Eunice? Remember any problems let me know and I'll weed them out."

"I know that Reg. You'll be my knight in shining armour and without doubt the first person I would turn to. But it's very unlikely."

Rightly or wrongly, Reg thought Eunice was giving him subtle hints. He mused; did she really say he'd be the first person she'd turn to?

Eunice began walking to the club as Reg watched her every step. She really was a classy woman. He kept thinking, was she really giving him the come on?

Reg turned back to walk to the changing rooms and spotted several of the players coming out of the doors and on to the outfield. Most of them were senior players with a small number of juniors from the under 18s and under 15s.

Walking over to Iain Redwood, Reg caught his attention. "Iain, I've arranged to pick Harold and Trevor up at quarter past six, so I'd better be on my way soon, but before I go, I've got young lad coming down for a trial. It's the nephew of Joey Bangla who owns the restaurant on Market Street. Joey reckons he bowls a bit of leg spin. Might turn out to be a useful player. Just keep your eye out for him and make him welcome till I get back. His name is Jimez Bangla but everyone calls him Jimmy."

"OK Reg. Are we still having the players meeting after nets, 8.30 in the concert room?" Reg span round and replied, "Yes, but make sure Eunice has finished her keep fat class. I don't want her girls upset by a load of leery cricketers."

Iain made his way to join the growing number of players around the nets whilst Reg jumped into the Austin Cambridge to make the short journey to pick Harold and Trevor up. The car pulled up outside the house where Harold and Trevor were staying. A medium sized semi-detached with a small tidy garden at the front. As Reg pulled up, he saw Trevor leaning on the dividing fence chatting to the Blower sisters.

"Hi Reg, how's it goin' matey? I'm just gettin' t'know the neighbours a little better. Lovely girls the twins," said Trevor. Harold appeared in the porch and acknowledged Reg. "We're both ready to go Reg, as soon as Romeo has finished with his patter to the twins."

"Leave it out H. Just doing my bit for Aussie-UK relations. I'll get my bag". This statement was accompanied by a rather obvious wink that wasn't intended to be discreet.

The Austin Cambridge purred along the short distance to the club. Trevor clearly wasn't impressed with Reg's choice of vehicle. "Hey, Reg, I reckon I've seen this motor in a few black and white movies. Must be at least 30 years old if it's a day. Wouldn't be out of place in the transport museum." Reg looked in the rear-view mirror and considered his response before delivering his reply. "It's nowhere near that old and it's been the most reliable motor I've had in years."

However, Reg's words were somewhat insincere. For quite a while now, Reg had been pondering a change of motor. The Austin Cambridge, whilst sturdy and reliable, didn't quite match Reg's new single man status. As Reg had confided in Dicky Hampton recently, he needed a motor which would impress and pull the birds.

The weekend before Reg had been down to Sid Lane's car lot. Sid was well known in the area and showed Reg a few second-hand cars he had on the forecourt. Reg looked at a gold Mark 4 Ford Cortina. He liked the look of it but didn't like the price. He then looked at a soft top MGB GT. Immediately he began imagining him and Eunice driving through some country lanes with the wind blowing through Eunice's hair. Sadly, this was also out of Reg's budget and Reg left in the Austin Cambridge.

Reg drove on to the ground and dropped the brothers at the changing rooms. After a few minutes they both walked out together and headed for the nets. Captain Iain Redwood gathered all the players together and spoke to the whole group. "Right lads we're all gonna get a bat and a bowl tonight plus some catching practice. Before we start though I'd like to welcome to our club our professional Harold and his brother

Trevor. Let's hope they can provide the extra quality I feel we need to push for trophies. I'm sure you'll remember Harold's ton against us last year and the five wickets that he took when Minton knocked us out of the Brunton Cup."

Following this speech from the captain he wrote down a batting and bowling order down. There was an air of anticipation in the air. Nobody would say or admit to it but all everyone wanted to do was see if Trevor was as fast a bowler as Reg had made out.

Trevor paced out his run up. It wasn't a particularly long one as he leapt the last pace. He then did a couple of stretching exercises before indicating to the batsman Iain Redwood that he was ready to bowl. Iain had taken the responsibility of being first to face Trevor. Not just because he wanted to be first to bat but because he didn't want to put anybody else at risk.

Acknowledging Iain was ready, Trevor ran in very quickly and delivered a ball at high speed which rapped Iain on the pads. His second ball was short of a length and cannoned into Iain's upper body. Trevor was bowling within a rota of four bowlers including Harold. Iain was impressed.

After ten minutes. Iain moved the rota along. Harold went to bat and was treated with the same hostility by his brother. Harold was a quality bat and demonstrated a wide range of classy shots.

Watching discreetly from the clubhouse, Reg decided to get a little closer and walked up to the practice area pulling Iain to one side. "What do you think of the lad? Looks tasty to me." Iain replied with enthusiasm: "He's quick Reg, no doubt about it. Got a great action and a good line and length. That's only on the practice wicket as well. I can't wait to see him in action on a hard track. I think we've found a gem here. I'm calling him by his new nickname, *Typhoon Trevor.* I'm impressed even though it's early days. He's next on the rota for batting. Might be worth hanging around for a while Reg."

Under normal circumstances Reg wouldn't have given that request a second thought. However, there was somewhere else where Reg wanted to be. It was approaching water break time at the bums and tums club and Reg was planning to 'bump into' Eunice as she herself took a water break. He'd caught a glimpse of Eunice earlier as he passed the function room from the outside and discreetly looked through the window. In a split second, and trying desperately not to appear leering, Reg spotted Eunice doing star jumps in a very trendy tight-fitting sky blue track suit.

Reg decided to stay at the practice despite his desire to engage with Eunice. With his pads on, Trevor marched confidently to the crease and took a middle peg guard. The bowler on the rota who had been selected was a second team opening bowler called Jim Mullineaux. With everyone watching and expecting the ball to go into orbit, Jim ran up and delivered a good length ball which cleaned Trevor's middle stump out of the ground.

For the next few balls Trevor produced a range of standard shots. His technique wasn't perfect, but he probably would improve with good coaching. Towards the end of his allotted time at the wicket, the call went up from Iain Redwood. "Last six Trevor." This indicated that Trevor was receiving his last six balls at the crease. Usually whoever was batting took the opportunity to slog each of the last six balls as far as they could.

Trevor was aware of this ritual and faced the first of six from Jim who had got him first ball. Almost effortlessly Trevor dispatched the ball clearing the changing rooms roof. This was a big hit by anybody's reckoning.

As the rest of the players looked on, four of the following five balls got the same treatment. Including one from his brother Harold. This was powerful, brutal hitting, carried out in an almost effortless manner. Iain Redwood was very impressed.

The practice carried on for a few minutes until a brand-new bright yellow Ford Granada pulled up on the car park. Rod 'The Cod' Norris was first to comment. "Jesus…that's a nice motor. There's a few bob's worth there". Two people got out of the Granada and looked lost. "I wonder if it's that Asian guy who Reg mentioned?" Rod squinted and looked over again. "Wait a minute…. that's Joey, the owner of Joey Banglas, the Indian Restaurant on Market Street. Wonder what he wants. Might be bidding for the contract for the teas?"

Iain Redwood took control of the situation, walked over to the car park and introduced himself. "Good evening. I'm Iain Redwood the first team captain. Is it Jimez?" he asked. The younger of the two responded, "Yes sir. I've been told to present myself tonight for a trial and practice. Am I too late? Please accept my humble apologies but I was working in my uncle's restaurant. And please, call me Jimmy. Everybody else does."

Iain immediately warmed to his polite manner and responded. "We are nearly finished but if you want to have 20 minutes bowling at me then I am quite happy to go to nets till it gets too dark."

Jimmy replied. "That would be most agreeable. Do I need to change into my whites, or will my tracksuit be sufficient?"

Iain replied, "Tracksuit is fine."

The pair made their way up to nets where the numbers had dwindled to a few of the juniors. Iain padded up and prepared to face the unknown quantity that was Jimez 'Jimmy' Bangla. Iain decided, before he'd faced a ball, that he was going to treat Jimmy with respect and not attempt to slog him out of sight. It quickly turned out to be a decision he didn't need to make as Jimmy sent a succession of more than decent deliveries. Some of them almost unplayable.

As the dusk gathered the whole net session ended with Reg, Iain and the potential new spin bowler Jimmy taking the nets down and placing them in Harry the groundsman's garage.

Iain approached Jimmy as he walked towards his uncle's car. "Jimmy. I think I could find a place for you in the first team. Would you like to sign for us. It's looking like we are going to be challenging on all fronts this season. We've got a great bunch of lads."

Jimmy seemed surprised. "I would very much like to play for your club but please understand I am only 17 years old, and my uncle will not let me do the drinking. Also, there might be times when I'm not available as I am in Bolton to learn how to be a businessman like my uncle."

"That's fine Jimmy. I understand completely. Can you write down your address and phone number then I can contact you. I'm sure you'll be playing in the first game on Saturday."

Iain offered out his hand to shake. At first Jimmy didn't immediately offer his hand in return. He was clearly not versed in the ways of the western world and didn't mean to offend. However, he responded after a few seconds, shook Iain's hand and the two parted.

In the function room, Eunice's gaggle of bums and tums members were slowly dispersing after the post workout weigh-in which served as a barometer of how much progress they had made since last week.

A queue of females of all shapes and sizes formed as Eunice took down the details of each attendee and they gingerly stepped up on the scales. Each one of the group receiving words of encouragement from Eunice.

The players began filtering in as the ladies weighed out. One of the larger ladies, Mona Critchley, approached. Mona was in her late fifties and was clearly in for a long spell at the bums and tums club if she was to lose some weight. Rod 'The Cod' Norris observed. "Crikey. Them scales are in for a stiff test. She's a heavy treader."

Mona took the scales to some encouragement from Eunice. "You've lost three ounces Mona. That's going in the right direction. Remember to leave the cakes alone. Better still don't put them in your weekly shop. Remove the temptation."

Eunice began to put all the equipment away in the storeroom when Reg appeared. "Need any help, Eunice. There's a half dozen fit and able lads here who'd be happy to help?"

"No thanks Reg. We've nearly done now but thanks anyway." With that parting statement Eunice walked the whole length of the room with Reg's eyes laser-like on their subject matter. The sky blue track suit hugging her body. Much to Reg's surprise and pleasure as she went through the door she turned round and said, "Have a good meeting lads. I'm going having a shower then a drink in the bar. Might see you later?"

Reg's mind went into overdrive. The thought of Eunice having a shower on the premises brought up all sorts of images in his mind. Was she giving him the come on? Once again, his mind drifted into fantasy world. He imagined he was a plumber and had been called out to fix the shower with an unknowing Eunice wrapped in the smallest of bath towels.

Reg decided that he was indeed going to have a drink in the bar later.

Most of the first team were in attendance for the meeting including Harold and Trevor. They sat around a couple of rectangular tables with Reg in an assumed position of power at the head of this lay out.

Reg decided earlier in the day he would do a kind of leader's speech and, so he wouldn't forget anything, he had written down a few prompts on a piece of paper he held in his hand.

Rising from his seat, Reg opened his speech with a joke to lighten the mood. "Well gentlemen, it's not the first time I've got up off a warm seat with a piece of paper in my hand!" Those who understood the joke laughed politely but the pun was totally lost on Harold and Trevor who stared at Reg and wondered what the hell he meant. Reg wasn't troubled by the Aussies reaction and carried on. "I'd like to thank you all for taking some time out tonight to come to this meeting and I'd also like to extend a particularly warm welcome to our two team members who have come to be part of what I hope will be a successful season. We've had a difficult few years but from what I've seen at nets tonight I think we've got something to build on. I want to use this meeting tonight as a platform for what we all expect from each other."

He then produced another piece of paper from his pocket. "I've drawn up a list of topics that I'd like us to discuss and then I'll open the meeting first of all to Iain our captain then to anybody who has anything to say. Any objections?"

Captain Iain Redwood responded. "That's fair enough Reg but let's not get too tied up in knots over trivial matters."

Reg took control of the meeting once again. "Right. You'll be pleased to know that you won't be directly filling the pockets of our old mate down at *World of Cricket*, Paul Tabler as we have reached a sponsorship deal with Butterfield's Bakery to supply you with a new short sleeved sweater, a new long-sleeved sweater, and a tracksuit top for all the first team. The gear is still coming from *World of Cricket* as it's good quality, but Butterfields will be funding it in return for sponsorship."

He then reached into a large cardboard box and pulled out a long-sleeved sweater and held it up for all to see. Across the front of the sweater was the club badge with the words underneath stating: *Butterfields Crumpets..Tasty Treats.*

The players looked tentatively at each other with Rod 'The Cod' Norris being the first to comment. "I'm not sure the Reverend Adrian Gawsworth will be too pleased with the message. You know how squeaky clean he is."

Reg was unmoved by Rod's concern. "Leave the Reverend and his disciples to me. Last thing we need is a bunch of God botherers getting in the way of progress. It's a cricket club after all. This sponsorship has saved the club and the players a fortune."

"Moving on, I've already extended a warm club welcome to Harold and Trevor, but they aren't the only newcomers to the ranks. As you may have witnessed before you all disappeared to avoid taking the nets down, we had a young lad come down for a trial and the first impression I got was we could have stumbled on a little gem. I'll let the skipper elaborate."

With that invitation, Iain Redwood took over the conversation. "Reg might be right there. I faced the young lad in the nets while you lot were combining dodging net duty with slavering over the females in the bums and tums club. He gives the ball a real tweak and I'd like to give him a start against Strolldon next week in the opening game. As you're all aware, a left arm leg spinner is a real rarity in this standard of cricket. Batsmen won't know what's hit them hopefully."

Iain kept control of the conversation and the topic and moved on. "Last but not least to receive a warm club welcome is our new wicketkeeper Jonathon Barrington. As most of you have known Jon or JB through his many years at our rivals and friends at Strollde, he won't need much of an introduction."

Iain was right. JB had been at Strollden for almost ten years and was a quality wicketkeeper. He had decided to make a move when Reg approached him in the aftermath of the club's long term wicketkeeper Dave Slack who was emigrating to Australia. There were rumours that JB was receiving a basket of assorted quality meats every week from skipper Iain Redwood's dad Arthur who was the local butcher and, as the sign said above his shop: *Purveyor of Quality Meats.*

Reg was quickly on the defensive when this rumour was brought up by the Reverend Adrian Gawsworth: "When you can find a trail of blood from Arthur's chopping board to JB's fridge then you can raise the questio."

Iain then continued. "I must be honest and agree with Reg when I say the club has lost its direction over the last few years. However, I really feel that with our new additions we can be a force in the league, in fact I think if we all pull together, we can challenge and win. In Harold we've got a proven professional in this league and with Trevor as an almost second professional we're immediately stronger in both batting and bowling. JB behind the sticks is a quality keeper and I'm quietly confident about the young trialist Jimmy contributing with his unusual spin. Although with Jimmy we may have to ease him in and not over bowl or overexpose him. He's only a kid. He's very timid and very polite. But that confidence could be shattered with sledging from the likes of Lee Hutton."

Lee Hutton was a player at Barnworth who, despite being a great lad off the field, had been for many years a nightmare for opponents on it. His constant chipping away at opposition batters had led to several unsavoury incidents nearly resulting in fisticuffs.

Iain continued and posed a question for Reg. "What's happening with the teas Reg now that Betty has gone to the great kitchen in the sky?" Betty Pollitt was the mother of Maureen Pollitt but more importantly, Betty had done the teas for almost 20 years. Sadly, Betty had passed away suffering a heart attack whilst shouting for a full house on the national link at the Buckingham Bingo.

Reg responded: "I've asked a few of the members, including treasurer Verity Tinkle and her daughter Felicity. They've not given me a final decision but hopefully she'll be in the club later and, fingers crossed, we'll have a new catering division. Although Betty will be a hard act to follow."

Iain decided to raise an issue which had long been a bone of contention. "Reg. Whoever gets the job of doing the teas is there any chance of having a change of food on offer?"

"Why, what's wrong?" said Reg.

"Well, the lads are fed up with the traditional salad tea, bread and butter, cakes, tea, and coffee. With the greatest of respect to Betty's efforts, which were much appreciated, the lads are fed up of eating rabbit nosh. We'd prefer to have pasta and pizza."

Reg was aware that Betty's teas were strictly from another era. But this was 1978 and food was becoming more cosmopolitan. The era of fast food and drive-through takeaways was quickly becoming a culinary way of life. Particularly with the younger ones.

"Let's see who gets the job first Iain. I'm sure you're aware doing the teas isn't the most attractive job in the club. We need to remember its done on a voluntary basis. I know Betty was probably past her sell by date, but we could always rely on her."

With no other business to be discussed, the meeting finished and most of the participants headed to the games room. Reg though headed straight to the toilet where he applied a coating of Hai Karate across his face. With the start of the season only four days away and his master plan coming into play, Reg had only one thing on his mind. Eunice in the shower...

7
First Match Preparation

The fixture list for the season had brought about a very interesting opening game. Visitors, Strollden Cricket Club were based only a mile or so away so there was a lot of rivalry at stake. In fact, they had been one of the league's most successful clubs in recent times, winning the league three times, the Brunton Cup twice and the Lancashire Knock Out twice.

Like most clubs in the league, they had a major benefactor who was usually a local businessperson who would either fund the payment of an unspecified number of players or provide them with extra 'benefits' for playing. Hence the provision of the meat hamper for Jon Barrington. At Easthoughton Cricket Club, local travel agent Gerry Tonge, would always throw in a week's holiday abroad at the end of the season for their 'special' players. Worley were probably the biggest spenders, with local scrap merchant Cyril Booth digging deep in his pockets in their quest for success.

In the case of Strollden they had a man who worked in the world of finance. His name was Fred Tinks and it would be fair to say he wasn't the most popular club chairman in the league. This was because he had overseen a period of success by paying almost every player on the team. Fred was indeed a wealthy man and cared little for the thoughts and opinions of others.

Reg decided he would go up to the ground mid-morning just to make sure everything was all okay. He thought about Strollden. They were indeed a good, strong team who hadn't changed much in personnel over the years. Unlike most of the other teams who, when recruiting a professional, went for West Indians or Australians, Strollden had enjoyed a large degree of success by recruiting players from New Zealand. The rumour was that Strollden had recruited a really good batting professional named Greg Madden.

The weather was unusually warm for the last weekend in April as Reg drove the Austin Cambridge onto the ground. It was only eleven o'clock, but it was clear there would be a full day of uninterrupted cricket which was indeed a rarity for the first day of the season.

As Reg drove on, he noticed a couple of things. First of all, Harry Flatley's grey VW Beetle was parked up next to the garage indicating his presence. Secondly, and more to Reg's displeasure, was the sight of one of Harry's dogs cocking its leg against the heavy roller which had been left at the top end of the wicket being used for today's season opener. Reg watched the dog for what seemed like a lifetime.

With Harry Flatley nowhere to be seen on the square or on the outfield, Reg decided he'd had enough and accelerated round to the garage, determined to castigate Harry for his lack of control of one of his two dogs. As he entered the garage door, he was thrown off topic by the bizarre scenario he was faced with. Harry was stood there in a brown check lumber jack type shirt, his now customary flat cap, wellingtons, and a pair of red and white Y fronts which had seen far better days. To Harry's right, hanging up on the hot water pipes which serviced the changing room showers and clubhouse, was Harry's work pants and socks. His wet boots jammed in-between the roof and pipe.

Momentarily Reg completely forgot about Harry's dog's indiscretion. "What are you doing Harry? Why are you mincing around the garage in your undies? Christ them Y fronts have seen better days. Anybody could have walked in!"

Harry responded quickly, going on the defensive. "The seal on the bloody hosepipe has gone. I turned it on, and the seal went with water spurting all over me keks. Wet through I was from the waist down, so I've hung them out to dry on the pipes. Shouldn't take too long. Not been my morning to be honest Reg. The heavy roller's conked out and won't move and I can't go out there in broad daylight and try and fix it with only my undercrackers on!"

The thought of Harry repairing the heavy roller bending over the engine dressed only in his Y fronts, shirt and cap meant

Reg had completely forgot about the dog's indiscretion and became concerned with the roller parked up in the middle of the square. He moved over to the corner of the garage where Harry had a desk/workbench with a metal vice on it. To the side of Harry's desk was a stack of three high metal office type drawers in which Harry kept his paperwork and machinery manuals.

Reg took the initiative and moved towards the stack of drawers. "Let's have a look in the manual for the heavy roller. I'm sure it can't be anything too complicated. I did a bit of work on the roller years ago when I was playing."

Harry was clearly concerned with Reg's intentions and moved quickly across to block Reg's access to the drawers. However, Reg beat him to it and tried to pull out the top drawer. It was locked. "Get the keys Harry. We need to get the bloody roller working and shifted. Game starts in a few hours' time. Let's find the manual."

"Er, I've left the keys at home," said Harry clearly unnerved by Reg's intentions. Out of the corner of his eye, Reg spotted a bunch of keys on a hook near the garage door and grabbed them. "Here they are!" said Reg, and as he said that he opened the lock and pulled open the drawer.

Reg was clearly not prepared for the collection of Harry's paperwork that presented itself. Instead of manuals referring to rollers, mowers, and assorted ground equipment he was confronted with a considerable amount of soft pornographic glossy magazines with titles such as *Razzle* and *Readers Wives*.

"Bloody hell Harry!" said Reg as he held up one of Harry's mags to the light and examined it from every angle. "No wonder you didn't want me opening your drawers. There's a right library in here. A real stash!"

Harry promoted an unconvincing defence. "They're not mine Reg. I confiscated them off the under 18s. I noticed them on the table in the dressing room when I went to fix a light a couple of weeks back. I meant to tell you, but I forgot. We don't want this sort of filth and depravity around the young lads."

Reg was still analysing the contents of Reg's collection and barely paid any attention to Harry's wafer-thin explanation. It seemed that Reg's attention had clearly shifted from the plight of the heavy roller to Stacey from Stockport in the *Readers Wives* issue he was examining.

He then returned to the drawer and pulled out a green Asda carrier bag. Reaching inside the bag, Reg pulled out a couple of VHS Video tapes, titled *Innocent Sinners* and *Deprived in Denmark*. Clearly these were not related to cricket. Harry was quick to defend this discovery. "They're not mine ether. I was minding them for Brains the barman. Brains didn't want them being left behind the bar, so he asked me to keep them safe He borrowed them off Brian Braithwaite. Apparently, Brian has a contact called Alf Tyson who owns a dirty book shop who deals with this sort of stuff. Not my sort of film. Give me a good war film any time."

However, Reg's thoughts were not with this complicated trail of excuses and blame. It was the thought that Eunice's husband had connections with the local soft porn industry. He wondered if Eunice was aware of this. If she was, then this could explain the very 'cosmopolitan' attitude Brian and Eunice Braithwaite had consistently demonstrated in their marital relationship. If she wasn't, then maybe someone needed to tell her.

After this temporary diversion, Reg's thoughts returned to the issue of Harry's dogs. Named Monty and Winston, they were small mongrels which Reg - to his credit - had taken from the dog rescue home.

Reg went on the attack and focused on Harry. "I come on the ground and what's the first thing I see? One of your two mutts pissing all over the wicket. Not just any wicket, but *today's* wicket. What do you think if anyone from Strollden had seen that mongrel splashing all over the wicket?"

Harry laughed and responded, "Won't do it any harm. It might come in handy for our new leg spinner Jimmy. You know spinners love to have a damp patch to bowl into. Nothing wrong with our Monty being the secret weapon!"

This wasn't the response Reg was looking for. "Get those

bloody dogs and put them under lock and key and let's get this bloody roller moving!"

The hint taken, Harry went back into the garage and took the trousers down off the pipe and put them back on. He then emerged from the garage clutching an old cloth shopping bag which contained a mixture of screwdrivers and spanners which had been selected to repair the static roller.

After some twenty minutes or so the sound of the roller starting up and emitting smoke and an accompanying regular engine chug meant Harry had indeed been successful. He put his fingers to his mouth and whistled to Reg who was speaking to Brains on the boundary perimeter road. "Jobs a good 'un!" Harry shouted raising his thumbs. Reg reciprocated with a similar thumbs up.

With this repair completed, Harry performed a mock salute to Reg, turned away from the roller and executed a military half turn. In a further attempt to mock it up, he placed his stiff brush on his shoulder. Unfortunately, as Harry completed his half turn, the brush head came into contact with the forward/reverse gear lever with devastating effect...

The roller set off on its own, heading across the square and towards the boundary with Harry running by its side. Suddenly Harry attempted something that was far beyond his agility and age. In an effort worthy of a failed James Bond stuntman Harry attempted to jump on to the moving roller. Sadly for Harry the roller had gained momentum and he fell behind it. Luckily enough falling behind the roller rather than in front of it ensured he wasn't involved in a nasty crushing accident.

Unattended and undisturbed like some big green monster, the roller made its way across the outfield towards the boundary with apparently nobody to stop it.

Instinctively, Reg and Brains ran across the square with Brains arriving side-on to the roller and, taking advantage of the ground's upward slope slowing the roller down, Brains managed to jump sideways on and put the gearstick into neutral bringing the menacing machine to a stop.

It was indeed a close call. If the roller had carried on

undisturbed it would have gone past the boundary and rolled down the sharp embankment on to Potter Road.

A clearly triumphant Brains announced: "Another job within a job that, as steward, I have taken on and completed successfully. Brains, master of everything from the bingo machine to heavy roller rescue. I've saved the club a few bob there Reg. If I hadn't had stopped the roller it could have caused havoc to the moving traffic and people on Potter Road. Not to mention the likelihood of the roller being severely damaged, maybe beyond repair. You don't replace the roller by running a couple of name cards. Cost hundreds it would. Remember that at the next committee meeting when you discuss my pay rise!"

Harry suddenly appeared at the scene. His relief at the outcome of event was reflected in his manner. "Nice one Brains. I don't know how to thank you". Brains nodded, basking in this short-term glory.

However, Reg was a little less unforgiving: "What were you playing at Harry? Pissing about doing a salute and knocking the roller into gear? You're forever telling us that it sticks in gear and yet it's you that nearly causes chaos. Add to that your 'orrible hound pissing all over the wicket, to say it's not been the best of mornings would be an understatement of biblical proportions."

With that Harry climbed up on the roller and engineered the machine back towards the wicket to complete the necessary amount of rolling. Time was moving on and the players were beginning to arrive. Some arrived in groups of twos and threes with some travelling singular. It was time for Reg's plan to take shape…

8

The First Match

Team captain Iain Redwood was one of the first to arrive in his recently purchased metallic green Ford Capri. As he pulled on to the car park, he carefully selected his space which was against the back-end gable of the clubhouse. This was a spot where it was impossible for any big hit to land on the car. Within a couple of minutes Reg appeared in his Austin Cambridge and parked it up for the duration, right next to Iain's Capri. Both club members knew their cars were almost 100 percent safe from damage in these spaces.

Reg took a couple of minutes to compare his Austin Cambridge with Iain's Ford Capri. There was no doubt that these two cars were a generation apart. The Cambridge, a black and white memory from a 1950s film with characters in grey gabardines with large belts, smoking and wearing unnecessary hats. Compared to Iain's shiny reflection of 1970s flash, fashion, and fulfilment. All it was short of was a member of *Pans People* sat in the front seat and some furry dice hanging off the rear-view mirror. Reg thought once again about changing his car. He decided that next week he was going to take another trip to Sid Lane's car lot.

The ground was indeed becoming busy. It was after all unseasonably warm, and this reflected in the number of spectators on the ground. The players from both sides had begun to knock up on the outfield combining batting and bowling with some muscle loosening exercises.

Strollden had two brothers who were long-standing players. Dave and John Jones had been at Strollden for years with Dave being captain. On the outfield they exchanged pleasantries with ex-teammate Jon "JB" Barrington.

Dave Jones spoke first. "How's things JB. Hope you're not putting too much weight on with all of them free sausages from Alf's butchers?"

JB took the remark on board and countered quickly. "Sausages? Peasant meat if you ask me. Nothing but the best steak for me Dave!"

With that the players retired to the changing rooms and the two captains went to toss up. Iain Redwood won the toss and decided to bowl.

After twenty overs Strollden were a comfortable but not exciting 90 for 3. The wickets being shared, one each for Rod 'The Cod' Norris, Jimmy Bangla and Harold the professional. Jimmy was indeed proving his worth, virtually tying one end down. However, ten overs later and with Strollden professional Greg Madden and overseas amateur Bruce Perry beginning to open up they had moved on a further 65 runs without looking in any trouble whatsoever. 155 for 3 with another 20 overs to bowl looked ominous.

With 20 overs left drinks were taken and the senior players gathered together to discuss tactics. Iain was worried, "If we're not careful we're going to be chasing 220 plus and I'm not sure we are capable of that."

JB chirped in with an idea: "Pepper the pro with some short stuff from Trev. We all know he can't resist a hook shot. Swap Jimmy to the Potter Road end and tempt the pro with a hook to the longer boundary off one of Trev's bouncers. It's got to be worth a try?"

"Sounds like a plan," said Iain. With that decision made, Iain undertook organising the necessary bowling and fielding arrangements. This involved bringing Harold on as the switch over bowler enabling Jimmy to swap ends and Trevor to come from the scoreboard end.

With Strollden's two best batsmen firmly ensconced it was a gamble worth taking. Something had to change quickly or else the game would go away from them.

On the second ball of Harold's over Lady Luck smiled on the professional. A ball short of a length brought an aggressive swipe from overseas amateur Parry. This resulted in a badly timed thick edge into wicketkeeper JB's gloves. Without waiting for the umpire's finger to go up, Parry turned and walked. The breakthrough had come, although it wasn't as planned.

The customary high fives and back slapping took place with vigour. Strollden still had a couple of useful batsmen who relied more on power than technique to come. Notwithstanding, Iain felt that if they could get rid of professional Madden, they'd be into the tail enders.

The change in bowling at the Potter Road end didn't bring any immediate benefits. However, the decision to put Jimmy on at the scoreboard end was proving to be a master stroke, albeit by default.

The next two incoming batsmen must have fancied their chances against this young unknown spinner who barely looked old enough to do a paper round. Both departed very cheaply. One a nailed-on LBW and one clean bowled to a ball that turned square. Jimmy now had four wickets for 28 runs off a tidy 16 overs.

On the boundary the triumvirate of Reg, Harry and Dicky Hampton stood next to the sightscreen. Earlier in play they had sat outside the clubhouse, but such was the effect that young Jimmy was having on the proceedings they decided to make their way to the opposite side of the ground. This was as close they could get to being behind Jimmy's arm to witness how much turn he was getting on the ball out of what was deemed as a batting track.

"I think we've got a good 'un 'ere Reg. Reminds me of when I was in me pomp. A squirter here, a tempter there. Batsman hasn't a clue what's happening," said Harry.

Reg responded "You're not kidding Harry. He's got a great action and almost a different ball every time. Even their pro's struggling to get him away."

Reg's remarks were interrupted by a loud and confident LBW shout off one of Jimmy's deliveries. With the umpire's finger in the air that meant Jimmy had now disposed of the professional Madden and he now had a four-wicket haul.

With Strollden now on 170 for 8 skipper Iain went for the kill, replacing wicketless Trevor and re-introduced the guile and craft of the pro Harold.

Within three overs it was all done. Harold and Jimmy both claiming wickets from catches in the deep from agricultural type shots from the Strollden tail enders. 190 all out was a great effort considering they were at one stage 155 for 3.

As the players made their way for tea, Reg spotted the brand new Ford Granada that Jimmy had arrived in on his trial night. "Ay up Reg., Jimmy's uncle's here. Shame he didn't see the lad bowling earlier."

Jimmy's uncle approached Reg, Dicky and Harry and politely nodded to them all. Joey was well known to the locals. His Indian Restaurant on Market Street had been the venue for many a late-night booze-fuelled feast after a session in Throbbers night club. Many of the club members dined out at *Joeys* and he was indeed a well-respected member and stalwart of the community.

Almost whispering Joey asked, "How did my nephew bowl?" Harry was quick to respond. "The figures speak for themselves. I've just had a look at the scorebook, and he's got 5 for 32. They just couldn't play him. Where's he got skills like that from? Not from rumbling up the curries in your gaff Joey?"

Clearly embarrassed and demonstrating a degree of humility, Reg and Harry could only dream about, Joey spoke softly and replied. "Well, back in Delhi he was fascinated with our national cricketing hero, Bishan Bedi who took a shine to Jimmy when he won a coaching scholarship at school. Bishan taught him everything but when my brother died suddenly Jimmy and his mother came to the UK to live with me. Sadly, Jimmy only has contact every now and again by phone call as Bishan is constantly on tour with the national squad. Hopefully we will have contact with Bishan this summer as our national team is touring this year in the UK. I am sure Bishan would be very happy at my nephew's bowling today."

Harry reached into his bag and pulled out a parcel that was wrapped up in some greaseproof paper that had once contained a loaf. As he opened the paper he spoke directly to Joey. "Fancy a corned beef and onion butty Joey?"

Joey politely declined Harry's offer. "No thanks Mr Flatley, for your gracious offer but I have already eaten. Please do not be offended."

Harry didn't look remotely offended as within three attempts the sandwich was catering history and he was tucking into one of his three pickled eggs.

"I don't know how you can eat three of them pickled eggs Harry," said Reg. "If I even attempted to eat them it'd play havoc with my guts."

Taking time out between covering the eggs with pepper and eating them, Harry responded, chewing as he spoke: "See these eggs? Staple diet in the desert in the desert battles of '41. All the lads would stick 'em in a jar in the belly hole of the tank and there they'd stay preserved as fresh as the day they were put in a big jar of vinegar. Sustained the troops through El Alamein all the way to Tripoli."

"I bet the inside of the tank stunk to high hell when you'd all been eating eggs though Harry?" said Dicky Hampton.

"You air force boys had it easy compared to us desert rats. We were away for months at a time whereas you glorified Biggles RAF boys just nipped down the airfield, flew across the channel, dropped a few bombs on the Nazis and were home for tea and tiffin at Biggin Hill plus a leg over from the wife or some floozie who'd fell for your leather fur lined jacket and patter. Not like us away for months at a time fighting Rommel and his crafty cronies."

Harry continued his culinary critique, "See that?" he said pointing to one of an assortment of biscuits in his lunch tin, "Next to the wheel this is without doubt man's greatest invention. The Jammy Dodger!"

These were of course the thoughts of a totally biased war veteran. Fortunately, ex RAF pilot Dicky Hampton had heard the exact same speech many times over the years and didn't react.

Dicky took a puff on his pipe and spoke to Joey. "You expect a busy night in the restaurant Joey? I hear *The Reg Coates Experience* are on tonight at Throbbers. They usually bring a crowd in. I know that Ronnie Blower's girls Susie and Shirley are going."

"Yes, indeed Mr Hampton. I'm hoping that we are busy, although with the right sort of customers. Last weekend we had more than normal customers thinking they don't have to pay and doing a runner. I myself caught two young men hiding in the sawdust skip at Mr Hagsford's timber yard. Most disrespectful." Joey explained solemnly. Turning his attention to Dicky Hampton he asked: "Will you be coming along Mr Hampton? Perhaps with your new lady friend?"

This question to Dicky immediately caused eye contact between Reg and Harry. Dicky Hampton was known to be a smooth operator when it came to women but was usually very discreet. Only those 'in the know' within the club knew about Dicky and Edna Pilling. For Dicky to be seen locally with another woman was not like him.

"Blimey Dicky," said Harry, "Not like you to be out with a bit of fluff locally. Was it Edna you were with?"

Dicky didn't answer and hastily switched the topic of conversation. "Not be long before we are out to bat. Are you staying on the ground Joey, or have you got to go?"

"It is most sad, but I shall have to leave shortly. I am staff down tonight and as you say with Reg Coates on, we will likely be most busy. I would be very grateful if somebody could call me later on with the result. Hopefully we can start the season with a win?"

With that statement Joey made his way to his Ford Granada and drove off the ground to prepare for a night's work at the restaurant.

190 all out wasn't going to be an easy run chase. Openers Dave Hedge and captain Iain Redwood walked out to the square. This opening pair had acquired the nickname 'tip and run' when at the wicket due to their ability to pick up the quick singles. They had opened the batting for many years.

However, the run chase suffered an early blow with a classic run out mix up which led to Dave Hedge departing without scoring a run. With 5 overs gone and the total on 12 for one it was a time for concentration and application rather than any exuberant displays of batting.

Skipper Iain Redwood was made for this sort of situation. A natural leader and possibly the most difficult batsman to get out in the whole league. He, in tandem with Barry Sandfield, took the total to 80 off 20 overs. With 111 required and 30 overs left things were ticking over nicely.

However, after the drinks break at 25 overs, disaster struck. With the score on 95 for one, Barry Sandfield was caught at first slip. This brought promising young batsman Stuart Hopwood to the crease. Sadly, Stuart only lasted one ball as he went for a golden duck bowled by John Jones. It was the turn of professional Harold Haltz to come out and face the hat-trick ball from Jones. With fielders crouching round the bat John Jones steamed in. The ball struck Harold on the pads which warranted a half-hearted but lacking in belief appeal for LBW that umpire Jim Price turned down.

At 95 for 3 it was a different game. Strollden, after being on the back foot for a large part of the innings, were now ready to turn the screw. The two batsmen walked down the wicket and spoke in between the over. Iain opened the conversation. "Let's just take it steady. There's no need to panic. We're around the right run rate so let's get to 191 and a winning score through graft and guile not glory."

"I agree skipper." Said Harold. "But if we do drop behind the run rate or lose a wicket, there's nothing to worry about. We've got our Trevor and JB who can both lay on a bit and score quickly."

This was true for both players. Although not the biggest wicket keeper/batsman who ever played the game, JB was stocky in build and many times down the years had scored quick runs by aggressive big hitting. Trevor's debut at Tuesday's net had left a healthy appreciation amongst his teammates that he also could score very quickly without any unnecessary running between the wickets.

The captain and the professional kept the runs ticking over until at 130 for 3, with 15 overs left, Harold was caught at mid-wicket.

Jonathon Barrington was next man in. Walking confidently through his ex-teammates who were not backward in coming forward when it came to sledging. "Fancy going playing for a team that finished bottom and playing for a meat hamper. Hardly a Kerry Packer contract. Not something for the back page of the *Evening News*! Can see the headline now: *Wicket Keeper swaps clubs. Sausages seal the deal*. Chirped Mark Benneton, the Strollden captain.

JB wasn't disturbed one bit and took his guard. A quick conference in the middle of the track. "61 off 15 should be achievable," said Iain. JB nodded his head, tapped the wicket with the end of his bat and took his guard.

With cautious batting, Iain and JB took the score to 175 for 4 when, in a momentary lack of concentration, JB tried hoisting one clear of the boundary. This sadly landed in the hands of the fielder at deep mid-on.

Next in to help guide the score to 191 was Trevor. The brother of Harold the professional and overseas amateur marched confidently towards the wicket. With 16 runs required it could have been a tricky passage of play. However, with brute strength applied by Trevor it was all over within five minutes as he hit one four and two huge sixes off the next over.

Skipper Iain Redwood was delighted. Not only had he remained unbeaten on 75 not out but more importantly the team had got off to a winning start against a decent team.

The atmosphere in the dressing room was good and skipper Iain Redwood decided he would seize the moment and make a speech. Standing bare chested and clutching a glass of lager he began to speak. "Lads. Let's enjoy the moment. Today we have taken on and beaten one of the favourites for the league title. Bear in mind we have had a much-changed team from the debris of last season. We all pulled together, and everyone should be proud of their contribution. I think it's fair to say that in a day of outstanding performances one player stood just that little bit taller than everyone else. In a new ceremony which will take place after each win, I will nominate the player of the match. This prize consists of ten free pints of bitter or lager for the winner. Bear in mind its only donated when we win. Today without doubt with bowling figures of 5 for 32 the winner is Jimmy Bangla."

With that the whole team broke not spontaneous applause with those stood closer to Jimmy giving him a hefty slap on the back. He was clearly humbled by this outbreak of congratulations.

"Speech! Speech!" came the cry from the rest of the players. Iain Redwood took control. "Jimmy. Would you like to say a few words?"

Jimmy looked like a boy amongst men. He wasn't physically impressive, stood there in his matching white vest and looking like one size too big underpants. If nobody had told you he was closer to 19 than 18 you would guess he was nearer 14 than 15. He was quite tall, but his body clearly had more room for natural development. With the beginnings of a tentative moustache above his upper lip.

Jimmy spoke quietly and demonstrated excellent delivery skills of the English language. "First of all, I want to thank all my teammates for making me most welcome and giving me a chance to bowl. I have really enjoyed myself today and hope I can be picked again. But I am sad to say that I cannot accept this prize as it is against my religion. I would like to pass this prize on to the whole of the team to share if that is OK with Mr Redwood?"

"That's no problem, Jimmy." said Iain Redwood.

The team got showered and changed and most of them headed for the clubhouse for post-match analysis and a few celebration pints.

Reg's master plan was gathering momentum...

9

More Confrontation

With a much warmer than usual April and May, the sun was certainly shining as the team sat top of the league with maximum points. Along with a first day of the season victory against Strollden came successive home victories against Aston Bridge and Harrick, with profitable away excursions at Eagleton and Storwich.

The weekend brought the season's first double header with Saturday's meeting with Worley being followed on Sunday by Beaton away from home in the Brunton Cup.

However, despite the success on the field, Reg was having trouble organising the *Miss Bolton* contest. Nobody it seemed wanted to help organise the competition. In a last-ditch attempt to rescue it, he asked for an emergency committee meeting.

A full turn out ensued. This surprised Reg who thought that the Reverend Adrian Gawsworth and treasurer Verity Tinkle would abstain on moral grounds.

The Braithwaites were both in attendance with Eunice looking delightful in a very tight-fitting cheesecloth blouse. Spread around the table sat the rest of the committee: Charlie Mather, Dicky Hampton, Queenie Hodgkiss, John Burrell and Norman Harris.

Reg opened the meeting. "As you're all aware, I have got a potential gold mine function in the making but I'm sensing a feeling of resentment from certain areas of the committee. I just need to know who and why there's such opposition to a great evening?"

The Reverend Adrian Gawsworth was quick off the mark and didn't hold back in his reply. "The whole idea is morally bankrupt. It's just a cheap flesh show for men of a certain age and persuasion. Plus, from what I am hearing, you have no structure to the event. Furthermore, the night you have potentially booked is already the subject of a double-booking mistake by Brains. So, the reality is Reg that you're third in the pecking order for this sordid and lewd production you're intending to promote."

This was news to Reg. He had no idea the room was already booked and as he'd already promised the date to a number of the female contestants it was crucial he had the date nailed for his beauty contest.

Reg went straight to the point: "What other two functions have been booked that are more important than a nailed-on room filler with punters who'll likely drink the bar dry. Thus, filling the club coffers with much needed lolly?"

Standing up to deliver his reply, the Reverend didn't pull any punches. "This is non-negotiable Reg. You're not going to use your arm twisting non-democratic bully boy tactics in this matter. First of all, there's my choir practice from the church to host here as the builders are in repairing the roof after the lead flashing and tiles got pinched a couple of weeks ago. The second of the double booking is Percy Crampton's 100th birthday bash. We still haven't worked out how we're going to break the news to Percy. Brains said his family may consent to using the games room as there's not likely to be a full house."

Reg wasn't amused by the Reverend's accusations and intentions. He could live with being accused of bully boy tactics. That was water off a duck's back for Reg, but the two functions given priority over Reg's beauty contest made his blood boil.

"You're having a laugh Reverend. First of all, you and your choir could go to St James for a one-off practice sing-along. I'm sure the Reverend Whittaker would let you use his gaff. All that fundraising last year for a new organ, well it would be nice for your singers too. They'd feel like they are on a tour kind of thing. Secondly, regarding Percy's birthday bash. If I were Percy's family, I wouldn't be ordering the balloons for that evening yet. That shindig could be cancelled at any time soon. I don't mean to sound cruel but from what I'm hearing old Percy might not make the party. He's not been well for quite a while now and could be one short of a collection on

99 if you know what I mean? I notice two of his sons have suddenly appeared on the scene for no reason after not seeing their dad for ages. Always remember the old saying: *Where there's a will there's a family.*"

The Reverend was clearly upset about Reg's cavalier attitude to the whole issue and focused his anger on Charlie Mather the secretary. "Are you going to stand idly by while one of our oldest and most respected members is conveniently dismissed as almost dead in order for this debaucherous, disgusting, steaming sordid flesh market to take place. What in God's name are we coming to? I wasn't aware the club's core focus had shifted from a cricket club to some seedy Amsterdam brothel. Or has the direction of travel for the club changed Mr Chairman?"

Charlie wasn't in the mood for this. This meeting had been called at short notice and collided with the darts and dominoes teams pre-season preparation which involved a friendly that evening against The Bears Head. Charlie asked The Bears Head captain if he could go on last. He was sure the meeting would have been over by then. To further complicate matters Charlie had indulged in his usual pre-match ritual of sinking five pints of Lion Bitter before he threw a dart.

Without giving it much more thought and his powers of reasoning clouded by the effects of the ale, Charlie decided the easy way out of this tricky situation. "There's only one thing we can do in a situation like this that needs quick resolve and that's to take a democratic vote on it. Now. Is everybody clear on the facts? If not, speak now."

Surprisingly the Reverend didn't object. He knew Dicky Hampton and Charlie Mather would vote for Reg whereas Verity Tinkle was a shoe-in for him. He thought that moral decency would bring John Burrell, The Braithwaites, and Queenie Hodgkiss on his side. Norman Harris could go either way.

Charlie asked for the vote. "All those in favour of Miss Bolton taking place on July 30th please raise their hand."

The arms went up. Reg, Dicky, Charlie, and the Braithwaites making a total of five.

"That's five in favour. All those against please raise your hand."

The Reverend Adrian Gawsworth, Verity Tinkle, John

Burrell, Queenie Hodgkiss, and Norman Harris all raised their hands.

"That's five against. We have deadlock so in accordance with club procedures I will ask Reg as Chairman to deliver the casting vote."

Reg tried to hide his glee and maintain a sense of dignity as he cast his vote. "I have to vote for the best interests of the club. Therefore, with respect to the other proposals, I have to go for the Miss Bolton contest."

The Reverend was clearly shocked. He'd gambled and lost when he thought he would win. Clearly the Braithwaites had been the votes that cost him this particular issue.

"Whilst I respect the core principle of a democratic vote, I am less than happy with the way this matter has been managed. I am going to request from the Chairman a full outline of how this meat market is going to run before it actually takes place, this includes dress code for the contestants and method of judgement."

"With there being no other business, I hereby call this meeting over." said Charlie as he lifted his large body out of the chair. The effects of years of overindulging in constant pints of Lion Bitter hadn't done Charlie's health or physical shape any favours. The rounded lounge chair was a tight fit for Charlie's expansive waist as he almost gyrated his way out of the chair, mopping his sweating brow with a handkerchief that was, to say the least, well used and had clearly not seen the inside of a washing machine for quite some time.

Once out of the chair, Charlie composed himself by putting his thumbs inside the waistband of his trousers and hitched his pants above his waist. Taking extra effort in a failed attempt to cover up his well matured protruding beer belly. He then removed his glasses, placed them in front of his mouth and breathed on them before 'cleaning' them with the very same handkerchief he'd mopped his brow. The sole objective being to ensure a clear view of the dartboard when on the oche. Charlie's pre match ritual was clearly back on track as he walked back into the games room, drank the remains of his fifth pint and ordered his sixth pint of the evening.

The games room was busy with the usual waft of blue haze floating through the room propagated by a non-stop supply from *Players Number 6, Embassy Regal, Benson and Hedges* and *Park Drive* cigarettes all being puffed and blown with great vigour.

Groups of men gathered at the top end of the games room. To a man true protagonists of the ideal indoor athlete with expansive waistlines, ruddy red-faced cheeks and yellow/brown nicotine-stained fingers.

The Bears Head team were captained by a man called Fred Mulligan. A seasoned drinker whose theory on drinking was borne out in a statement which he often repeated. "I drink in moderation me. One at a time and three at last orders." When referring to Fred's complexion, Charlie described him as having a face "like the surface of Mars."

Charlie went over to Reg and said, "Don't you think you might have pushed the boat out with this Miss Bolton lark? I mean whose going to help you with it?" Reg responded confidently, "Let me get this weekend out the way first. We've two big games and on Monday I'll put a strategy and format together."

In the corner of the room, Reg spotted captain Iain Redwood and made his way over to him. "Sorry I missed selection meeting tonight, had some lumber with God's anointed man on the committee. Anyway, how did selection go tonight? Any problems or dropouts?"

Iain responded. "The only problem we have is that young Jimmy Bangla can't play Saturday. He has to work in his uncle's restaurant. Apparently *The Four Tops* are on and he's expecting to be rammed out."

Reg was less than amused. "What! I don't believe it. The game will be well over by the time the Four Tops start warbling. I'll have a word with his uncle and get that sorted."

"If you could get Jimmy to play it would be a huge bonus. He's been a real find for us," said Iain.

With that Reg left the club and headed to Bangla's restaurant where after 20 minutes of discussion Reg got what he wanted. That being Jimmy's name on the team sheet and a beef vindaloo half rice/half chips.

The weekend approached with no sign of a break in the unusually warm weather.

10
A Big Weekend... Double Header

Saturday came along and began with a league fixture at home to Worley, a club who were relentless in their pursuit of trophies. They had several players on the payroll which was financed by local scrap metal merchant and self-made millionaire Cyril Bootle. Worley were a strong team who were the only club in the league who had a team manager in the shape of Chris Dennis whose son Steven opened the batting. On the field they were led by a ruthless and very talented captain Chris Lowell and had a West Indian professional called Sylvester Duran who was without doubt one of the biggest if not the biggest hitter ever to come from the islands. Add to that Pete Barry, a stylish number three, plus three of the best amateur cricketers in the league in David Black, Craig Digby and Steven Dennis. Also, within the Worley ranks was a long seasoned slow/medium pace bowler called Malcom Whitlock.

Whitlock was around 50 years old. Nobody actually knew his real age and it was subject to much speculation around the league. To his credit he had regularly topped the league bowling averages.

To the unknowing eye Whitlock would be classed as a veteran "pie chucker". However, the statistics over many years told a different story. His main source of victims falling to a well-supported almost choir-like team appeal for LBW. An appeal that rendered around the ground at least once an over whilst he was bowling. A lot of people were of the opinion that he worked on the theory of percentages. If he appealed enough surely the umpire would get fed up and give the decision in his favour. Every time the ball hit the batsmen's pads would result in a well-orchestrated appeal.

Some of Whitlock's methods of appeal and subsequent reaction were pure theatre. A confident appeal would see him jump up in the air whilst executing a half turn that a seasoned

Moscow ballerina would have been proud of, leaving him facing the umpire with a convincing expression on his face.

Whereas a turned down appeal resulted in one of several poses. One being a descent to a squatting position as he stared down the wicket. Another well-rehearsed failed appeal reaction was to stare wistfully at the batsman whilst stroking his chin in bemusement at the not-out decision.

In fairness to Whitlock, he was a great example. A man of his age still being recognised as a bowler who had earned a lot of respect.

After winning the toss and electing to bat, Worley made good progress with openers Digby and Dennis quickly moving the total up to 50 without loss after only eight overs. After 15 overs they were still at the crease with 90 on the board and looking in no trouble whatsoever. Both batsmen playing the ball confidently to all parts of the ground. Scoring at six per over and ten wickets in hand things were looking good for Worley.

The alarm bells were beginning to ring as even if a wicket was to be taken, one of Worley's strengths was their depth of batting which posed some type of threat, with all down to ten being able to make a contribution with the bat. The last man being the veteran bowler Malcom Whitlock who his teammates described as a 'specialist' number eleven.

After 24 overs the much-needed breakthrough came with young Jimmy Bangla trapping Digby with a confident appeal for LBW. This brought the stylish Pete Barry to the crease. A supremely confident batsman who was one of several on the 'secret payroll' at Worley.

On the boundary edge benches as usual sat the triumvirate of Reg, Dicky and groundsman Harry. Reg was no lover of the way Worley structured their team. Paying several players wasn't good for clubs in his opinion. As Pete Barry marched out to the crease following the dismissal of Digby, Reg couldn't hold his contempt for the Worley cash-based model. "See him that Pete Barry? Wouldn't be seen dead at Worley if Cyril wasn't weighing him in every week. I heard Cyril pays him 30p per run. Same as Malc Whitlock. 30p a wicket. Bloody mercenary each and every one of them."

Dicky Hampton responded "Well that's the way they've always operated Reg. And I must admit it works for them. I'm not saying it's right by the way. I don't think we could work that way at our club."

With a hefty touch of sarcasm Reg replied, "We'd never get payments of that magnitude past the God squad on our committee. I sometimes think the Rev and his bunch of bible bashers think the club runs on thin air, hymns and prayers. Remember a bit back when all the lead went missing off the top of the church and he asked for a donation? I reckon a quick trip with the local plod to Cyril Bootle's yard would have recovered all that lead. Never mind putting the begging bowl out for donations from the club. I mean, think of it, Worley are being funded by the lead off the church roof which we donated to replace. Madness!"

Groundsman Harry Flatley changed the topic of conversation as he reached into his bag and lifted out a large plastic Tupperware food container. "See this Jammy Dodger? Well, after the wheel, it stands second as man's greatest invention. Best enjoyed after a smoked mackerel barm cake with a load of pepper on. Delicious."

Both Reg and Dicky looked at each other and simultaneously shook their heads. "You must have iron guts with the stuff that you chuck down your throat, God only knows how your other end copes. It's hardly a balanced or well thought out diet," said Reg.

Suddenly the debate on Harry's diet was abruptly brought to an end as a loud appeal for caught behind was rewarded with Pete Barry being given out off the bowling of Harold the professional.

Next in was professional Sylvester Duran. An imposing figure both physically and mentally. He wasn't one for taking his time and playing himself in. He strutted out to the wicket with the full-sized bat tucked under his arm like a small twig. Duran didn't walk quickly. It was as if he was making a silent statement of presence.

He took a leg and middle guard and surveyed the field via a 360 degree turn whilst waving his bat around like an overpowered windmill. Sylvester Duran looked in the mood and with Worley in a strong position with the score on 120 for two with twenty overs to come the stage was set for a brutal onslaught by the West Indian.

On the boundary bench Harry finished eating his Jammy Dodger and made several observations and comments. "Like him or not, this guy is pure box office. Look how many people have just come out of the club house just to see him bat. How do you think he'll treat young Jimmy Bangla? He could ruin him if he gets his eye in. If I was skipper, I'd take Jimmy off and put Trevor on, if there's one thing Sylvester Duran doesn't like it's a fast-paced hostile spell bowled short at him."

Harold had two balls left to bowl which surprisingly enough Duran just pushed back and the over ended with no further alteration to the score.

The next over saw no change in the attack with young Jimmy Bangla bowling to Steve Dennis who was well past his half century and looking to get his first century of the season. After two dot balls the batsmen took a quick single leaving Jimmy bowling at the professional Duran for the remaining three balls of the over.

Jimmy consulted his captain and made several fielding alterations. It was obvious that both captain and bowler were agreed that professional Duran was smelling blood and was hungry for a session of big hitting. Jimmy turned and delivered a ball which turned slightly and rapped Duran on the pads. Jimmy appealed along with the wicket keeper and one remaining slip fielder. The appeal met with a head shaking response from umpire Jack Parks.

Duran scowled at Jimmy with a look of contempt. How dare he appeal against the most high-profile professional in the league? Did he not know who Duran was?

On the boundary benches Harry made a cynical observation regarding the umpire. "Jack Parks. Friend to the stars. He'd never give Duran out first ball. Whatever the appeal he'd find a reason to give a not out decision. Why, if Jimmy bowled him all three stumps, he'd call no ball even if Jimmy had bowled from the sightscreen. You watch in the bar after the game. He'll be all over Duran. I played a couple of seasons with Parksy. He's bent as a butcher's hook."

Back on the square Jimmy prepared and delivered the fifth ball of the over which Duran took a huge agricultural swipe but totally mistimed the pace of the ball spooning it high in the sky. Jimmy shouted loudly: "Catch it!"

The ball went high above mid-on where Rod Norris had ample time to position himself waiting for this prize catch with his hands cupped. It seemed like the ball was in the air forever, but then disaster struck. The ball went straight through his hands and landed on the square. Young Jimmy wasn't prone to showing his emotions, but his guard dropped as he kicked the ground in anger.

This could prove to be game changing. If Rod Norris had held on to the catch the most destructive and dangerous batsman in the whole league would have been dispatched for a duck. The body language of the whole team told the story of a missed opportunity.

Watching from the boundary Reg was fuming. "Why didn't the wicket keeper take the catch? The ball was in the air long enough for him to claim it and take position for an easy catch. That could cost us the game!"

Reg's worst fears were confirmed as over the next six overs Duran bludgeoned his way to a quick fifty with the other batsman, opener Steve Dennis, merely playing a supporting role pinching quick singles at every opportunity enabling Duran to keep the strike. Duran was particularly brutal with club professional Harold Haltz being dispatched for several sixes.

There was tension on the field as mild harmless banter began to escalate. Club professional Harold Haltz and his younger brother Trevor were typical Australians who were never short of a few words. Trevor in particular had been very vocal in ensuring everyone on the ground including spectators was aware he thought that Duran was "Just a lucky slogger".

With 14 overs left to bowl and Worley on 180 for two skipper Iain Redwood opted for a change in the bowling.

After a four-man consultation by the senior players, amateur Trevor was brought on to see if he could break the vice like grip that Duran and Dennis had enforced.

Trevor was a more than useful bowler who generated pace and bounce. He ran in off his run up and predictably dug one in short which flew between Duran's peak on his cap and his raised hands clutching his bat. Such was the bounce generated by Trevor that wicket keeper JB was at full stretch as he stopped it going for four byes.

The gloves were clearly off in this two-man contest of bravado and bravery as the second ball was a replica of the first with Duran taking evasive action by ducking down underneath the delivery.

A call to Duran from the Worley changing rooms asking him if he needed a protective helmet was met with a dismissive shake of the head. Duran was clearly rattled, and his mood was being tested to the limit by the fielders closest to him constantly chipping away.

However, the tension and mood of the game increased dramatically when Trevor ran up and delivered the third ball of the over. Instead of following with another short, pitched ball, Trevor released the ball early and ended up sending a "beamer" down at full speed which just about missed Duran's head.

Duran was understandably furious and began marching down the wicket brandishing his bat in a menacing pose. Trevor stood at the bowlers end with his hands held up in an apologetic manner. Several players ran to the wicket and stalled Duran who eventually stopped his march a couple of yards from where Trevor stood.

"So sorry Syl…so sorry. I didn't mean to beam you matey. Please believe me. It came out my hand too early," said Trevor. Whether this was the truth only he would know.

Duran wanted his say though and responded with a waving of the bat: "Listen man, if you can't play by the rules, you clearly can't play. Bowl properly and I hit your bowling outta the ground. Bowl another beamer and I hit your body out the ground with this bat!"

Umpire Jack Parkes chipped in "Now lads, lets cool down. Trevor's apologised and I'm going to issue him with a warning." The umpire turned his attention to Iain Redwood and beckoned him over. "Captain, one more beamer and you will have to take him off and he won't bowl again today. You all understand?"

The rest of the over went by in an almost surrealistic atmosphere. No short balls, no appeals and most importantly no confrontations.

The next over saw Duran return to type, hitting young Jimmy Bangla for two successive sixes. One went out of the ground with the other bouncing off the club house. However, Jimmy gained his revenge and a big wicket when he bowled Duran with one that kept low.

Harry Flatley was enthusiastic about the young spin bowler. "He reminds me of myself when I was in my pomp. He's not afraid to give it some flight. My *Tempter* ball was exactly the same. Sloggers like Duran can't resist having a dip. I got plenty out with my *Tempter*.

The last twelve overs saw Steven Dennis reach his hundred with Worley reaching a total of 227 for six at the end of their allotted overs.

At the tea interval Reg made his way over to the club house. On the way he encountered his nemesis in the shape of Chris Dennis the Worley team manager. Chris Dennis was a very confident bloke who was a smart dresser in a sky-blue polo shirt and smartly ironed grey slacks. Digging his hands into his trouser pockets he rustled his change and offered his opinion. "I think we've forty too many for you today, Reg. In fact, I think we let you off lightly if truth be known. Another couple of overs with Syl at the wicket and you could have been staring at 250 plus."

"We'll see," said Reg. "We might not have as big a hitter like your man Duran but don't forget our professional Harold H is a stylish batter. Nobody gave him 1000 runs last year. Plus, his brother Trevor can hit big if necessary. If we can get a good start, it'll be game on. Especially if what we hear about Dave Black is true."

"What you heard about Dave?" Chris retorted. "Don't believe everything you hear." Reg sensed that Chris was on the defensive. "Well, we heard he wasn't fit enough to bowl after having his foot run over by a bread van in Melling's yard where he works."

Chris Dennis replied to Reg's statement. "I won't deny he got his foot run over at work but that was over a week ago and he's had some private physio off Cyril's physio Dr Mambu and he's responded well.

Reg couldn't hide his indignation at the fact that one of the Worley cricketers had been afforded in effect the luxury of private health care courtesy of the local scrap metal merchant. He tried for a few seconds but couldn't resist expressing his dislike of the Worley money-based model.

"I tell you what Chris, the way you run your club isn't right. Filling the pockets of players who come as the finished article and care nothing for the club. I'll ask you a question. If Cyril pulled out his money how many of them would stick around and play for jaff all? Plus, it stops the progress of the younger players who can't break into the first team."

Chris Dennis seized the moment. "Young players not breaking through! What are you talking about Reg? The two openers today are products of our junior system. One of them scored a century who also happens to be my son. He's only twenty-one!"

Reg realised he was a little off target with some of his accusations and opinions as the Worley team manager was spot on with his comments. He shrugged his shoulders and made an offer of a side bet on the game: "I'll tell you what Chris, I'll stand you two pints the end of the game if you win and likewise, you'll stand me two pints if we win. What do you say? Can't be any fairer than that can I?"

Chris Dennis replied in a confident manner. "No problem, Reg. We'll shake on it now and meet back in the club house at close of play. With that the two men shook hands and Reg made his way to the club house.

Inside the club house it was quite busy. The unusually good weather and the chance to see Worley professional Sylvester

Duran in full flow had certainly brought the spectators out. The club was indeed thriving. As Reg made his way to the kitchen to see if there were any leftovers from the cricket teas, he noticed a couple of things. First of all, Eunice was behind the bar giving Brains a hand. Secondly the larger than life character of a well-known figure from the local community, Alf Tyson was leaning on the bar chatting to Eunice as she placed pint pots in the glass washer.

This set alarm bells off in Reg's brain. Alf Tyson was the owner of a small shop next to the bus stop on Victoria Road. However, the goods on offer were strictly for the over eighteen-year-olds. Appropriately named *Alf's Books and Mags* it dealt with materials in the shape of books, magazines and films that were strictly for the adult market. Reg asked himself what would a fine woman like Eunice want with Alf Tyson?

However, Reg hadn't enough time at his disposal to start making enquiries. He needed some food and also, he didn't want to miss the start of play after tea. He turned it over in his mind again. Just what was Eunice talking to Alf Tyson about?

Reg walked out of the club house and made his way towards where Dicky Hampton and groundsman Harry Flatley were sat. Harry had managed to eat his way through his tupperware box full of food and was finishing off with a jumbo bag of cheese and onion crisps. Dicky sat next to Harry and lit up his pipe.

The two opening batsmen had occupied the opening places for a number of years now. Both skipper Iain Redwood and David Hedge were known throughout the league as being the quickest opening pair running between the wickets.

The Worley opening bowlers were as expected. At one end was Malcom Whitlock with David Black at the other. However, it soon became clear that David Black was still suffering from having his foot run over and after five overs he took his cap and was withdrawn from the attack.

This was a severe blow to Worley. They were after all a stronger batting than bowling team who relied on being able to bat teams out of the contest.

The removal of Black from the attack meant an early introduction from professional Sylvester Duran who bowled a standard off spin.

Both Redwood and Hedge made steady but not spectacular progress and despite Whitlock's regular appeals for LBW, they laid the foundations for a possible successful run chase.

After fifteen overs the openers were still at the wicket with 50 on the board. Harry Flatley was less than impressed. "We're getting bogged down by being too cautious. We need to be more aggressive. This bowling attack could be taken apart with a bit of application. They're giving too much respect to Mal Whitlock. For goodness sake he's lobbing meat pies down and we're padding then back to him. Anybody would think it was Richie Benaud bowling!"

Mal Whitlock bowled another maiden over which even by his standards was overloaded with appeals. With the score not moving at the desired rate, even Dicky Hampton expressed concern. "Harry's got a point Reg. We really need to move the score along. We're not even taking the quick singles. If I was Malc Whitlock I'd keep my gob shut and stop appealing. If these two stays put, we'll be 110 for none at close of play. That's no good to us."

Five more overs passed with only 10 runs added to the total when Iain Redwood lofted an attempted-on drive into the hands of Stephen Dennis. Harry passed a caustic comment. "If that would have been me in the field, I would have dropped it on purpose. I bet Worley skipper Chris Lowell is fuming."

The incoming batter, young Stuart Hopwood, had played at every level from under tens to what was now his first season in the first team. Hopwood stood very tall at the wicket and took his guard. A round of applause rendered round the ground as Hopwood drove both remaining balls through the covers moving the score on by eight very valuable runs.

The next ten overs saw an acceleration in the run rate as Stuart Hopwood in particular got to grips with the Worley attack, scoring freely. With the score on 110 for one Dave Hedge fell to an LBW appeal which was pure theatre from Malc Whitlock.

There had obviously been some head scratching and discussion in the dressing room as the next man in was the pro's brother Trevor Haltz. Normally batting later down the order, skipper Iain Redwood's instructions were crystal clear as he pulled the young Australian to one side. "This bowling is food and drink to you Trev. Both of them are tiring physically and mentally. Go after them from the first ball and see if you can rumble up a quick fifty and get us within spitting distance."

When Trevor walked out, the change in batting order was greeted with universal approval by Reg, Dicky, and Harry. With the groundsman Harry being more supportive than usual to the club captain.

Trevor took his guard and gently pushed back the remaining two balls of the over which passed without appeal or incident.

The next ten overs saw Trevor follow his captain's instructions to the letter. The loss of David Black clearly weakened the Worley attack. Usually, Black would pitch in with around 15 overs for none too many runs. Both Mal Whitlock and professional Sylvester Duran were clearly not used to or indeed relishing these lengthier spells of bowling.

Feeling confident, Trevor quickly settled in and moved effortlessly past fifty. Taking particular pleasure at dispatching the Worley professional Syl Duran for three successive fours and a six in one over as the Worley professional flagged.

With the run rate easily restored and passed, victory was in sight and despite losing Stuart Hopwood for a very useful 43 and Trevor for a match-winning 87, victory was confirmed with four overs left to bowl.

Reg was ecstatic. "That's without doubt probably the biggest challenge we've faced all season; Worley are a tough team to play, and we've chased them down with six wickets in the tent and four overs to bowl!"

Dicky Hampton was a little more circumspective in his analysis. "Don't forget Reg, they were missing Dave Black from their bowling attack. There's no doubt it would have been a different game if he would have been bowling."

With the game over, Reg, Dicky and Harry made their

way over to the club house. En-route Reg noticed Alf Tyson over on the far side of the ground near the entry gates. Next to the gates was a patch of spare land with an old garage type building which used to be the storage place for Harry Flatley's ground equipment. It was now empty as it had now been superseded by Harry's new garage which was built three years ago.

Reg wondered out loud to both Dicky and Harry. "What's Alf Tyson doing mooching around your old garage Harry? Hope he's not after storing some of his mucky books and films in there. The Reverend would have a heart attack."

"I don't know Reg," said Harry "But knowing Alf it'll be something dodgy. I hear he had a court order issued on him telling him to tone down the content of his shop window. I was passing the other day when I went for a bottle of milk. It's very near the knuckle stuff but you know what Alf's like, he doesn't give a hoot."

On the steps of the club house stood the Worley team manager Chris Dennis. He made eye contact with Reg and as they both approached each other they engaged in a robust and sincere handshake. "The fruits of our bet are paid for with money in the till," said Chris Dennis. "Looks like you're going to take some stopping this season. But it's still early doors yet. You could be aiming at a cup and league double, who you playing tomorrow, Reg? I forgot."

"We're away at Beaton in the cup, could be a tricky tie. They have had some work on the square this winter and it's not played well at all. Who have you drawn Chris?"

"We've drawn Greenhill at home. Shouldn't be too difficult as they have won only one game and the pro has gone home." Said Chris.

"Well good luck tomorrow then Chris and maybe we'll meet in the final?"

With that parting statement both men went their separate ways. Reg headed for the clubhouse and held a silent private debate in his head. Should he take his car home and get a taxi back to the club or should he take his time and maybe only have three or four pints. Reg was sure his constitution could both absorb four or five pints of Lion Bitter and pass a breathalyser should he get pulled. He was indeed in a dilemma.

His mind was made up when he saw once again that Eunice was assisting Brains behind the bar with no sign of her husband anywhere. Reg decided that he would drive home, get a quick shower, throw on some Hai Karate and get himself dressed up should the opportunity to have a chat with Eunice transpire.

It took Reg just half an hour to get changed. He ordered a taxi from Mortax for 7.30pm. However, at 7.45pm the taxi still hadn't arrived, and Reg was fuming. He rang three times in ten minutes, each time the message was the same from the lady at Mortax: "He's two minutes away cock."

The taxi finally arrived at ten past eight. During the ride Reg made it clear he was unhappy with the taxi driver's punctuality. Each passing minute meant that he had less time to spend with Eunice.

The taxi pulled up at the club and Reg left without leaving a tip. He called in the gents on the way into the club house and ran the tap over his hands. This was so he could dab his hair into place. Before leaving he took a quick look in the mirror and added some final adjustment to his receding hair.

Walking into the club house he noticed that it was very quiet. Especially considering the team had pulled of an excellent win over close rivals Worley.

Reg cast his eyes to the bar where Brains was reading the local sports paper The Bruff. Brains called Reg over. "Hey Reg. There's a big feature on the club in this week's edition. Have you seen it?"

"No, I can't say that I have" Reg replied and then shifted focus to what he'd really rushed back to the club for. "Where's Eunice gone Brains? I thought she do you was giving you a hand behind the bar?".

"She left about ten minutes ago with Alf Tyson. They said something about going to some club. Don't know what 'er husband would make of it. They must be going somewhere special 'cos I heard her say she would have to go home and put her best hot pants on."

Reg was devastated. Just when he was looking forward to spending some time with Eunice, she had decided to depart the building with Alf bloody Tyson. Reg wondered where Eunice's husband was. He was hardly at the club these days. It was indeed a strange marital arrangement in Reg's opinion.

Skipper Iain Redwood was still in the club. He made his way over and spoke to Reg. "Same team for tomorrow, Reg. We've just had a meeting in the changing room, and everyone is confident. I'm just hoping that Jimmy's not too tired after bowling today and also working tonight at his uncle's restaurant."

"What do you think tomorrow, Iain? Beaton can be an unpredictable team. The pro is a top bowler," said Reg.

"I think the form we're in will carry us through. Don't forget we're unbeaten so far this season and its mid-June. The spirit in the club and the team has been brilliant. I have to say that I had my doubts at the start of the season, but everything is panning out better than I could have hoped" Iain beamed.

He reached for his cricket bag and said his farewells to the remaining members in the club house and left. Reg was on his lonesome sat at the bar and he decided that he would have another pint and then make his way home. But first he decided he was going to make some enquiries into Eunice's lifestyle. In Reg's opinion there was nobody better to ask than Brains the club steward who lived on the same street as her.

"What do you think of Eunice and her husband?" Reg began. "Seems like she spends a lot of time on her own. I know he works away a lot, but we rarely see him at weekends whereas Eunice is never off the premises. Is she totally a woman of leisure?"

Brains' reply took Reg by surprise. "She has a part time business doing massage from home. Why only a couple of weeks ago I went for a series of massages on my back. She sorted me out big style and only charged me a fiver for three fifteen-minute sessions. She's looking to expand her business, but the house isn't big enough to have a full massage table and all the equipment she needs to do the sessions.

It was then that the penny dropped regarding Alf Tyson. Almost automatically when a situation involving Eunice developed, his mind began to wander. Maybe Alf Tyson was offering Eunice a business deal involving her renting one of the two large rooms in the back of his shop on Victoria Road.

"She's a good looker Reg," said Brains as he wiped several wet pint pots. "I could do with her doing more shifts to be honest. All the blokes like her. She's very easy on the eye."

"So, she definitely got into Alf's car did she? Let's hope he took her all the way home with no sordid side trips down Crommy Lodges."

Reaching for his jacket, Reg decided it was time to go. There was no point hanging around. With nobody to talk to he rang for a taxi and made his way home.

"See you tomorrow Reg." said Brains, "I might try to get up to Beaton tomorrow. That's if I don't get stuck here all day. It's going to be busy tomorrow what with the joint birthday party for the Blower twins. Every man jack in the town will be here. Especially at night."

The Blower sisters were popular girls around the town's pubs and clubs and a lot of people had promised to attend. DJ Jimmy 'Spangles' Spanner had once again been hired to spin the discs.

The second day of the weekend was dominated by a Brunton Cup fixture at Beaton. They were a club who were based in the posher part of town who were perennial challengers but hadn't won any silverware for many years. The ground was set in a very picturesque setting. The only problem was it was possibly the smallest ground in not just the league but in all of northern cricket. This meant that if you had a big hitter who got his eye in a score of 250 plus was achievable.

The weather was glorious as Reg parked up the Austin Cambridge right next to the club house. As Reg closed the door, he spotted an old foe and friend, Beaton stalwart Warren Milner. They both instinctively walked towards each other, embraced and shook hands in a genuine demonstration of high mutual respect.

"How's my old mate Reg?" asked Warren. "It's great to see you. You're looking well my friend. Let me buy you a drink!" Reg didn't need asking twice and followed Warren into the bar.

Warren Milner and Reg were one club men who didn't just play for their clubs but also contributed valuable time and efforts off the field. Warren Milner had played at all levels for Beaton and had stayed several times despite being offered money for playing elsewhere.

Both Reg and Warren were still in the bar when the players took the field. Beaton had won the toss and had elected to bat.

Warren was a well-respected member of not just Beaton Cricket Club but of the whole cricketing community across the league. He was more than a little eccentric in his way of life but was indeed an engaging character. His mind was a vault of cricketing memories that he could date and time with impeccable precision.

As the game played out in front of these two local legends, memories of matches were played out with smiles and shaking heads.

Reg's attention was diverted towards the club gates as the sound of Harry Flatley's VW Beetle made its entrance on to the Beaton car park. Despite Harry's attention to detail and maintenance schedule, the fifteen-year-old Beetle had clearly seen better days.

"Is that Harry Flatley?" asked Warren. "I see he's still driving the old VW. Sounds like a bloody combine harvester. I take it he's still looking after you ground Reg?"

"It is indeed the legend that is Harry Flatley and yes, he is still looking after the ground. I must be honest he does a terrific job, but I'd never tell him that to his face." Reg mused.

Up on the car park Harry lifted a small folding canvas summer seat out of his boot and began to make his way around the boundary edge to where Reg and Warren were sitting. Harry was clearly dressed for the warm weather in his khaki shorts, Hawaiian short sleeved shirt, and sandals.

Reg looked Harry up and down and couldn't resist a remark on Harry's attire. "Jesus Harry…you look like a cross between an extra from Hawaii Five 0 and Montgomery with that shirt and those khaki keks!"

Harry was unmoved as he unfolded his chair and placed his shoulder bag containing his various culinary selections for the afternoon in the shade under the bench.

His next move was a surprise as he unbuttoned and removed his brightly coloured shirt, folded it neatly and placed it over the back of his folding chair leaving him stood in his white string vest. Harry then reached into his bag and produced a plastic tube. He then gave the tube a squeeze into his palm and proceeded to rub its contents onto his forearms.

Having failed to get Harry wound up first time around, Reg decided to try again. "All the years I've known you Harry, I didn't know you were a sun worshipper. Making yourself into a sun-kissed God for all the women at Queenie's Bingo Night. Better watch out for the tabloid reporters and photographers. I can see the headlines in the Journal now: *Bingo beauties and the groundsman's secret love nest!* Reg was almost beside himself laughing loudly at his jibes at Harry.

Harry responded, keeping his temper. "It's nothing to do with trying to get a tan. It's a case of looking after your skin. I remember being in the African desert with Monty in 1941. The sun was relentless. We had to put old vegetable oil on our skins to stop the burning. When we were chasing Rommel up Tripoli way, the lads suffered terrible sunburn. What with that, the prickly heat and the desert snakes…bloody torture. When I see these medallion men with their suntans posing it makes my blood boil."

"Mind if I now join you gentlemen?" said Harry. As he pulled his fold up chair next to Warren.

"Not at all" replied Warren. "Any friend of Reg's is a friend of mine. Nice to see you my good friend." Both Warren and Harry had played against each other many times down the years and were not unfamiliar with each other.

Warren then took the opportunity to not only boost Harry's importance and ego but also sound out Harry for some advice. "Harry," said Warren, "You know we had a lot of work done on the square this winter but we're still having trouble with the wicket. We've not got the biggest square in the league so there's only four tracks. Trouble is at the wicket ends, where the bounce is, at best, erratic. You got any ideas?"

Harry thought for a few seconds before he gave a reply. "Well, you may laugh at this but when we had wicket trouble a few years back I took some advice off Ted Norris. You must remember Ted? He used to be head groundsman at Old Trafford. He told me to put a big bowl of milk and cornflakes on the wicket ends once a week. I thought it was a potty idea at the time but guess what? It worked! Ted reckons that the milk attracts the stray cats who then pee on the wicket. Brought some life back in the wicket big style. More bounce than Maureen Pollitt's mattress!"

Warren chuckled as he thought about Harry's response "Well Harry I've never heard that one before but I'm willing to try anything. Won't be till this winter though."

On the field the game was taking place and Beaton had reached 135 for 6 with ten overs left to play. On the face of it this didn't look like this was looking to be a total to worry too much about for Iain Redwood's men. With professional Harold Haltz bowling a particularly tight spell, things were looking good for the fielding side.

The sixth wicket fell as young Jimmy Bangla claimed his third victim of the day. This brought to the wicket Amil Kharzi, the Beaton professional. An Indian chap who was more of a spin bowler than an accomplished batsman. With only eight overs to bowl he had decided that the best policy was all out attack.

This led to the last two balls of Jimmy's over being hit over the boundary ropes for six runs each time..

After a brief but eventful innings, the Beaton professional was dismissed for 25 and the rest of the Beaton tail end batsmen contributed very little as they finished their innings on 169 all out.

Reg and Warren vacated their seats on the boundary and headed for the club house where Warren had demonstrated generosity by insisting that Reg had what Warren described as a "proper cricket tea." The teas at Beaton were generally regarded as the best in the league and today's offering didn't disappoint.

After tea and a chat with some of the Beaton club members, Reg and Warren made their way back to where Harry was tucking into the contents of his sandwich bag. Reg sensed a smell of fish as he sat down and took an inquisitive look into Harry's bag. "What are you eating today, Harry? Smells a bit fishy." Harry didn't respond straight away but carried on chewing. After swallowing his food he cleared his throat and said, "Smoked mackerel and mustard barmcakes. Lovely. I've got a couple spare if anyone's feeling hungry?" Unsurprisingly nobody took up on Harry's kind and genuine offer.

The usual opening batsmen Iain Redwood and David Hedge started well and raced to 50 after nine overs. Warren Milner wasn't given to waving the white flag but commented on the state of play as the two openers took the total to 80 without loss after 14 overs. "I think this is going to be over before the pubs open at seven. These two don't look in any difficulty at all."

"It's a funny game Warren. Although I must admit it that if I was a gambling man, I'd be putting my money on us," said Reg.

Suffering only the loss of skipper Iain Redwood when the total was on 121 and also Stuart Hopwood on 157 the total of 169 was comfortably achieved with seven overs to spare.

As the winning run was driven to the boundary Warren stood up and shook both Reg and Harry's hands and passed on good wishes for the next round.

After saying their goodbyes to Warren both Reg and Harry made their way to the car park. Harry turned to Reg, "You at the Blower sisters' joint birthday party tonight, Reg? The club will be packed to the rafters."

"Yes, I'll be there Harry. Should be a good do. There'll be plenty of fluff there tonight you'll see. Them Blower sisters have loads of mates of all ages. You never know Harry there might be a bit of old gold waiting for you to pounce. Save you keep referring to them magazines in your garage. You can't beat the real thing. Beware though Harry. I'll be on the prowl tonight myself so you may have to get behind me in the queue."

Harry didn't respond and the two club stalwarts made their way to their respective cars and left.

Reg made his way back home and contemplated the season so far. It was clear to his way of thinking that all the decisions made either by himself or engineered though committee were all correct. And who could argue with that assumption? The first team were unbeaten and were in the second round of the Brunton Cup. Furthermore, due to the exceptional weather, the club was indeed thriving, particularly on match days. All was well in Reg's world and tonight he was going to attend the Blower sisters' party. His mind wandered from cricket to the party that evening. He wondered if Eunice would be there with her husband Brian. If not, he had already made his mind up that he was going to make some kind of advance on Eunice to make her aware of his feelings towards her. All he needed was just one chance...

11
Party Night... and the Night of the Lost Keys

After having a shower Reg looked in the hallway mirror and liked what he saw. A black polo neck sweater and a pair of grey flared slacks combined with a pair of wet look loafer shoes gave him a sharp look. He contemplated wearing a grey silk cravat but decided to leave it as he thought it was a little over the top.

The popularity of Susie and Shirley Blower was evident as Reg walked in to the club. The car park was full and there were plenty of people outside enjoying the last couple of hours sunshine that the day had to offer. The sisters had selected the evening carefully and although it was a Sunday night it was a bank holiday the following day so everyone could let their hair down as there was no work.

Inside Spangles was spinning the discs as DJ for the night and although it was early on in the evening the dance floor was busy to the sounds of the summer of 1978.

Looking round the room Reg noticed that there was a lot of strangers present and also that most of them were female. This wasn't lost on several members of the first team. In particular the professional Harold and his brother Trevor who were chatting with both Blower sisters.

Susie Blower was making some enquiries into Trevor's life back home in Australia. "So, what do you do apart from playing cricket when you're back home in Australia?" Trevor took a confident swig on his lager before replying: "Well, it's a kind of dangerous job. I work as a medical assistant at the local wildlife conservation park. I'm messing with and handling all sorts of creatures from koala bears to kangaroos to crocodiles and snakes. Why, just before I flew out here, I ended up wrestling with an escaped Lesser Spotted River

Snake down in the lagoon. Was pretty tough I can tell you. Although those rascals aren't poisonous, if they get you in a squeeze, they can cause a lot of pain and injury. They can easily crush a small child or dog. I grabbed him by the throat in the end and pinned him up against a tree before the guys came along in the Land Rover and bagged him up. Got my picture in the local paper. Said I was a local hero. Although I didn't think anything of it at the time. It was kind of a natural reaction."

Trevor paused for a few seconds to allow Susie to digest his story. She was obviously impressed at his heroics. Demonstrating unusual humility for a self-assured Australian, Trevor raised the same question to Susie "So what you do for a living Susie. Anything interesting?"

Susie hesitated before almost apologetically replying, "I only work as a machinist down at the Drake Mill factory. Both me mum and our Shirley work there. We make all sorts of garments like raincoats and stuff. Pretty boring really but the money's pretty good with the bonus chucked in. There's a lot of our mates here tonight. Most of them single or divorced and on the lookout for a man."

Trevor took some time to reply. He found Susie very attractive and didn't want to spoil his chances by saying something crude and unsuitable. On the other hand, he needed to make it obvious he was interested. As the sounds of *Night Fever* continued to pump out of Spangle's speakers, Trevor spontaneously grabbed Susie by the hand and led her to the dance floor. She didn't refuse and for three and a half minutes Trevor and Susie were John Travolta and Olivia Newton John. Susie was indeed impressed.

Spangles followed this up and introduced the next tune: "Here's one for getting intimate pop pickers. A nice slow burner like the lamp of love..here's Wishing On a Star by Rose Royce!"

Both Trevor and Susie didn't hesitate to accept Spangles' invitation and were soon wrapped around each other exchanging lip to lip contact which became longer as the song played on.

Watching from the edge of the dance floor was Harold H, Trevor's brother. Like most of the male attendees to the party he was also looking for some female company and was impressed but not surprised at his younger brother's rapid progress with Susie Blower. Turning to Susie's sister as Spangles placed another classic - *Band of Gold* - on his flashing turntable rig, he asked Shirley to dance. The response wasn't exactly what Harold had been expecting as she told him she couldn't dance because she was recovering from a verruca on her left foot. Harold felt his night was doomed. However, it was then that he got what he considered the green light in his attempt to make the evening a little more intimate. Shirley squeezed his hand and whispered into his ear: "It's a bit too warm in here for my liking. How about we get some fresh air later. After the pastie and peas maybe? We could go for a ride somewhere. What do you think Harold?"

Harold thought it was a terrific idea, but it had one problem. He didn't have a car. He quickly debated his potential options. Maybe he could borrow Brain's Hillman Imp. Not exactly big enough for what Harold had in mind and hardly mechanically reliable. The suspension being regularly over stressed during Brain's daily trips to the cash and carry.

Maybe Dicky Hampton's Austin Maxi. Now there was a motor that had the desired space for what Harold was hoping for. The folding down back seats would provide the necessary room for any extracurricular movements or activities.

Skipper Iain Redwood's sporty Ford Capri came to mind and although he'd look as cool as a cucumber cruising down Market Street, it was definitely not blessed with the space Harold was anticipating he'd need.

With Reg leaving the Austin Cambridge at home he decided to ask Dicky Hampton about borrowing his Austin Maxi.

Dicky was as ever dressed very smartly in his royal blue blazer with gold-plated buttons and gold handkerchief in his jacket breast pocket. He was in conversation at the bar with Brains but broke off the conversation to speak to Harold. "Great weekend all round for the club on and off the field Harold. I thought Beaton would be a bit of a stiffer task, but the team played well don't you think?"

"For sure," agreed Harold, "If we carry on playing like this the league and cup double could be on. We've got a great team spirit and a genuine all-round team."

"Can I get you a drink Trevor?" asked Dicky. "No thanks." Came the reply. Harold decided it was now or never and asked the question. "Dicky. I need a favour mate. I couldn't borrow your motor for an hour or so, could I? You see I need to run a couple of errands and I've only had a couple of pints. I'll drive dead careful."

Dicky took a couple of puffs on his pipe accompanied with a wry smile. He knew what Harold was up to and responded, "I'm sorry Harold but I'm going home early tonight. In fact, in about half an hour's time so I don't think that'll be enough time to run your errand."

Dicky wasn't telling lies but was being a little bit flexible with the truth. He was indeed leaving a little early, but he wasn't going straight home. Within the next 45 minutes he'd left the club and had parked the Austin Maxi a short but discreet distance from Edna Pilling's house. Her husband Eric was on nights at the gravy granule factory over in Bury.

Harold decided to ask Brains about the availability of his Hillman Imp but once again got no joy as he confessed to Harold that he was driving his motor round without an MOT and wasn't prepared to take a chance.

However, Brains came up with a suggestion. "Why don't you have a word with Arthur Butterfield about using his work's transit van? I know his lad Frankie has come here tonight but as he's drinking, he's leaving the van on the car park all night. Plenty room in the van for what you've got planned Harold." Brains ended the sentence with a more than obvious wink and smile.

This seemed like a good idea to Harold who looked across the room and spotted the proprietor of the local cake shop. Arthur Butterfield was well known in the community for many charitable gestures but was also regarded by a lot of females as a bit of a dirty old man who used his gestures as a smokescreen for his indiscretions. Harold explained what he wanted the van for. It was pointless trying to lie to an old timer like Arthur, who straight away told Harold to get the keys off Frankie.

Meanwhile Reg was sipping on his second pint of Lion Bitter. He had decided he was going to pace himself early in the evening. There was one thing troubling Reg. It was almost nine o'clock and there was no sign of Eunice or her husband. This was indeed unusual. In the short time they had been members of the club the Braithwaites had never missed a social event. Eunice especially never passed up on the opportunity to demonstrate her dancing skills along with her well-toned body.

Reg was propping the bar up and talking but only half listening to the Reverend Adrian Gawsworth who was expressing concern at the fact that club secretary Charlie Mather had allowed Alf Tyson to rent the spare piece of land and old garage down near the entry to the club. He'd done this without consulting the rest of the committee. Reg wasn't paying much attention to the Reverend's concerns and lost interest completely when out of the corner of his eye he saw Eunice come through the doors.

Eunice looked amazing dressed in a silver one-piece low-cut party dress with a split up both sides. However, his joy was short lived as almost immediately behind her was Alf Tyson. Reg's heart sank as he asked himself just what was a decent lady like Eunice was doing appearing publicly with a bloke like Alf Tyson.

The very same Alf Tyson who had no scruples whatsoever when it came to the way he conducted business, who he conducted business with and more importantly the nature of the business he was in. Even to a man with Reg's questionable morals, Alf Tyson's were in Reg's opinion lower than a snake's belly in a wheel rut.

The Reverend Adrian Gawsworth once again spoke to Reg and urged him to approach Alf Tyson directly about the rental of the disused spare land and garage. "What's he up to Reg? Ask him."

Reg decided to take the Reverend's advice and decided on a polite and dignified approach as he didn't want to cause a scene whilst Eunice was in the company. He offered his hand and smiled, "Good evening, Alf. Nice to see you in the club tonight. Good to see local businesses supporting the club. How's things?"

"Ay up Reg. I'm feeling great thanks. Couldn't be better in fact. Business is good, got a brand-new Austin Princess on the drive back home and just booked a fortnights holiday in Torremolinos. I'm looking at buying another bookshop in a prime location on Market Street at the bus stop. Add to that my new health club that's just re-opened down Cawdor Street and yes, things are looking good."

This was typical of Alf. Not one thought for anyone else but himself. He was the epitome of the 'all about me' character. Reg despised Alf right down to his afro bubble style haircut favoured by much younger and trendier young men. Even more so now he was seemingly making a successful play for the affections of Eunice.

But Alf hadn't finished with his boasting and continued. "Yes, and I've just done a nice little bit of business with your Chairman Charlie. Rented the spare land and old garage at the front of the club I have. Putting money in the club's bank and also providing part time employment for local girls. Add to that the income tax they'll be putting into that blood sucking leech of a Chancellor of the Exchequer Dennis Healey's coffers and it's winner, winner, chicken dinner all round!"

Reg's mind went into overdrive as he wondered just what Alf was planning. One thing was for sure, Reg needed to know and quick. However, when he posed the question and asked him outright what he was planning, what Alf said next was completely unexpected.

"Topless Car Wash!" came Alf's reply. "It's a great idea Reg. What do you think?" With that Alf produced some business flyers. On one side of the brightly coloured piece of A5 paper were the words, "Fancy a great hand job?" This was accompanied by a picture of a scantily clad young girl in a black bikini with a bucket and shammy leather. The other side of the flyer featured a different girl in a red bikini bending over polishing the car bonnet and leaving little to the imagination. The wording on this side of the flier said: "Have a great hand job whilst sat in your car from one of our trained and qualified car wash experts…from Reliant Robin to Rolls Royce no job is too small. Call at Alf's quality hand wash on Potter Road."

This wasn't what Reg had expected. But Reg's surprise was nothing in comparison to the Reverend Adrian Gawsworth who was clearly in a state of shock.

"Why on earth has this disgusting venture been sanctioned?" Asked The Reverend. "This can *not* be allowed to take place!"

Alf Tyson was unnerved and unmoved. "What's the problem Reverend? This could lead to more people coming into the club and spending money."

"We don't want *that* sort of money coming into the club. It's money gained from the exploitation of young girls. It's downright disgusting, depraved and dirty." the Reverend retorted, almost in a state of hyperventilation.

Alf was clearly prepared for the Reverend's reaction. "See them girls on the flyers? Well, they were two selected from an applicant list of twenty four when I ran the advert in the Journal. None of them were forced into working for me. Also, I pay well more than the national minimum wage. Anyway, there's no going back now. I shook hands with Charlie the Chairman and we're opening for business next week when the first team are at home."

What Alf conveniently forgot to inform Reg was that Charlie the Chairman had borrowed £50 off Alf six months ago and used this as leverage on Charlie when he spotted the car wash opportunity. Although this meant leaving Eunice at the mercy of Alf Tyson he had to make further enquiries with Charlie the Chairman.

Meanwhile Trevor and Susie were part of a throbbing dance floor throwing shapes to DJ Spangles' selection of *YMCA* by The Village People. As the pasties and peas were being served, Trevor noticed that Susie wasn't eating. "Why you having no food, Susie?" he asked. Susie replied: "I can't eat the pastry. It gives me heartburn. And the mushy peas…well don't ask. Trouble is I'm starving."

Trevor saw a chance to get Susie on her own in more favourable surroundings where there would be only the two of them. "Tell you what Susie. We can call at the chippy and go back to mine. You won't have far to go home when we've eaten."

As the professional and his brother Trevor were living next door to the Blower sisters, this was indeed convenient. With a knowing smile and silent understanding of what was likely to happen, Susie agreed. "Let's give it half an hour on the dance floor then make a move to the chippy, I need to build up my appetite if you know what I mean."

Trevor agreed as they took to the dance floor as DJ Spangles issued a not to be refused invitation: "Come on all you hustling boys and rustling girls and step out on he dance floor of desire as me The Spangle plays for you the love master, The one and only Barry White who says he Just Can't Get Enough of Your Love. Mmmmmmm baby!"

In the meantime, Harold and Shirley had set off for a ride in the Butterfields Bakery Ford Transit Van. Harold knew the area quite well as during his first season in the UK he had managed to get a part time job driving a small truck for Hagsfords, the local timber merchant.

The van and its two occupants made its way down the local bypass and Shirley broke the silence as she stroked Harold's left leg. "Where are we going to Harold?" Harold looked over at her and smiled. "We're going to the country park at Tumbles reservoir. We can sit in the van and watch the sun go down."

It was at this point in the conversation that Shirley moved her hand away from Harold's rapidly expanding groin area and gave Harold a reply he certainly wasn't expecting. "Bear in mind Harold Haltz that the sun is the ONLY thing that will be going down. My knickers don't double up as ankle warmers. Least not on the first night. And I certainly won't be looking for the van keys if they go on the van floor. I'm sure you know what I mean. So, let's be clear about that. I don't mind a bit of a fumble but that's as far as it goes. Are we clear on that Harold? And if we do make it to the next step then make sure you bring a Johnny. I've heard all about what happened with the scorer at Minton last year. There's no way your getting your leg over with me then hot footing it back to Australia leaving me with a screaming sprog. Do I make myself clear Harold?"

Harold was shocked at the bluntness of Shirley's statement. Whatever romance or sexual advance he had planned by watching the sun going down over Breightmet in the front of the Bellamy's confectionary van had clearly disappeared. In an attempt to rescue the moment and clear his name he responded with an allegation about the Minton club scorer from last season. "I wasn't the only bloke who went with her. She was as loose as a bag of bolts. Could be anybody's kid. Anyways I have offered myself for a blood test and nobody's been in touch to arrange it. That speaks volumes in my opinion."

Shirley was clearly unconvinced. "Well it's all history now Harold. But I'm no Maureen Pollitt when it comes to hanky panky, so think on. If you want to make me and you an item just for the summer with no strings attached then you're going to have to wait a while. Let's go back to the club, my dad is going to do a speech for me and our Susie and it would be rude to miss it."

With that last statement in mind Harold knew that his plan of sunsets and sex was doomed. He wasn't too upset as he thought that Shirley had given him enough hints about what could happen very shortly if he played his cards right.

Harold started the van up and began the journey back to the club. During the ride back Shirley began to stroke Harold's leg and whilst waiting for the traffic lights to change leaned over, squeezed his groin area and kissed him on the lips for several seconds.

They arrived back at the club and Harold ordered drinks. Seeing Susie and Shirley's dad, Harold asked if he wanted a drink. Ronnie Blower was totally oblivious to Harold's request until Brains the steward reminded Harold that Ronnie was indeed as deaf as a post.

DJ Spangles was keeping the dance floor busy but, as arranged for 10pm, made an announcement.

"Ladies and Gentlemen, Boys and Girls. Could I take this opportunity to invite both Shirley and Susie up to the stage along with mum and dad to celebrate these two lovely girls' birthday!"

With that both the twins and Ronnie and Joan made their way up to the stage where a large cake had been placed with the twins' names on it.

Ronnie took control of the microphone and began to speak. "I'd like to thank you all for coming along here tonight to celebrate the twins' birthday. When we found out 21 years ago that Joan was up the duff there were lots of people who said we were daft going through with it. I'd lost my job on the council gardens and Joan was only 16. "Get rid," they told me. In fact, I'll let you into a secret. Joan's dad gave me a good hiding behind the launderette, but I never told anyone. It made me and Joan stronger. Here we are, 21 years, later still married and barely a crossed word between us. Plus, we were blessed with two beautiful girls. So, let's join together and celebrate!"

A rather hurried chorus of *Happy Birthday To You* and its concluding three cheers merged into Abba's *Take A Chance On Me,* and the dance floor quickly filled up.

Now Trevor was ready to take his chance too. Harold took him to one side and told him about his ride out in the van with Shirley. Trevor was confident he was going to have better luck in his exploits with Susie. It was no secret in male conversation around the club that Susie was a little more receptive to romantic overtures and advances than her sister, who was a little feistier.

Trevor then made a suggestion: "I think it's time we hit the chippy, Susie. What do you think? We can make a discreet exit via the back fire door and I'll meet you outside the club near the telephone box. I'll let Harold know we'll be in the house, so we won't be disturbed. If you know what I mean?"

Susie agreed. "Sounds like a plan to me. But make sure nobody sees you leaving. I'll go first. Just let me do a bit of mingling and thank people for coming. I don't want to just disappear into thin air. Keep your eyes on me and when I've hopped it give it a couple of minutes and you can follow me."

The plan went well and, sure enough, five minutes later, they met at the phone box. It was at this moment that Trevor thought his luck was really in. As he arrived, Susie pressed her lips directly onto Trevor's for at least fifteen seconds, wrapping her arms around his shoulders. Trevor was surprised but didn't disengage from the kiss. Susie pulled away and gasped, "I've always wanted to kiss a real snake catcher, and I wasn't disappointed!"

Trevor, confident in manner and reaction, was never lost for words. "That's the best neck twister I've had for a long time. You got some more of them babies in store?"

Susie laughed and linked her arm in Trevor's. "You still fancy the chippy Mr Snakecatcher? I must be honest I'm not too bothered after smelling them pastie and peas at the party," said Susie. "We could go back to your place. I've not seen it since it was done up by the builders. You could give me a tour if you want?"

This last statement from Susie definitely had a provocative undercurrent that Trevor picked up on straight away. "Sounds like a great plan!" he replied.

With the chippy idea being cancelled, they made their way to where Harold and Trevor were staying for the summer which was a semi-detached right next to where Susie and Shirley lived with mum and dad Ronnie and Joyce.

Susie and Trevor walked up the drive to the aluminium framed door and Trevor reached in his pocket for his keys. After 30 seconds he still hadn't managed to find them. "What's the problem? Can't you find them?" Trevor continued to fumble in his pockets with no joy. "Jeez..I've no idea where they are. I swear I had them when I came out earlier on."

Sensing his big chance with Susie was fading fast, Trevor proposed a somewhat desperate plan. "We're going to have to go back to the club and I'll borrow our Harold's key. He wont mind, if he knows what it's for."

It was at this moment that Trevor's planned night of passion which was, on the face of it, dying a hasty death, was thrown an unexpected and very encouraging lifeline by Susie.

"No chance!" said Susie. "By the time you've been there and back me mum and dad will be ready for home. Me dad can't spend too much time in the vicinity of Spangles Disco because of his partial deafness. He can't hear the tunes, but the silent feedback waves affect his ears. No, I've got my keys, so we'll go in mine if you're happy with that. I reckon we'll get an hour or so on our own Mr Snakecatcher. Maybe I'll turn into Mrs Snakecatcher if I look in the right places!"

With a cheeky and very suggestive grin, Susie led Trevor to the front door of the Blower household. Trevor decided to take a check on how game Susie might be once inside and squeezed her bottom as they walked up the path. "Oohh Mr Snakecatcher you are a naughty man. You won't find any snakes there will you? But you have a lovely grip!"

They entered the house and as Susie closed the door, they grabbed a quick kiss in the lobby before making their way into the front room. The room was a large one which had a large wooden sideboard/bookcase/cabinet complete with a state-of-the-art Hitachi music centre as a main feature along with a large selection of LPs. Added to that was a large fruit bowl and a row of books plus a dozen or so wine glasses.

Underneath the window was a new television which had a huge table lamp on top of it and another bowl of fruit along with several picture frames featuring members of the Blower family.

The carpet felt new and was wall to wall. A brown background with a circular tangerine and yellow hooped pattern effect. This was supplemented by a white sheepskin rug, placed with precision right in front of the wall-mounted gas fire.

"Nice music centre," said Trevor "Although I'm guessing your dad doesn't get much entertainment from it with him being partially Mutt and Jeff."

"No. You're right but me and our Shirley get our money's worth. We got it from Bennetts Music shop on Market Street." replied Susie.

Trevor enquired, "We going to listen to some tunes then? I'm sure there's something in that pile of LPs that'll put Mr Snakecatcher in the mood!"

Susie selected a record and placed it on the turntable. "We can have it on as loud as we like as there's nobody in next door and even if my dad comes home, he won't hear the music."

With that the sounds of *Too Hot To Handle* blasted out of the speakers and Trevor sat on the leather settee right next to Susie. He couldn't have been any closer if he had tried.

Meanwhile back at the club, the party was in full swing. Spangles the DJ was a master at managing his audience and had the floor full, dancing to *Night Fever* by The Bee Gees. Reg looked on as Eunice danced to the tune imperiously. It was one of the tunes that was a regular at her bums and tums weightwatchers night and as such she knew every move off to a tee. Reg looked round to pinpoint Alf Tyson's location, but he was nowhere to be seen.

Over at the bar Harold sank another pint and had a proposal for Shirley: "How's about we take a walk to your mum and dad's? They'll be here for a while yet and at yours the coast will be clear. Our Trevor's in our house with your Susie."

Shirley was remarkably receptive to the idea. "I'll tell my mum I'm going, and we'll head off home." She conveniently forgot to mention she was leaving with Harold.

Harold and Shirley made quick excitable progress to the house. As they approached the two semi-detached houses Harold commented, "Crikey Bob, there's not a light on in ours. Our Trevor must have made some quick progress. Randy sod!"

"Hmm. I sometimes worry about my twin sister's morals. She certainly isn't as fussy as me when it comes to entertaining men." Shirley then made an observation: "That's strange. The lights are on in the stairs and hallway. I'm sure we turned all the lights off before we went out."

Harold and Shirley walked up to the door and Shirley reached for her keys. Harold's heartbeat was gaining momentum in anticipation of an anticipated night of sexual gratuity despite the failure earlier in the evening whilst watching the sun go down. Shirley was still rummaging in her bag for the keys to the house but having no joy. "I can't understand it. I'm sure I had my keys. I'm guessing that dad's got a lift home while we've been walking. I'll have to ring the bell."

Harold's heart sank again, it looked like his night of passion had once again slipped away as Shirley reached for the doorbell.

Meanwhile inside the house, Trevor had come up with a plan to consummate his desires for the evening. With the lights dimmed and after offering an introductory few minutes of kissing on the settee, this would be followed by a gentle but not dangerous roll off the settee onto the sheepskin rug in front of the gas fire. A few gentle prods and rubs in the right places would then lead to a controlled removal of Susie's red jump suit and any associated underwear.

All was going to plan, with Susie down to her underwear and Trevor only his purple Y-fronts, when all of a sudden, the huge lamp residing on the top of the TV began flashing on and off. Trevor jumped up frantically, leaving Susie on the rug.

"What's with the lamp? What's going on? Is there a fire?" Susie was unusually cool and as she quickly put her jump suit on and offered an explanation. "There's someone at the door. The light on the top of the telly is for me dad when there's no one in. As he's deaf he can't hear the doorbell so when someone rings the doorbell its wired up to the lamp and flashes intermittently. Me dad can see the lamp as he always sits near the telly. Mind you I can't think who's coming round at this time of night unless mum and dad have left their keys. Let me see who it is."

"Jeez…let me get my keks on before you let anyone in…. you want me to back door it and get out the way?" Trevor replied, still flustered from the rude interruption.

Susie didn't reply and went and opened the front door. Standing there were Shirley and Harold.

"Well, you'll never guess who was planning of a night of private passion while no one was looking. It's my twin sister and your brother on the doorstep. You not got your keys Shirley?" Susie enquired with a wry smile.

"Think I've lost them out of me bag while I was dancing in the club earlier," replied Shirley.

"That's two sets of keys gone missing in one night. Really put a downer on the evening." said Susie. "Never mind, I'm sure there'll be other opportunities to get to know each other a little better."

At that moment the conversation changed as a taxi pulled up outside the Blower's home with both Ronnie and Joyce climbing out. Ronnie was clearly the worse for wear having had one too many pints of Guinness. Joyce was a little giddy but not drunk. "Been a great party tonight. Really enjoyed it, and to come home to two handsome, bronzed, six-packed Aussies in my house is almost a dream come true. Shame I've got your dad in tow!" The fact that both of the Aussies were seeking sexual solace with Joyce's daughters and not her was totally lost on Joyce as she made a complete fool of herself.

The two Australians, both clearly embarrassed, looked at each other. "I think I'm gonna call it a day. It's been a busy weekend and I'm getting tired." said Harold.

"Yeah mate. I'm gonna hit the hay as well." said Trevor as he got up off the settee which ten minutes earlier had been the starting point of his plan of seduction.

With that both Harold and Trevor walked the short distance to next door. Without speaking they both contemplated what might have been.

Back at the club the twins' party was still in full swing despite their absence. DJ Spangles was in full Tamla Motown mode as he spun *Move On Up* by Curtis Mayfield to a still full dance floor.

Reg had spent the night trying to establish some form of contact with Eunice but due to the presence of the despotic Alf Tyson, had by choice, kept his distance. Eunice had spent almost all the evening dancing to the well delivered tunes from Spangle's turntable.

Throughout the evening Reg was aware that Eunice's husband hadn't turned up. It was now 11.30pm and he still hadn't shown. Alf Tyson had left the club around 11.00pm so Eunice was now on her own. The problem was though that when she wasn't dancing, she was in the company of the majority of the female workforce of the sewing room from Drake Mill factory. This was, in Reg's opinion, a veritable nest of toxic female vipers where one misplaced comment or intention could be generated into something on a scale of a *News of the World* scandal.

As he leaned on the bar, he caught Brains' eye. "How's the till faring tonight, Brains? By the number of people who's been here tonight I reckon we'll have taken a couple of grand."

"I reckon we've gone past two grand," said Brains. "The women from Drake Mill have given the shots some hammer."

Reg felt a tap on his shoulder as he was finishing his conversation with Brains. He turned round and to his surprise Eunice was stood right next to him. "Well Reg, how are you? Are you buying me a drink before Brains closes the bar or are we in for a bit of an after time giggle? Either way, you know the slogan: I'd love a Babycham!"

With that request, Reg dug deep into his pockets and produced a 50p coin, "Look at that. Exact money. Must be your lucky drink from a lucky fella who's glad to be in your company!"

Behind the bar Brains rolled his eyes and shook his head at Reg's very obvious play for Eunice's attentions. He thought it was over the top and a tad embarrassing. Brains had three concerns as a good friend of Reg who he knew was keen on Eunice.

If she was so keen for Reg's attention where was her husband, the seldom-seen Roger? Also why did she arrive with Reg's arch enemy Alf Tyson? Finally, why did she leave it so late in the evening to make contact with Reg?

Brains smelt mischief at play. As much as he disagreed with Reg on all sorts of matters, he valued Reg as a good friend who had frequently supported him in club and personal matters. Especially when Brains' wife left him for the captain of The Brittania's women's darts team. He didn't want Reg being led a merry dance and being made into a fool by Eunice.

Dancing in the Streets by Martha and the Vandellas was the next offering from Spangles and Eunice took the opportunity to grab Reg by the hand and lead him to a bouncing dance floor which was heavily populated even at this late hour by members of the Drake Mill sewing room. All were in the late stages of intoxication as they gyrated to the bouncing sounds of the selections of Spangles.

Reg didn't make any attempt to rebuke Eunice's invitation and spent the next twenty minutes attempting to match up to her far superior timing and movements. The fact that Reg had no co-ordination whatsoever wasn't lost on Brains who once again shook his head in embarrassment. Whatever the tune, Reg did exactly the same movements. It could have been *God Save the Queen* or the North Korean national anthem. Reg would do the same moves.

After twenty minutes Reg was clearly flagging. His forehead was becoming heavily populated with beads of sweat. Although his black nylon polo neck was mildly effective at disguising most of his perspiration it was less effective in the arm pit area which song by song, gyration by gyration and dance by dance displayed rapidly expanding sweat patches. These sweat patches seemingly locked in battle with Reg's anti-perspirant deodorant that had been in applied/sprayed on several hours earlier.

Both Reg and Eunice headed back to the bar. However, Reg's request for another couple of drinks was surprisingly interrupted by a request from Eunice as the evening took an unexpected swing to the favourable. "Reg. Could we skip the drinks and share a taxi home? I'm getting tired now and don't want to be left on my own at the mercy of S and B Taxis."

Reg couldn't believe what he'd heard. Even more the situation he was now in. What an evening and (possible) change of luck. Here was an evening that started with Eunice entering with toxic Tyson and looked like ending with Reg leaving the premises arm in arm with the beautiful Eunice. "You sure about this Eunice? Do you want to get a taxi on your own or for me to drop you off on the way to mine?" enquired Reg.

"Oh no. Only order one taxi Reg. No need for two taxis when we're both almost going the same way. I can trust you can't I Reggie?" replied Eunice.

"Of course, you can Eunice. My integrity is totally without question. You want to go straight away then? If that's the case, I'll order one now." said Reg.

Reg made a quick trip to the bar and questioned Brains "Have you got a two pence piece for the phone? I don't seem to have one". Brains obliged and the taxi was ordered. The ordering of one taxi for these two prominent members of the club didn't go unnoticed by several members of the Drake Mill sewing room staff who were waiting in the club lobby area for a minibus.

Reg wasn't bothered though. In fact, he was quite happy to be seen in such glamorous company. It was certainly a boost to his ego which several hours earlier was in a state of deflation. More important was the fact that Eunice was quite happy to go home accompanied by him.

The taxi arrived and once again the driver was Jock Tuck who was still moonlighting whilst the workers at the battery factory remained on strike. Jock asked the question: "Well Reg, is it one drop off or two? Either way it makes no odds to me. My lips are sealed." Reg didn't have chance to respond as Eunice answered the question for the both of them. "That's enough of your matchmaking Jock Tuck. We'll drop me off at mine and you can drop my Reggie off afterwards at his house."

Reg was disappointed. He had thought that given his meteoritic change in fortunes in the last hour or so that he may have at least received an invite in for a coffee or indeed a nightcap of some alcoholic description. It did appear that any further luck, for that night at least, had indeed run out.

The taxi pulled up in the cul-de-sac where Eunice resided and Eunice made a two-pronged request to Reg and Jock: "Jock, whilst you're turning your car round is it OK for my Reggie to walk me up to the front door? As you can see it's a bit of a walk and I don't like walking on my own in the dark."

"That'll be no problem my wee hen. You take your time Eunice." replied Jock in a manner that Reg considered was a little too over-familiar.

With that Reg got out of the car and held the door open for Eunice to alight. Unfortunately, due to a combination of too much alcohol and all-round giddiness, Eunice made a very undignified and unladylike exit from the vehicle. This resulted in both Reg and Jock receiving a welcome glimpse of Eunice's stockings and suspenders as her dress rode up her legs.

Jock's eyeballs, already a deepening shade of pink through years of whisky abuse, nearly popped out of his head as he gazed for what seemed like a lifetime, but was actually a split second, at Eunice's exposed legs.

Reg was a little more dignified but didn't exactly cover his eyes in embarrassment. Eunice however was well aware of her indiscretion and began giggling uncontrollably before asserting some control of her balance and dignity.

"Oooh boys..what am I like? I'm not fit to be out on my own. Take me to the front door please Reggie," said Eunice. With that Reg linked arms with Eunice and walked up towards the front door. Halfway up the path Reg stopped and posed a query to Eunice regarding her husband. "Are you sure your husband will be happy with another man walking his wife up the drive?" Eunice hesitated before looking Reg straight in the eye and replying, "Reg. First of all, Roger's not here and secondly, there's a lot you don't know about us. You will in due course, I promise. Now get back in the taxi and I'll see you tomorrow. I've had a lovely evening."

Just as Reg was turning to go back down the path Eunice threw her arms round Reg and they kissed passionately for over 20 seconds before Eunice broke away and said, "See you tomorrow my Reggie, my knight in shining armour!"

Reg's mind was in turmoil. He had two options. Should he roll the dice and try and get over the front door and send Jock (and a lot of gossip) on his way, or should he be the perfect gentleman and bide his time? It was clear that Eunice had some kind of feelings for him. In a split second he decided he wasn't going to risk all the goodwill and feelings from Eunice that had suddenly transpired.

Reg turned round and headed back to the taxi. Before he got in, he blew a kiss to Eunice who was stood on the doorstep. It was a gesture that was immediately reciprocated by a smiling Eunice.

Reg got in Jock's taxi and before Jock could engage first gear he was straight on to Reg. "Blimey Reg, did ya see her sussies? She's some hot crumpet, and guess what? I'm sure she's got the hots for you mate. I saw the little snogging session before you left as well. That wasn't a good night peck on the cheek. That was an *I'm gagging for it* full blown snog. Yeah. You're for deffo well in there mate!"

Reg sat in the back of the taxi. He was only half listening to Jock as he reflected on the events of the last couple of hours. A couple of hours which had seen his stock with Eunice rise spectacularly. Why she'd even referred to him as *her Reggie* on several occasions.

The taxi pulled up at Reg's house. As he got out, he was reminded of a conversation that took place in that very same cab several weeks ago: "Hey Reg, don't forget my place on the Miss Bolton voting panel. I'll make sure I'm available!" Jock said eagerly.

"I'll bear it in mind Jock, but don't get your hopes up. Everything I'm trying to do is being sabotaged or blocked by the Reverend Adrian Gawsworth and his God squad. I'll be in touch." Reg explained.

He walked up his drive and all was good. It had been an eventful evening. He was going to get his pyjamas on and have a brandy nightcap before retiring to bed and thinking of his next move involving the lovely Eunice.

12
The Break-in

Reg didn't fall asleep straight away. He lay in the dark and wondered how he could further develop his relationship with Eunice. Maybe a weekend away in Rhyl at his sister's caravan, though that might be a bit too ambitious for a first date. Possibly a meal down at Smithills Coaching House which was a posh eating location on the other side of town. It would certainly be a better bet than Joey Bangla's Indian restaurant on Market Street where groups of young men who were eating there were instructed by a sign in the window to remove their footwear. This wasn't in respect of some Indian religious ritual, but a way of making sure the said gangs of men didn't hotfoot it from the premises without paying.

All sorts of scenarios and options went through Reg's mind before he eventually dropped off, only to be woken at 5.15am by the telephone next to his bed.

"Reg Birtles speaking. Who's calling at this unearthly hour?" Reg mumbled blearily, in an attempt to inject some sarcasm into the call.

"I'm sorry to bother you Mr Birtles. It's Police Constable Bob Gordon here. I believe you're one of the nominated committee members who's on the keyholders list down at the cricket club?" enquired the stern voice on the line.

Reg sat up straight, suddenly wide awake, "That's right officer. What's the problem?"

"Well, there's been a break-in at the club. It's a bit of a mess to be honest. But basically, we need someone to come down and make the premises safe." Officer Gordon explained. "Can you come down to the club and sort it out?"

"I'll be there in the next fifteen minutes officer. Will that be OK?" said Reg. "That should be fine," Officer Gordon replied abruptly, "but try not to be much longer. We've only got two panda cars out on patrol tonight. I'm in one of them and Police Constable Huggins has got one stuck in a ditch with a flat battery down Crommy Lodges. He's on patrol trying to stop some unsavoury nighttime activities. God only knows why the battery is flat. He must have knocked the lights on by mistake. Anyway Mr Birtles, I'll see you down the club as soon as. Goodbye for now."

As he shuffled out of his pyjama bottoms, Reg wondered about what damage might have been caused. Moreover, he hoped that the safe had been secured at the end of possibly the busiest night at the club for years.

Reg drove through the club gates and noticed there were several other committee members in the vicinity. These were also key holders and on the police alarm contact list. This included Brains, the Reverend Adrian Gawsworth, Treasurer Verity Tinkle, Charlie Mather, Dicky Hampton, and John Burrell.

Reg surveyed the damage. The doors had been pulled off the hinges by attaching a tow rope to the back of a stolen car and were lying flat on the floor. Skid marks on the grass showed the considerable force that had been used in order to pull off the doors.

Brains and Reg walked alone together inside the club. There wasn't a lot of wilful damage. The burglars had no interest in unnecessary destruction unless it came in the way of their targets. Those targets being the safe, fruit machine and cigarettes behind the bar.

Turning his attention to Brains, Reg asked glumly, "Well, give me the good or bad news. Did they manage to get in the safe?" Brains' response was music to his ears. "Yes, they got in the safe, but I've got something to tell you. Instead of leaving all the takings from the twins' party in the safe, I trousered two and a half grand, took it home in the taxi and slept with it under my pillow. It's still there now. I left about £250 in the safe and obviously the burglars took that. Lucky really as I nearly took an offer for a late coffee from Maureen Pollitt round at Heartbreak Hotel."

Reg was made up with this news. It wasn't the first time Brains had taken this course of action following a heavy bar take.

Thinking quickly on his feet Reg made some subtle enquiries to Brains. "Did the Plod see the damaged and empty safe Brains? And between you and me which other members of the committee know you took most of the takings home with you?"

Brains was feeling good about himself and gave Reg more good news: "Yes, the copper saw the damaged and empty safe and wrote it down in his notebook. And I think there's only you and Dicky Hampton know I took most of the lolly home. Although I think the Reverend may have overheard me as he was sat in trap one when I told Dicky. We were both having a squirt in the bogs and didn't realise till the Reverend pulled the bog chain. Still, I don't think he heard all of what we said as the cistern in trap two is knackered and makes a loud hissing noise."

"Have you still got the till rolls for last night Brains? Between you and me if the two till rolls add up, we can submit a claim for the total taken." Reg enquired pensively. Brains knew the direction of travel that this conversation was taking and looked at using it to his advantage. "Look Reg, I'm not party or influential in any committee decisions regarding claims of finance. I'm willing to go along with any stories, description of events or figures you submit for claim as long as you support me in my next pay rise review. The Hillman Imp's on its last legs and I've seen one of them new Lada Estates down at Grahams Lada dealers."

This proposal from Brains wasn't a surprise at all to Reg. Brains knew how to think on his feet and react to his advantage in this sort of situation.

"No problem, Brains. I'll see what I can sort out." said Reg.

This cosy analysis was interrupted by the appearance of PC Gordon who entered the bar area. PC Gordon was the epitome of the local bobby. Known personally to Reg when he'd had a very brief and unsuccessful dalliance with The Masons and by almost everyone in the town more for his out of uniform and off duty activities rather than his crime fighting skills, achievements, and innovations. He was more suited to giving out clips round the ear to potential juvenile criminals rather than solving major international crime. PC Gordon cared little for the Police promotional ladder preferring to stroll his way to retirement rather than get too involved in any difficult matters of crime.

When it came to the thorny topic of solving criminal activities, PC Bob Gordon had two stock-in-trade answers to most of the crime committed in the area. These being, "It's an open and shut case," which meant he wasn't going to spend any more on the enquiry. The other being, "We haven't got the resources," which meant (once again) that he wasn't going to spend any more time solving the crime.

In fact, during his ill-fated days with The Masons, Reg had been an accessory to one of PC Gordon's out of uniform 'crimes' when the constable took to the wheel of his Sunbeam Rapier after a heavy session at The Cumberland Club. Despite driving erratically and being followed by the police along Blackburn Road, PC Gordon was left to drive on interrupted. When Reg mentioned this the day after on the phone, he received some 'advice' from PC Gordon. "The boys in the traffic police spotted my conveniently placed policeman's helmet on the back shelf. That's a secret sign between us members of the force that a fellow PC is at the wheel and therefore won't get a pull."

PC Gordon was an ex-Grenadier Guard who in his prime stood at an imposing six foot plus. Sadly, for PC Gordon those days were a distant memory due to a combination of too much Tetley Mild and making sure his beat was undertaken from the comfort of the passenger seat of a Ford Anglia Panda patrol vehicle instead of his sweat-inducing pushbike with three speed Sturmey-Archer gears.

Completely and conveniently dismissing even basic detection methods, PC Gordon offered his solution to the problem of the break in. It wasn't a theory based on anything he might have learned from any novels of Sir Arthur Conan Doyle, let alone the Lancashire College of Detection from which he graduated some 18 years earlier in 1960.

Shaking his head, PC Gordon expanded his theory: "Looks like an open and shut case Mr Birtles. If I were you, I'd make the place secure and be firing in a claim for the takings from the bar, the one-armed bandit and the ciggies you've had stolen. I believe you had a good night last night takings wise?"

"That's right officer," Replied Reg "we're looking at almost £3000 that they got away with. Plus, a full one-armed bandit and ciggies."

PC Gordon took a sharp intake of breath and shook his head. He then posed a question: "Don't think the insurance will pay out on the one-armed bandit. Why wasn't it emptied and put in the safe at the end of the night?"

Brains replied and for once hadn't thought it through what he was going to say before replying, "It's too much trouble emptying it every night."

Reg rolled his eyes as PC Gordon laughed and said "Too much trouble! Too much trouble! It wasn't too much trouble for the burglars!"

The conversation was interrupted as PC Gordon's walkie-talkie came to life. "Ford Anglia mobile 1 to Ford Anglia mobile 2. Are you receiving me?" PC Gordon fumbled in his tunic, found, and spoke into his walkie-talkie. "Ford Anglia mobile 2 receiving. What is your position?"

Once contact had been established the conversation became a little more informal. The voice on the radio was clear and more than a little frenetic. "What's my position. What's my position? To be honest Bob, I'm still stuck in this bloody ditch. The lads at the garage with the tow truck aren't responding and this bloody park is rammed with all sorts of sexual deviants. There are more bloody flashing lights than Blackpool Illuminations. Plus, a few of them have got their eye on me - and not just the women. I tell you what Bob, I'm genuinely fearing for my life down here. How long you gonna be?"

PC Gordon waited and then offered a delayed response, "Not be long down here at the cricket club. Just tying a few loose ends up. Don't worry, they mean no harm. Mind you, they do like a man in a uniform so I'd keep the car doors locked and don't let them see your hand cuffs!"

This latest instruction from PC Gordon was accompanied with a hefty wink and mischievous smile in both Reg and Brain's direction who both offered a genuine laugh.

"Right then Mr Birtles," said PC Gordon, "I trust you can make the club safe until you get the doors properly fixed? I'd better go and rescue PC Huggins from Crommy Lodges."

With that PC Gordon made his way to his Ford Anglia Panda car and began to leave the scene of the crime. Such was his concern for PC Huggin's plight that he lit up a Players Number 6 Filter and smoked it all the way through before heading off to rescue his beleaguered colleague.

Brains and Reg made their way to the function room where the rest of the committee were gathered. Reg opened the post break-in debate. "Right, we need to get some sort of step-by-step plan of action. The front doors need re-hanging. Charlie, can you get your lad to come down sometime this morning? I'm sure he can take some time away from his council woodworking duties to come and fix the doors. Tell him there's a couple of pints in it for him." Charlie nodded his head and said he would give him a ring.

Next up was the tricky subject of the insurance claim. Reg was mindful of the fact that club treasurer Verity Tinkle was very unlikely to be party to any financial shenanigans or mischief when it came to claiming on the insurance for monies stolen. He decided that he would be totally honest and see if that approach would fall on sympathetic ears.

"Regarding the claim for monies stolen..." Reg began cautiously, "I'll be perfectly honest with you all when I tell you that, thanks to our beloved steward thinking on his feet, we are now in a position of some financial strength. You see, Brains took most of the takings home instead of leaving it in the safe. However, as witnessed by PC Gordon this morning, there wasn't a brass washer in the safe. A fact that he made important reference to when compiling the crime report which we will attach to our claim for monies lost. We have two till rolls which total together around three grand. So, I say in, front of you all, we claim for the three grand to Horrocks Insurance. If the police are happy with the claim, then what's to lose? All we need to do is gradually feed that money back into the coffers week by week. Especially as we have a few big dos coming off like the Miss Bolton Night. Three grand is a lot of money to a little club like ours. What do we think?"

It was then that this unofficial meeting took a surprise twist, with Treasurer Verity Tinkle voicing a surprising opinion. "Believe it or not - and despite our many disagreements on club policies and issues - I am not unsympathetic to Reg's take on this matter. I'm sure the police will produce a favourable report when it comes to our claim for stolen monies being submitted, However, let's not kid ourselves here. If we are to submit such a claim, then all involved must remain tight lipped. I am no fan of Horrocks Insurance Brokers as the Reverend will no doubt confirm."

Reg was pleasantly shocked, and straight away focused on the Reverend Adrian Gawsworth. "If you don't mind me asking Reverend, what happened?"

The Reverend shook his head and began explaining ruefully, "I had dealings with Horrocks Insurance Brokers last year. Remember the great storms we had? Well, they caused some of the lead on the roof of the church to become loose. However, before we had time to secure the lead, two nights later the whole lot got pinched. The church submitted a claim for stolen tiles and the proprietor Walter Horrocks turned it down. He said it was an act of God and therefore the claim was invalid. I got him to come down and see the footprints and the ladder that were still in the graveyard. I said to him that if it was an act of God, he was wearing Dunlop Wellingtons and had left his ladder in the graveyard. Why, even PC Gordon, who we are dealing with over this break-in, came to do a report and said it was an open and shut case. We had to pay for the roof to be repaired out of the new church organ fund. I was so angry at Walter Horrocks and his attitude. Therefore, I am sure that the Good Lord would look down from Heaven favourably at any contribution via Horrocks Insurance. Maybe £500 would be an acceptable contribution in the eyes of the Almighty. What do you think Reg?"

Reg delayed his response and thought about the situation. It was clear that this £3000 was being slowly carved up. First of all, Brains with his eyes on a new Lada and secondly The Reverend Adrian Gawsworth with his organ fund. He wondered if it would have been better had he been dishonest and split the cash between himself, Brains and Dicky Hampton and nobody would have known any better. In that scenario Reg, Dicky and Brains would have been a grand better off in cash each and the club would still receive a full £3000 pay out. But here he was giving concessions to others who were benefitting through his proposed dishonesty with Horrocks Insurance. This didn't rest easy with Reg who's only interest in this proposed case of grand fraud was the club itself.

However, the deed was now done, with the evidence of the decimated safe and its lack of contents being key to the claim for stolen cash.

Charlie Mather was the next committee member with a suggestion for utilisation of a slice of this unplanned financial windfall. "I tell you what Reg, the darts and dominoes teams are now competing in the Lancashire Super League this coming Autumn. Travelling to such far away exotic and unknown locations as Barnoldswick Railwayman's Club. The standard is very high, and we could do with our own flashy club darts shirts. Like the ones worn on the telly by Eric Bristow and Jocky Wilson. They'll look dead smart and give us a sense of identity. I reckon if we can have a word with Joyce Blower then she'll get some decent shirts made up with a bit of knocked off roll of fabric from Drake Mill. The girls could make them on their dinner hour. I reckon a bung of £100 between the girls involved should sort it. We'll be the smartest set of darters on the northern oches!"

Reg decided he was going to get a slice of this cash cake before it all but disappeared. As he had apparently been nominated as chancellor elect over the three grand, he made his suggestion which he knew may meet some initial resistance but was sure would meet with eventual democratic approval.

"In a couple of weeks, it's the Miss Bolton Night. Now there's room for eight candidates and to be fair we've not had a bad response. However, the winner's prize of a weekend away at my sister's caravan at Happy Valley Caravan Park in Rhyl plus £15 in vouchers hasn't exactly attracted the cream of the Bolton female species. Don't get me wrong, me and Dicky have vetted a lot of girls and will have enough contestants. However, some of the talent we've interviewed leaves a lot to be desired. I feel if we could add a fifty pound cash prize and maybe up the quality of the prize on offer then the quality of the talent wanting to enter will improve. I can speak to Terry Fiddler from Battersby's Travel and see if he'll throw in a weekend at one of his chalets at Pontins Morecambe. If it comes off it will be a double win as the roof on the caravan is leaking and there's no guarantee it'll be fixed in time. What do we think?"

Dicky Hampton voiced his thoughts. "I'm with you on that Reg. I must be honest and agree about the quality of potential contestants. The one who wanted to be Miss Breightmet had done two stretches in the nick. The last one for assault on the estate milk man when he alleged she hadn't paid her milk bill. The other who wanted to be Miss Great Lever. Well, to say she was a big girl would be an understatement of biblical proportions. She certainly knew he way to the fridge. I second Reg's idea about increasing the prize on offer."

This was an unexpected piece of good fortune. Reg and Dicky hadn't told anyone, but they were really struggling to attract quality talent for the Miss Bolton Night.

"Right then," said Reg, "We'll have a push on the publicity and get a few posters made up and put in strategic locations. We'll hit the nightclubs such as Scamps, The Neptune Club, Brando's, Blighty's, Rumblers and Copperfields. That should attract a better class of candidate!"

The sound of a car pulling up on the car park close to the entrance to the club doors prompted Reg to look through the window. It was Eunice stepping rather gingerly out of her new bright red Hillman Avenger. She was clearly still suffering from the previous night's intake of Babycham.

Despite suffering from overindulgence, Eunice (in Reg's eyes) still looked magnificent. Dressed in a tight-fitting pair of Falmers loon style denim jeans and jacket complimented with a bleach white Fruit of the Loom tee shirt under the denim jacket. However, it wasn't the jeans, jacket, or tee shirt that Reg focused on. It was very obvious that Eunice had decided to go without a bra that morning for whatever reason. She really was a sight for sore eyes.

Reg moved his eyes away from Eunice's chest and focused them onto her eyes. She smiled as if she knew dammed well what had been passing through Reg's mind and it wasn't Lion Bitter or any other alcoholic pleasure that Reg would enjoy.

"How are you this morning Reg? I'm guessing you could have done without this hassle after such an enjoyable evening. I had a lovely evening." It didn't go unnoticed by Reg that Eunice hadn't addressed anybody else but him, despite there being almost a full committee present.

"I think we're almost done here," said Reg, "time is moving on and Brains is planning to clear his beer lines and bottle up. If it's okay with everyone I'll explain about the safe to Eunice later on today. Any objections?"

With no response whatsoever the committee went their own ways leaving just Reg, Brains and Eunice in the club. Reg went into a detailed explanation about the safe and was surprised at Eunice's response. Discarding her denim jacket onto the back of the chair she had Reg almost spellbound with her lack of a bra. "Well Reg, that little windfall of three grand would come in useful for my bums and tums club. I'm sure I could increase the membership if I could acquire some more equipment. A couple of those new crosstrainer type machines would go down well with my ladies. I reckon I could get three of them for a grand. What do you think Reg?"

What Reg was thinking at that time was clearly nothing to do with crosstrainers. As Eunice presented her case for new equipment she was very active, with her boobs swinging about as she gesticulated whilst stating her case. Reg was putty in her hands and in an effort to bring him out of his trance she repeated herself. Fortunately, second time round Reg managed to absorb most of Eunice's proposal. She could have been asking for a North Korean rhino skin overcoat and Reg would have approved. The night of the break-in had indeed proved to be an unlikely source of good luck financially and, in Reg's case, significant progress in his pursuit of the lovely Eunice, but he wondered what Eunice meant when she said there was a lot that nobody knew about her and husband Brian. He had to find out...

13

Preparation - Miss Bolton Night

It was the afternoon prior to the Miss Bolton Night and several members of the committee were present at the club preparing the function room for what Reg described as 'the glitziest night that Bolton would ever see!'

Charlie Mather's lad Archie was a joiner on the council and had been presented with the task of building the catwalk for the contestants. However, the timber which was required hadn't materialised from the council yard and Reg was becoming worried.

"What time's Degsy coming with this wood Archie? Time's moving on." he enquired, tapping his wristwatch exaggeratedly.

Archie was confident in his reply: "Don't worry Reg, we can't nail Degsy down to a fixed time when he's pinching it. He'll be here before five, don't you worry."

Reg replied with a request. "OK Archie. I'll take your word for it. In the meantime, while you're waiting, can you give me a lift to get the stand-up organ out of the storeroom and place it on the stage where your uncle Maurice will sit?"

"Jesus. You're scraping the barrel using uncle Maurice aren't you? He'll be bladdered before the contest starts!" said Archie.

Archie had good reason to question Reg's choice of organist for the evening. Maurice Mather (better known as Mo) was the older brother of club secretary Charlie Mather and for many years when it came to drinking, he had been in a league of his own. It wasn't unusual for Maurice to sink anything between 12 to 15 pints of Lion bitter when he was in his pomp. Although these days his consumption was reduced as this excessive drinking was indeed catching up with him. Unfortunately, when Maurice had more than three or four pints his bladder control was minimal at best. This had led to the unfortunate nickname of *Trickle Pants* as his trouser fly area frequently displayed proof of Maurice's poor and unfortunate lack of bladder control.

Sadly, Maurice had, in the last twenty years, made no conscious effort to curb his excessive drinking which had been part of his life. Many of the members blame an incident which took place sometime in the mid 1960s when Maurice was a very promising dart player on the local circuit. However, his dart playing days were brought to an end after a drunken attempt to create a pre-bedtime snack in the form of a corned beef and mustard sandwich. During its preparation, Maurice tried quite vigorously to open a tin of Fray Bentos corn beef with the sharp metal key on the side of the tin. This resulted in a cut, subsequent loss of blood and severe nerve damage to three of his fingers. This marked the end of his dart throwing days as he could no longer grip his darts.

Maurice however had other talents. He could still play the piano and any other keyboard to a more than acceptable standard. Indeed, he had been part of the club's backing band resident trio in days gone by with Walter "Wally" Walsh on drums and Billy "Fibber" Fitton on guitar. Billy acquiring this name through his claim that in the 1960s he was instrumental in launching "some unknown bloke from Wales called Tom Jones" when he played a season at Butlins, Pwllheli in his backing band.

The days of Maurice playing the organ now though were strictly limited. In fact, Reg had approached the Reverend Adrian Gawsworth about using the church organist Gertie Thurrock who knew every tune in the Book of Psalms but understandably had no experience in beauty contest tunes.

This request for Gertie's services was turned down before she had the chance to consider the offer. The Reverend acting like some local Colonel Tom Parker. In his words he was "protecting the virtuous Mrs Thurrock from this disgusting, un-Christian exhibition of the flesh."

Therefore, with local DJ Spangles otherwise engaged and unable to provide suitable backing music, a deal was struck, involving Maurice playing the organ and getting free pints of Lion Bitter for his services.

Archie's attention was diverted as the arrival of the catwalk timber was announced and Degsy appeared in the room.

Wearing a precariously perched baseball hat which sat on hair that could only be likened to a beehive, Degsy shouted to Archie: "Come and give us a lift with this timber. I loaded it myself, but I could do with a lift as its bloody heavy and there's plenty of it."

As Archie and Reg started unloading the timber, a request for further assistance to Brains fell on stony ground with him declaring he didn't want to 'agitate his bad back.'

Archie enquired to Reg, "Where do you want this catwalk to run to and from? You need to give it a bit of thought Reg."

"I've decided that we'll have all the girls behind this screen, and I'll introduce them one by one." With that, Reg pointed to an old three-piece hospital screen on wheels which opened up and formed three parts of a square.

"You're having a laugh Reg!" said Archie, "You're not expecting the contestants to get changed behind that flimsy contraption? Knowing the type of blokes we're likely to have in the audience, one push on that screen and all will be revealed. It's nothing to do with me Reg, but I'd run the catwalk from the changing rooms through the games room past the snooker table and through the double doors into the big room. You just need Maurice to be on cue with his organ catwalk intro."

Reg looked thoughtful and rubbed his chin. "I think you're right Archie, We need the girls to be interviewed close to where the judges are sat at the front, but out of touching distance for Maurice on the organ. We need him to focus on his hands tinkling with the keyboard, not on the contestants."

"OK Archie, that sounds like a better plan. Start in the function room and use the good timber from there, working backwards towards the changing rooms. If you run out of the good timber, then there's a few pallets in Harry's garage you can finish off the catwalk with. None of the punters or judges will see the pallets."

Work on the catwalk began with Archie and Degsy putting together a more than decent effort, consisting of five by three inch timber struts plus a dozen plus sheets of plywood eight feet by four feet in size.

Reg was busy overseeing preparation work. John Burrell had put his skills as an electrician to good use and was assembling a number of strategically placed lighting towers, one of which featured a hand-operated mobile spotlight. The job of spotlight operator had been delegated to its creator John Burrell.

All was going well, and Reg decided that he would have a pint as he oversaw preparation for the big night. However, Reg's enjoyment of his pint was soon curtailed as he looked at the floor of the nearly-constructed catwalk. Stamped in bright red writing on every sheet of plywood were the words "Property of Bolton Council. No gas or electric on these premises."

"What's this Archie?" said Reg, "We can't have that on our catwalk. Turn the sheets over! One of the guests tonight is the Mayor Arnold Wetherby. Looks well if we're using knocked off timber from the council yard at a function he's attending!"

Frowning awkwardly, Archie replied. "We can't Reg. It's the same on both sides. They're used for the board ups on the houses where the absconders have left."

Reg was beside himself and beginning to panic. "Jesus, it's not just the mayor who's coming tonight, but also Felicity Drinkwater of the *Bolton Evening News* and Jeremy Temple from *The Journal*. God only knows what the headlines will be. You can imagine: *Local beauties strutting stuff on stolen rate-payers' timber* What are we going to do?" The room fell silent, apart from the sound of Tony Blackburn waffling on Radio One with Cliff Richard singing about his *Devil Woman* in the background.

Suddenly, Archie broke the silence: "Visqueen! Visqueen! That's what we need! If we can get a roll from Hagsfords we'll be fine!"

Reg was confused, not being familiar with this material and posed the question, "What the hell is Visqueen?" Archie replied with a smile: "It's obvious you're a shop floor factory worker Reg and know nothing about the building game. Visqueen is thin black plastic sheeting that comes in rolls.

It's a bit like a roll of carpet but it's black plastic. A roll of Visqueen will do the job. All we need to do is keep the catwalk straight with right angle corners and no bends in it. We can cut the right length for each section of catwalk and then staple the roll of sheeting onto the plywood. I think it'll look pretty good as well if you ask me."

Reg was worried. He looked at the catwalk and rubbed his chin. "OK then I'll trust you on this one Archie. Can you get Degsy to run down to Hagsfords and bring a roll of this stuff…whatever it may be. And get a move on. We're racing the clock here."

Archie and Degsy left the room, leaving Reg and John Burrell who had finished the lighting tower and spotlight. Reg surveyed the tower and spotlight and was impressed. Smiling, he asked John about the range of the spotlight in particular.

"It will reach the doors to the room won't it John? I want it to be on each contestant as they strut down the catwalk." As he spoke Reg walked towards the start of the catwalk and instructed John to focus the spotlight on him.

John climbed up and sat on the aluminium step ladder and switched the spotlight on. True to John's word the spotlight went right to the end of the catwalk. Reg was delighted. So much so he decided he would indulge himself in another pint of bitter.

Within 15 minutes both Degsy and Archie appeared and began placing the Visqueen on the catwalk. Once again Reg was pleased with the outcome and decided he would treat himself to another pint.

"Has Maurice arrived yet?" asked Reg, "I told him to come down this affy so we can organise the timings. Where's he gone?"

Degsy had just returned from the men's toilets and provided the answer to Reg's query. "He's sat in trap one curling one out by the sound and smell of it. Jesus, I don't know what he's been eating but I'd steer clear of the bogs for a while if I were you."

Work on the catwalk continued with Archie and Degsy doing a sterling job. "Where do you want the catwalk to finish Reg?" asked Archie. "Do you want it to join up to the stage area?"

Reg downed the last mouthful of his third pint of the afternoon and walked towards the stage area. "Yes, that's a good idea. I'll conduct the interviews to the left of the stage with the panel of judges in the middle and we'll stick Maurice and his keyboard way over on the right."

Almost on cue, the organist for the night Maurice walked into the room. He was a big chap with a big beer belly. His 60-year-old body being formed through 45 years or so of excessive drinking and poor diet.

"How's it going Reg?" asked Maurice "Are we gonna have a dress rehearsal or what?"

Reg replied: "Right Maurice. Sit yourself down and we'll do a dry run, we…."

With the words barely out of his mouth, Maurice quickly interjected and stopped Reg in full flow, "No dry run yet Reg. I'm gasping for a pint. You know the deal we struck. No room for backing out now Reg. I just need a pint to calm me nerves."

"Alright!" said Reg impatiently, "But remember, it's a big night tonight. We don't want you legless and playing some bum notes!" With that Reg went behind the bar and returned with two pints. One for Maurice and another for himself.

Reg gathered his fellow workers and began to organise the rehersal. "Right, I think it best if I announce the contestant and as soon as I finish saying, 'let's give a big club welcome to Miss Moses Gate' or whoever, you strike the organ up Maurice with a big da-da-da-da-da daaaaar. The contestant will then start walking down the catwalk as you play something like that tune they walk on to on the Michael Parkinson show, Opportunity Knocks or something similar. I'm sure you've got something in your repertoire off the telly?"

Turning to John Burrell, he gave out further instructions: "John, you get up in your bird's nest and follow the contestant all the way up the catwalk till they reach the stage podium where I'll be waiting with the microphone to carry out the interview process. Now we need a contestant for the dry run. Degsy, go to the changing room and as soon as you hear Mo on the organ strike up the entry tune, start walking down the catwalk. But walk slowly. Don't rush."

Degsy was happy to oblige, using his selection to poke some fun at Reg. "OK Reg. Seeing as it's a dress rehearsal, where's me swimsuit and high heels?"

"Very funny Degsy. Just go up the dressing rooms and wait your call…are we all ready? Everybody assumes positions."

With that instruction everybody got into position and awaited Reg's introductory prompt.

Reg then cleared his throat and announced, "I'd like to give a warm club welcome to the lovely Miss Moses Gate!" Maurice produced a perfect introductory da-da-da-da-da-daaaaaaa. Degsy started a slow walk down the catwalk right on cue, as Maurice continued the intro with a well-known tune from TV. However, Reg wasn't happy. He knew the tune but couldn't quite place it. But whatever Maurice was playing it wasn't suitable for Reg.

"Hold it, hold it!" Shouted Reg. "What's that bloody tune Maurice? We can't have it whatever it is!"

"It's the theme tune to Dr Who. You said something off the telly. Don't you think its suitable?" said Maurice slightly perplexed.

"No, I don't, and neither will the contestants. Dr Who is full of ugly monsters. The girls won't want that as intro music. Can't you think of something else?" said Reg.

Maurice took a drink from his pint and scratched his nose. "What about *Telstar* by The Tornados?" And without prompt Maurice played the intro to the tune which had been a number one in the charts some 16 years earlier.

"That's fine Maurice. Absolutely fine. Now let's re-assume positions and go again," said Reg.

Everybody got back into place and Reg made his announcement: "Introducing the lovely Miss Moses Gate… Mildred Granby!" Maurice hit the intro tune perfectly as Degsy strutted down the catwalk camping it up with two tea towels stuck under his jumper. On the lighting tower John

Burrell followed Degsy's strut down the catwalk with inch-perfect precision on the spotlight.

Reg was pleased. "Thanks everyone. All back at 6.30pm for the real thing. Maurice, do us all a favour and try and keep off the beer this affy. I know the Brittania doesn't shut, and you can get in through the back door with the not-so-very-secret knock, but try and leave it alone today."

"No worries, Reg." replied Maurice. "By the way, is that Eunice on the panel of judges? She's hot fluff for her age. She ought to be the club's entrant as she'd win it by a mile. A body like a racing snake in a nice tight bikini...there's a thought."

"You be careful with your thoughts Maurice," said Reg, "You'll be coming out in a rash. Remember when we went to that topless splash fun pool party in Morecambe a few years back on the lads trip out? You came out in a rash with your face looking like a sheet of bubble wrap. This is a respectable beauty contest with no bikinis."

Reg locked the club doors with one thought...Eunice dashing and splashing her way down Blackpool front...in a bikini...

14
Miss Bolton Night

Reg left the club at around half past four and planned to return at six thirty. Having already had several unplanned but very enjoyable pints during preparation that afternoon he was a little tired and had, as they say, 'a wobble on'. He decided that he wasn't going to cook any tea but would have a short nap in the chair and nip to the chippy about half six.

He sat in the chair and very quickly nodded off dreaming about all sorts of situations. All of them involving Eunice. Most of them in very compromising positions.

At six thirty the alarm went off. Reg rubbed his eyes and managed to pull himself out of the chair. However, he didn't feel like going to the chippy as he felt the chips would be too greasy and this would limit his capacity to drink as much as he would like.

After a quick shower Reg dressed himself in front of the full-length mirror. His sole purpose that night was to put on a good show. He was compere for the evening, and this was an opportunity to impress the lovely Eunice who was one of the judges.

Reg ordered a taxi. He stood in the lobby and hoped that the driver wasn't going to be Jock Tuck who had been pushing for a place on the voting panel.

Fortunately, the driver wasn't Jock and wasn't known to Reg. After a short quiet journey Reg arrived at the club.

As he was a little early and still a bit tipsy from the afternoon's drinks, Reg was in good spirits as he walked in the club. Seeing Brains behind the bar, he made his way over. "Evening Brains. How's things going? Have any of the contestants arrived yet?"

Brains replied, "As well as can be expected Reg. No contestants here yet. Got extra beer on tonight as I think most of the audience will be blokes. By the way, Maurice has told me he's on a free bar and has had about four pints. Is that all right?"

"I have made an agreement with him, but it didn't involve him drinking the cellar dry," replied Reg. "I'll go have a word with him. The last thing we want is Mo going all leaky at the wrong time."

The room was filling up and as Brains had correctly predicted most of the audience were men of a certain age. There was at least ninety in the room, with the other twenty or so spaces filling up very quickly. The contestants had been instructed to report to Brains who would direct them to the warmth and privacy of the changing rooms.

The room was set up well. With several rows of tables and chairs either side of Archie and Degsy's catwalk leading up to the stage area. On the left-hand side of the stage, Maurice sat down behind his keyboard. On the right-hand side of the stage there were four chairs for the judges, facing outwards towards the end of the catwalk and the audience. In front of the stage were eight strategically placed chairs for the contestants to sit after being interviewed.

At precisely eight o'clock the evening began, A blue haze of cigarette smoke wafted down the room to the background noise of clinking glasses and the mumbling undercurrent of idle chit-chat and male anticipation.

With military precision and musical timing that defied the effects of his consumption of four pints of Lion Bitter, Maurice hit a perfect *da da da da da da daaaaa* from the keyboard as Reg strolled up the catwalk in a style that Bruce Forsyth would have been proud of. Reaching the stage and acknowledging the audience's applause he completed a very camp pirouette.

Pressing his fingers to his lips Reg continued to milk the applause as he basked in the moment, bowing to the audience.

Preferring to hold the microphone than rest it on the stand, Reg began his well-rehearsed welcome: "Ladies and Gentlemen, my name is Reg Birtles, and I am honoured to be your host and compere for the evening. I'd like to wish you a sincere good evening and welcome you to what is going to become the highlight of the Bolton social calendar. In years to come, you lucky people will have the honest privilege of being able to say that you indeed were present at the inaugural contest which is sure to become the must-see event of the year. Welcome to Miss Bolton Night. Kindly sponsored by Arthur Butterfield of Butterfields Bakery. The winner will have the honour for the next 365 days of being the proud title holder of Miss Butterfields Crumpet 1978."

Pointing to where the judges were sat, Reg encouraged a round of applause for Arthur Butterfield who, without any prompting, instruction or encouragement, stood up and waved his hands above his head like a latter-day Julius Caesar would acknowledge his faithful admiring crowds.

As the applause for Arthur Butterfield died down, Reg once again took to the microphone. "Not twenty yards away, waiting in the changing rooms, are eight of Bolton's most beautiful ladies. All waiting to demonstrate to a lucky - and dare I say lustful - audience, the characteristics and charm to qualify for the title of Miss Butterfields Crumpet 1978."

The audience offered another round of applause as Reg surveyed the audience. He wanted to be able to identify any potential troublemakers. Suddenly his eyes were drawn to the far corner of the back of the room where, sitting at the top of that particular table, was taxi driver and battery plant shop steward Jock Tuck. Reg avoided eye contact but was nonetheless worried about how Jock would behave after several shots of Bell's whisky. Jock was indeed a popular man at the moment and was enjoying a free night courtesy of his workmates having secured a large pay-rise following industrial action down at the battery plant.

Reaching again for the microphone Reg continued his introduction. "Before our beauties stake their claim for the title of Miss Butterfields Crumpet 1978, I'd like to introduce our panel of judges. Looking beautiful as ever, can you give a warm welcome to one of the hardest working ladies on the committee. Please take a bow, Eunice Braithwaite..."

Eunice acknowledged a vigorous round of applause, stood up and bowed to the audience. Wearing a tight pair of leather pants and a tangerine blouse with possibly one too many buttons unopened she indeed looked very easy on the eye.

However, this round of applause for Eunice was punctuated by a shout of, "Go for it, Reg's fluff!" This call, without any doubt, emanated from the corner where Jock Tuck was sat with his pals from the battery plant. Reg looked over at this potentially rowdy bunch but, rather than make a fuss which could lead to a possible confrontation, he decided to press on with the introduction of the judges.

Reg took to the microphone again and continued. "Our third judge for the evening is a much respected not only member, or should I say, leader of our community. Please welcome our Lord Mayor the Right Honourable Mr Arnold Wetherby..."

Once again there was a comment shouted from the corner of the room where Jock and his gang of battery plant workers were ensconced. "More like the dishonourable Arnold Wetherby...what about the allegations in the Journal a couple of months back?"

Reg had to think on his feet very quickly or his glamour evening would soon descend into disaster and chaos. He was well aware of the allegations of the Lord Mayor being accused of being spotted in the sauna at Alf Tyson's recently opened 'health' club wearing nothing but a dog collar and leather lead.

The mayor had been the subject of a recent *Journal* three-page exposé regarding the comings and goings at Alf Tyson's recently opened *Rubbers Health and Fitness Centre*. His excuse that he was on an undercover fact-finding mission on behalf of the community didn't go down very well with his constituents.

Reg had anticipated that there may be a bout of barracking when the Lord Mayor was announced. During the dispute at the battery plant the mayor had made a public relations gaff by coming out in support of the plant management and stating publicly that the striking workers were already "on a good thing."

However, Reg had what he considered two aces up his sleeve. The first was a gamble in which he would threaten to call the whole thing off there and then. This would end up depriving the battery workers of viewing all the contestants. Secondly, he had appointed Archie and Degsy as doormen and crowd controllers for the evening. Archie in particular was a handy lad at six feet plus and not to be messed with.

Reg rolled the dice and gambled with his following statement. "Ladies and Gentlemen. Could we please refrain from barracking our judges who are giving their time and services for free. I have to say that should there be any further discourteous barracking I will have no option but to stop the contest before any of our beauties set foot on the catwalk."

This warning from Reg was greeted with unprompted applause and a few 'Hear, hear!' calls. The evening was back on track.

Reg continued, "Our fourth judge for the evening is a much-respected former player and member of the committee for many years. I would like you to give a warm welcome to Richard - better known as Dicky - Hampton."

A polite round of applause followed as Dicky stood up from his chair and took a dignified bow. Dressed in a royal blue blazer with gold plate buttons and canvas-coloured slacks, an immaculately-ironed white shirt complimented with a red dickie bow and pocket handkerchief, Dicky looked really dapper. As ever his pipe was placed precisely between his lips in the right-hand corner of his mouth with a constant flow of smoke rising from the pipe pot.

Dicky sat down and Reg continued: "I'd like to introduce our final judge for this wonderful event. Please give a big club welcome to our first team captain. A man who certainly has an eye for a beautiful lady, Mr Iain Redwood!"

Once again, the audience broke into a healthy round of applause. Iain Redwood was a committed one-club-man who had been at the club since his early teens and despite being offered money to play elsewhere had always stayed loyal. He was a popular man as both a social member and player. Reg's comment regarding Iain having an eye for a beautiful lady wasn't without foundation. Over the last few years Iain had indeed been leading the life of a fully qualified bachelor having had several long - and short-term - relationships with ladies who could easily qualify for the final stages of Miss Bolton.

Reg was feeling confident and boisterous, fuelled by several unplanned but very enjoyable pints of Lion Bitter during the afternoon which had only partially worn off. He wasn't drunk, but was certainly merry, and a little leery. He was, in his own mind, going to be Bolton's answer to Eric Morley and if that meant pushing the barriers, then so be it.

As Iain sat down, Reg resumed with the microphone: "Well ladies and gentlemen, it's nearly time to start. However, I'm sure you'll be interested in how our judges are going to make the difficult decision to decide who indeed is going to be crowned Miss Butterfields Crumpet 1978."

Reg paused, walked up the catwalk and explained, "We have eight beautiful contestants all from our home town. In the interests of fair play, they will be introduced alphabetically. All our contestants will walk the catwalk and then be asked the same questions by myself. When all eight of our ladies have been interviewed, our panel will retire to the sanctuary of the games room where, undisturbed, they will make a decision. If indeed there is no clear agreement, then I as compere will have the authority to delegate the casting vote. So without further ado, let's welcome our eight beautiful contestants for their pre-interview walk where they will take to the catwalk and return to the changing rooms before we have the almost impossible task of interviewing them personally and deciding who is Miss Butterfields Crumpet 1978!"

Reg reached for his clipboard and began the introductions. "From Astley Bridge, please welcome Beryl Bainbridge. From Breightmet, a warm club welcome to Karen Hilton who is Miss Breightmet. Next up is Janet Walsh who is Miss Deane and Derby. Following Miss Deane we have Penelope Singleton-Warren who is Miss Egerton..."

While Reg continued with the preliminary introductions, the contestants walked from the changing room along the catwalk and bowed before returning. With Maurice playing immaculate background music and John Burrell using the spotlight with pinpoint precision, everything was going well. Except, due to the heat in the room and a dodgy tummy, Reg was feeling queasy...

Despite this, Reg felt he would improve as the night progressed and continued with the pre-contest introductions. He really wanted to take his tie off, but felt that wouldn't be appropriate or professional.

"Next up we have Julie Codsbury who is Miss Farnworth and following Julie we have Donna Milford who is here tonight as Miss Halliwell..."

Each contestant's pre-contest walk was accompanied by polite applause as the last two took to the catwalk to Reg's introduction: "...and last but certainly not least, we have Hazel Hughes who is Miss Heaton and Mavis Tickle who is Miss Tonge Moor."

Walking towards the front of the stage, Reg continued with his contest introduction. "Let's get this show on the road as I'd like to introduce our first contestant. Please put your hands together and welcome Beryl Bainbridge who is Miss Astley Bridge 1978."

With that announcement, Beryl Bainbridge emerged from the changing room and walked slowly up the catwalk. Included in the applause were a number of shouts of "Go for it Beryl!" coming from supporters and family of Miss Astley Bridge. Another shout of "Make 'em bounce Beryl!" came from Jock Tuck's table in reference to Miss Astley Bridge's tight swimsuit and the display of ample cleavage that went with it.

It would be fair to say that Beryl was a popular female in the Astley Bridge area. Wearing a black swimsuit showing off her tidy figure and followed by John Burrell's spotlight she walked to the end of the catwalk as Reg approached.

Miss Astley Bridge was clearly no stranger to events of this nature and waved to the audience who in turn responded with welcoming applause. Reg stood next to Miss Astley Bridge and opened the conversation. "How are you this evening? Not too nervous I hope?"

"No Mr Birtles. I'm just so pleased to be representing Astley Bridge and taking part in this prestigious event." she replied.

"We're delighted to see you, Beryl. The pleasure is indeed all ours," said Reg. "Now in the interests of fair play after finding out a little bit about each of our lovely ladies we're going to ask the same questions to each contestant. So, tell us a little bit about yourself first Beryl."

Beryl confidently replied, "I'm 24, I'm single and work at Woolworths in Farnworth on the toffee, chocolate and pick-and-mix counter. I started initially as a cleaner but took the offer of promotion to the pick-and-mix counter when I was 20. It's my dream to one day take over as manageress from Mona Dougall who's been off for three months with shingles. Although I wish nothing but good health to Mona, who I know has friends here tonight." This statement brought a polite round of applause, prompted by Reg.

"Well then Beryl, here's the first of our questions tonight. Do you have any hobbies?" Reg enquired with convincing enthusiasm.

Beryl was well prepared for this question. This was due to the fact that in the changing room Reg had left the list of questions for the contestants to peruse pre-contest.

"Well, I love going to the Wrighton Stadium on a Saturday afternoon watching the wrestling. I go with me mum and we always sit near the front. Mum gets ever so nervous and has to do her knitting to sooth her nerves as sometimes she gets carried away with herself. We both love the wrestling and I know most of the top wrestlers. I have a scrap book going back to when I first attended when I was twelve. It has loads of pictures of the wrestlers."

"Have you any particular favourite wrestlers Beryl?" Asked Reg. Beryl smiled and replied, "Both me and mum love Bob Royal. He's from Bolton and always comes over and says hello. I'm the secretary of the Bob Royal Fan Club and always wear my membership badge. Except for tonight of course. I couldn't very well pin my Bob Royal badge on my cossie could I?"

Beryl giggled and continued, "In fact, for a few years mum used to have permission to go in Bob's changing room after a bout. Mum's a first aider at Drake Mill where she works and if Bob got any muscle strains in the ring he would ask for her medical expertise. I used to have to wait in the foyer having an ice cream while she made Bob feel better. She always brought a nurse's outfit with her just in case. Bob said she couldn't do first aid on him unless she had the right and official outfit on. Something to do with the health and safety my mum said."

Reg couldn't resist a chance to have a bit of smutty fun. "I believe Bert recently had a bout where he was losing but came from behind and licked his opponent all-round the ring!"

This pun drew a slight tremor of laughter, particularly from Jock Tuck's table but the punchline was largely lost on the rest of the audience, and in particular Miss Astley Bridge.

The heat from John Burrell's spotlight was clearly having an effect on Reg's head. Several times during his conversation with Miss Astley Bridge he reached for his handkerchief to wipe his brow.

Reg continued his dialogue with Miss Astley Bridge. "Well Beryl, I must say you look resplendent in your swimming costume. But I have to ask you where would you most like to go on holiday and put your cossie to good use?"

Beryl replied, "Well Mr Birtles, we used to go to Butlin's Skegness every year There was me, my younger sister Elaine and my mum and dad. But since I left school, I haven't been anywhere on holiday. Dad's been on the dole and I couldn't afford it saving on my own. That's why the first prize of a weekend in Morecambe would be brilliant. I'd take my sister with me."

Reg mopped his brow once again and continued, "Well what a lovely thought that is. They do say travel broadens the mind. To take that quantum leap from the sights, sounds and serenity of Skegness to the mysteries of a majestic, mystic Morecambe would indeed be an experience of a lifetime. A cultural experience you could only dream of…that is of course if you are indeed selected to be Miss Butterfields Crumpet 1978. Ladies and gentlemen, give a big round of applause to Beryl Bainbridge. Also known as Miss Astley Bridge 1978."

With that Reg took Miss Astley Bridge's hand and led her to one of the strategically placed seats at the front of the stairs where the contestants were all on display.

Reg continued with his dialogue. "Is everybody sitting comfortably? I hope so. Its warm in here tonight and lads…its going to get a little bit warmer as I am now going to introduce our next beautiful contestant. Ladies and gentlemen please give a warm club welcome to Karen Hilton who tonight is here as Miss Breightmet!"

Maurice hit the keyboards perfectly in time as Miss Breightmet strutted down the catwalk. A small gathering to the left of the stage voiced encouragement with shouts of "We want Kaz. We want Kaz!"

Sporting a red costume Miss Breightmet wasn't exactly the stuff of Miss World contests. She wasn't the tallest of girls and it had to be said she had an aggressive look about her. Her hair was tight to her head in an almost boyish style. A small tattoo decorated each of her shoulders. One was a dagger with the name Eddie on it. The other had four capital letters separated by dots with the acronym ACAB which stood for *All Coppers Are Bastards*. Reg took a good look at her and reasoned that Miss Breightmet could be quite a handful. He wasn't wrong….

The combination of the heat and the unplanned drinking whilst setting up that afternoon was clearly having an effect on Reg. So much so that it led to him loosening his tie.

"Good evening, Karen and welcome to our contest. How are you tonight?" said Reg. The reply wasn't the one that Reg was expecting. Speaking in an accent true to her local roots she responded.

"I was all reet till I started gettin' me ready and that bar man sneaked in the changing room as I were just tekkin' me drawers off!"

The whole room was in shock. A chorus of orchestrated booing came from Jock Tuck's table along with shouts of "out of order!"

Fortunately, Brains was anticipating this and, from his position behind the bar, delivered a response without invitation: "Before anybody jumps to any conclusions, let me tell you all what happened. The fire alarm went off in the changing rooms and I had to check whether it was a genuine or a false alarm. I publicly offer my apologies to Miss Breightmet and hope they are accepted in the spirit they are offered."

The evening was under threat of descending into chaos. Reg took the initiative and thought on his feet. Mopping his brow, he delivered a few words in a speech that he hoped would save the whole evening: "I don't know what everybody else thinks..." Reg then paused deliberately, opened his arms and offered his hands. He continued, "But I personally feel that is a genuine, from the heart sincere apology from our steward Brains. I'll add to that the fact that we've been having trouble with the fire alarms going off with no need, But I suppose the final word to accept or decline of the apology rests with our lovely contestant Miss Breightmet. Karen, the ball's in your court."

Possibly thinking she might gain some points in the final count up by exercising a degree of mercy to Brains, Miss Breightmet delivered her decision: "Aye... I suppose so. Long as he gets me a drink int' bar after't contest. No funny business though or else. Fire alarm or no fire alarm. Any hanky panky and it'll be the ambulance that'll be rucking up."

Mopping his head once again Reg decided to take his jacket off and host the rest of the evening in his waistcoat. He really felt uncomfortably hot and a little off colour. Reg resumed his dialogue with Miss Breightmet. "So, Karen. Tell me about yourself. I'm guessing you've lived an interesting life. Where do you work and what do you do for a living?"

Miss Breightmet didn't pull any punches. "I'm 25 year old and I'm on't dole at the moment. I used to work at the gas board dealing with meters but after a raid on the Withins Estate there were 54 meters that were traced back to our depot that were piping gas in illegally. It were nowt to do wi' me but they sacked the lot of us including my partner Dwayne. They said Dwayne had nicked them from the depot. Load of codswallop."

Reg quickly absorbed this information. He certainly wasn't prepared for this response and was looking for a route out of this criminal conversation. As soon as Miss Breightmet finished speaking, Reg attempted to get the dialogue back on track. "After your departure from the gas board are you looking for a career change now Karen?" The response, again, wasn't as expected. "No…I get some money off the council and social services for being the chief organiser of the estate's Single Mothers Society and Unemployed Support Group."

Reg couldn't resist and jumped in, "Withins Estate Single Mothers and Unemployed Support Group, eh? You'll never be short of members on Withins Estate, both old and young. I bet you've got your work cut out doing that job?"

Miss Breightmet wasn't fazed and despite being the subject of some fun by Reg, she then impressed the judges with what she said: "We work hard on the estate. There's a lot of poverty around and we need to help the girls at the bottom of the social ladder to bring up their kids. There are loads of young kids who fall into the trap of unplanned pregnancy and badly planned crime resulting in absent fathers in prison or AWOL and fatherless children. My sister Veronica is a perfect example of how tough it can be on the estates with three children by three different fathers and the last one of these fathers is in the nick after pinching a load of lead off the church roof..."

This brought out a strong round of applause. It was clear Miss Breightmet was a woman with a social conscience.

Reg picked up the dialogue with another attempt to lighten the tone off the evening. "So, Karen where's your dream holiday destination?"

Karen replied "Me an' me partner Dwayne would love to go to somewhere in't wild west. We both love watching cowboy films. 'E loves anything wi' John Wayne in it. I know that we'll never be able to go to the Wild West, but someone told me that Morecambe's got a theme park called Frontier Land. We'd love to go spend a load of time there if I win."

"That's a lovely thought Karen," said Reg, "There is indeed a Frontier Land Theme Park in Morecambe. I've been there myself. Just imagine two days in Morecambe's equivalent of the wild west supplemented by two nights in the heart of the entertainment metropolis of the north which is Morecambe. I was told last week that Peters and Lee are doing the season at the Pier Ballroom."

Reg then turned to the audience and said, "Ladies and gentlemen, please put your hands together for the lovely Karen Hilton who tonight is Miss Breightmet, but may leave as Miss Butterfields Crumpet 1978!"

The audience clapped as Miss Breightmet made her way to the chairs in front of the stage and sat next to Miss Astley Bridge.

Reg reached for his pint of Lion Bitter. He was indeed feeling very hot and very uncomfortable. He once again mopped his brow with his handkerchief and carried on with his introductions.

"Next up on the catwalk will you give a warm club welcome to the lovely Janet Walsh who tonight is Miss Deane and Derby." A very robust round of applause greeted Miss Deane and Derby as she strutted confidently down the catwalk in a white swimsuit. She had clearly brought along some supporters for the evening. Such was her confidence that as she reached the end of the catwalk, she gave Reg an unrehearsed kiss on the cheek. Miss Deane and Derby was clearly a few years older than the rest of the contestants. Notwithstanding that fact she clearly had taken the time and effort down the years to look after herself. Particular evidence in the shape of a healthy if artificial suntan and the extreme likelihood of an implant operation having taken place in the chest area.

"Good evening, Janet and welcome to Miss Bolton night. Please tell us all a little about yourself." Miss Deane and Derby replied confidently: "My name's Janet Walsh, I'm 28 years old and I'm the manageress of Rubbers Health Club down at Moses Gate."

Reg realised very quickly that Rubbers Health Club was indeed the location of the alleged indiscretion of the honourable mayor Arnold Weatherby. The same Arnold Weatherby who was sat not three yards away on the voting/

judgement panel for the evening. The last thing Reg and the mayor needed was a possible embarrassing situation on this big night. Rubbers Health Club was of course owned by Alf Tyson who was blamed by the mayor for this incident. The mayor said it was a huge set-up propagated by Tyson because the council, led by the mayor, had refused planning permission for the conversion of the old carpet shop into another of his chain of health clubs.

However, Jock Tuck and his pals were determined to highlight the mayor's alleged indiscretions. Shouts of "Where's your doggie Janet?" along with barking noises were heard all round the room.

Reg chose not to engage in what he perceived as mischief-making as it could develop into unwanted confrontation, possible fisticuffs and worst of all the whole topic of the right honourable Arnold Wetherby and the sauna/dog lead being resurrected by the local press.

In an attempt to move the conversation away from the tricky topic of Rubbers Health Club, Reg moved towards the safe topic of holidays. "Well Janet…although you already have a lovely suntan where's your dream holiday and have you got any holidays planned?"

"Well," replied Janet, "I've nothing planned but I was talking to my boss Mr Tyson the other day. He's setting up a new holiday business called Swappers. It's only in its infancy at the moment but he's already made some contacts in Europe. It's adults only with no kids involved. He told me that at the end of this month he needs me to go with him and meet some business contacts in Amsterdam and Ibiza. He told me a lot of business is conducted around the pool so to bring a few of my skimpy bikinis."

Realising he'd managed to navigate to what could have been a difficult exchange, Reg once again shifted the topic of conversation. "So, Janet, it sounds like you're an important part of Alf's growing business empire. Do you have any time for hobbies?"

Janet replied "My body is my hobby. I treat it like a temple and have a strict fitness schedule. I also love swimming and jogging and don't eat any junk food. I mean when I'm out and see the state of some people I despair. Alf said to me that when he gets the renovations done at Rubbers, I can start my own keep fit classes. Mixed ones as well."

"That sounds great." said Reg "It's good to see women getting involved in business. Who knows Janet. You could be on the way to being Alf's CEO."

With that statement Reg decided it was time up for Miss Deane and Derby. The last five minutes had proved to be very tricky. Reaching for the microphone he made an announcement. "Thanks to the lovely Miss Deane and Derby...could you please put your hands together for the lovely Janet Walsh."

Another round of polite if not exuberant applause accompanied Miss Dean and Derby taking her place at the front of the room. Reg thought everything was going well apart from the rowdy crowd who constituted Jock Tuck's entourage.

"And so, lets introduce our next contestant in the competition to be Miss Butterfields Crumpet 1978. Would you please give a warm club welcome to the lovely Penelope Singleton-Warren who tonight is Miss Egerton." The obligatory round of applause greeted Miss Egerton who was dressed in a leopard print costume.

It was obvious before she even spoke that Miss Egerton was a little bit classier than the contestants seen so far. Demonstrating good poise with a straight back and neck and walking in a very upright manner, Miss Egerton virtually glided to the front of the stage where Reg was waiting.

"Good evening, Miss Egerton" announced Reg, "Welcome to the Miss Bolton night where you tonight will have the chance to be crowned Miss Butterworths Crumpet 1978. Should I call you Penelope or Penny?"

"I'd prefer to be called by the name I was christened with at the Holy Catholic Church of St Stephens which is Penelope." she replied abruptly. Despite being from the same area, it was clear to even the untrained ear that she spoke in a totally different accent and dialect then any of the previous contestants. Some would call it "posh". Others would call it educated. None the less, Miss Egerton oozed class.

"Well Penelope," said Reg, "can you tell us a little bit about yourself?"

Before Miss Egerton had the chance to reply more noise came from the corner of the room where Jock Tuck and his cronies were sat. "Posh Fluff Reg…your out of yer depth now mate!" along with, "Go for it Lady Penelope. Do a Parker on him. Stick your stiletto in on him!" in a reference to the puppet character Lady Penelope from the children's TV Series *Thunderbirds*.

Before Reg could give a thought to his next move in this moment of mini-crisis, Miss Egerton grabbed the microphone from his hand. Looking over to where Jock Tuck and his gang was sat, she delivered a well thought out response. "Let's hope the energy from the men from the battery plant isn't wasted on idiotic remarks and gestures this evening rendering them short of power when they get home to their wives and girlfriends."

The audience responded with loud cheering and clapping which silenced the men from the battery plant.

Despite being the target for most of the sarcastic remarks, Reg didn't want to appear to take sides. He reckoned it wouldn't take much to light the blue touch paper and the contest to descend into a cauldron of chaos. He decided not to comment on the behaviour of Jock and his rabble, but to press on with the questioning of Miss Egerton.

"So, Penelope can you tell me a little about yourself?" "Well Mr Birtles my name is Penelope Singleton-Warren. I'm 25 years old and I live at home on mummy and daddy's farm in upper Egerton. I have a boyfriend called Percy Smitherton who is general manager of his daddy's company which is Smithertons, the BMW Dealers."

Miss Egerton paused for breath then continued. "I work for daddy on the farm principally with the horses. We have several horses that race over the jumps, and we've had a few winners this season. Also, we have a contract with Granada TV to supply the horse for the TV programme Black Beauty. It's a very physically demanding job but I love it."

"That's very interesting Penelope," said Reg. "Did you ever watch the American TV show Mr Ed? They got the horse to speak using sugar cubes. He was very funny." This pun was clearly lost on Miss Egerton who stood motionless with a blank expression.

Reg re-ignited the dialogue with Miss Egerton. "What do you do for holidays Penelope. Where's your favourite or dream destination?"

"Well," said Miss Egerton. "As we were so busy on the farm last year, we only had time for three holidays. We had four weeks at mummy and daddy's villa in Barbados, plus three weeks skiing at Chalfont's Resort in Switzerland. We also got a little bit of winter sun with a mini two week break at daddy's other villa in Tenerife."

"Sounds like you get full use of your passport!" Said Reg, who was curious as to why a lady of Miss Egerton's financial position was entering a contest that offered a weekend in Morecambe for first prize. Feeling confident and buoyant Reg pursued this line of enquiry.

"Miss Egerton, dare I ask you a question?" He held his breath and waited for a positive reply. Miss Egerton replied with a clever play on words, giggling as she spoke. "Of course, Mr Birtles…as long as it's not too coarse."

Reg took the chance he was offered and asked: "What's a girl as well-heeled and well-travelled as you are doing in a beauty contest that offers a weekend in Morecambe?"

Miss Egerton replied. "It's like this Mr Birtles. I do a lot of work helping under privileged families in the Bolton area. Amongst these people are a lovely couple called Steve and Linda Baines who have a daughter called Angela. Sadly, Angela is severely handicapped from birth and requires 24/7 round the clock attention. If I win the contest, I would not only donate the weekend in Morecambe to them but also provide them with £100 spending money plus fully qualified 24 hour care for Angela so they can enjoy some well-earned respite. Also, my boyfriend Percy will provide them with a free BMW hire car for the weekend with a free tank of petrol".

Without any prompting from Reg the audience broke into spontaneous applause with shouts of "Bravo!" and "Good Luck Miss Egerton!" coming from, in particular, the corner where Jock Tuck and his cronies were sat.

Reg let the audience continue with their extended applause and took the opportunity to wipe his brow and take a mouthful of his Lion Bitter. Despite the evening going well Reg was feeling far from well.

"What a fantastic gesture from Miss Egerton. It just shows there are indeed some decent folks in our community. However, judges, please don't let that gesture colour your final judgement of Miss Butterworths Crumpet 1978. Ladies and gentlemen will you give a warm round of applause for Miss Egerton."

Reg ushered Miss Egerton to the front of the stage to join the company of Miss Astley Bridge, Miss Breightmet and Miss Deane and Derby.

Reg continued, "Well we've reached the halfway stage and what a wonderful evening we are all having. We're going to continue with our next contestant. Would you please give a warm club welcome to Eileen Codsley who tonight is here as Miss Farnworth, hoping to become Miss Butterworths Crumpet 1978."

Miss Farnworth was obviously a popular contestant judging by the cheering that accompanied her walk down the catwalk. Tall, with genuine ginger hair, she was a very good-looking lady who clearly relied on natural good looks rather than excesses of mascara and eye liner.

Reg took control of the moment "Good evening, Eileen. Welcome to our contest tonight. It's clear you're the local girl given the cheering from the audience. Nothing wrong with that of course but can you tell me a bit about yourself?"

Miss Farnworth replied, "Good evening, Mr Birtles and thank you for that warm Farnworth welcome from all my friends in the audience. My name for those who don't know me is Eileen Codsley. I'm 24 years old and after working at Fishers Fishing Tackle and Pet Shop for six years I am currently suspended on half pay after a dispute with the new management."

Reg decided he needed to delve further and asked "Whatever for? I can't believe a lovely lady like you would be suspended. Dare I ask what's led up to this sorry situation?"

"Yes, I can explain," she replied, "It all happened when the old owner Mr Fisher sold the shop, and some new younger owners took over. One especially kept pestering me for a bit of how's-your-father. Said that if we were to keep the name of the shop as Fisher then I should wear fishnets. Kept going on about how he'd love to show me his tackle and how sensitive to touch his new rod was. But I'm not daft. I knew exactly what he meant. Well, Mr Birtles, I had enough of his fumbling around where he shouldn't have been, so I put a bag of maggots in his butty box. He wasn't best pleased I can tell you, said I was sacked on the spot, but I went to the Citizens Advice and they're fighting my case. I don't want me job back but the Citizens Advice reckon I've a good case for some cash compo though..."

"What courage!" said Reg, interjecting before Eileen's account became too letigious, "I'm sure that was a very distressing experience."

Undeterred, Miss Farnworth continued, "It used to be a lovely place to work. Mr Fisher was a real good mate of my dad's. Come to think of it, he was such a good mate to my dad that he often came round when dad was away to do all sorts of jobs for us. He was good at do it yourself and all that. I remember overhearing him telling his mates that he had been round to our house and serviced the old boiler. He often called when dad was at work and made sure mum was all right when dad was on nights. A lovely man that Mr Fisher."

Despite feeling sympathetic towards Miss Farnworth's plight, conscious of the increasing volume of giggles that were spreading around the audience, Reg reckoned the conversation needed to go in a different direction. "What do you do in your spare time Eileen?" he asked.

"Well, I do voluntary radio work for Radio Horwich. Along with co-host Boris Harris I front the agony aunt and uncle helpline at midnight till two in the morning. I don't think people are aware of all the problems that are out there. We get loads of calls. We always end the show with a new feature called *Our Tune*. It always makes me cry."

"That's interesting then. I wonder if anyone else knew you were an aspiring Majorie Proops or if there's anyone in this room who's rang you on the agony line? Not that we're asking for confessions from the audience of course."

Reg was feeling very queasy. Not only was he very hot but he was now sweating profusely, and his heartbeat was racing. He looked at the clock on the wall in the bar. Quarter past nine was the time and with half the contestants already interviewed he reckoned he was running behind by about fifteen minutes. This wasn't too much of a problem though. The pastie and peas had yet to arrive so there was no chance of the food going cold whilst the interviewing of the contestants took place.

Despite Reg feeling unwell he decided that the show must go on and politely thanked Miss Farnworth and ushered her to her seat with the rest of the contestants.

Suddenly, as Reg turned and made his way towards the stage, he lurched forward and fell onto the stage right in front of Maurice Mather's keyboard, dropping his microphone close to the amplifier causing uncomfortably loud feedback.

Maurice reacted quickly and immediately switched off the amp. Dicky Hampton and Eunice were sat in closest proximity in the judge's area and lay Reg flat out on the stage. Eunice was clearly upset and shouted to Brains behind the bar. "Brains…hurry up and order an ambulance. I think Reg has had a heart attack!"

Brains had already started dialling 999 and fortunately got an answer after three rings. Trying to stay as calm as possible, Brains gave out the answers to the pre-set questions from the lady on the phone. She assured him that an ambulance was on its way.

On stage, Eunice took control. "Degsy, Archie. Get over here and help me put Reg in a safe position. He needs to be sat on the stage with his back resting against the wall. Don't try and sit him up on the chair. He might fall over. Brains, where's the medical box? Have we got any aspirin?"

It was at this point that Maurice Mather chipped in, "Are you sure he'll be okay with drugs Eunice... he's had a few pints today. I mean he sank about four pints this affy."

Eunice replied, "We've got no option. It helps to thin the blood." Turning her attention to Degsy and Archie she supervised a controlled re-location of Reg.

Reg looked helpless but was still conscious "What's happening Eunice? How we going to finish the contest?"

"Reg, don't worry, it's all under control. I think you're having a mild, yes only mild, heart attack. I'm going to come with you to the hospital if that's okay with the ambulance man."

Dicky Hampton gave further assurance to Reg. "Try and stay calm Reg, the ambulance will be here any minute. Don't worry about the contest. That's the last thing we need to be concerned about."

The sound of the siren becoming louder by the second indicated the arrival of the ambulance. It parked up as close to the club as possible and two grey-uniformed attendants made their way to the front of the stage where Reg was propped up. After opening his shirt, they carried out some quick tests and decided that it was indeed a mild heart attack.

Without further ado they brought in the stretcher and carefully loaded him into the back of the ambulance.

Eunice climbed into the back of the ambulance and sat down. One of the ambulancemen asked her a difficult question. "Are you his wife love?" Eunice replied, "No, I'm just a very close friend. There's nobody here tonight who is family, and we are very close friends.... if you know what I mean?"

The ambulanceman looked at Eunice and decided she could come along in the ambulance to the hospital "Just hold his hand love. You'd be surprised how much that can help. Just give him an occasional squeeze. A kind of subliminal injection of a feeling of love."

Reg was still just about conscious. Eunice squeezed his hand as hard as she could regularly during the short journey. As the ambulance turned into the emergency area she gave him one last hard squeeze, looked at him, smiled returned the smile and gave him a kiss.

Reg smiled, then lost consciousness....

15

Hospital Visits, Contemplation and Future Plans

Reg was gradually coming round. His vision was blurred, and he wasn't quite sure where he was. He was aware there were several tubes coming out of his body, although he didn't know what they were actually taking out or pumping into him - chemicals or fluid-wise. Sat upright in last night's string vest and Y fronts, he felt vulnerable.

He was feeling tired and totally unaware of his surroundings and decided to close his eyes and try to re-live the last few moments before he lost consciousness. He remembered introducing Miss Farnworth and then falling over but the events that followed were all a bit hazy. Was he dreaming or did Eunice actually come to the hospital? Did she actually intimate that she was his "closest friend" in the club? Did she really travel in the ambulance with him to the hospital? Did she actually squeeze Reg's hand as an expression of love and affection as instructed by the ambulanceman?

It was a lot to contemplate in his current condition. As he wondered exactly what had happened and tried to put the pieces of this jigsaw together and make some sense of it all.

Suddenly he felt a warm hand squeeze his left hand. He opened his tired eyes and, although his vision was blurred, he soon recognised that it was the woman he had been thinking of prior to him opening his eyes in response to his hand feeling a squeeze. Eunice was sat to the left of his hospital bed and was leaning over him, smiling but not speaking.

"Eunice...Eunice..what's happened and where am I?" Said Reg. "You're in good hands Reg, at Townleys Hospital. You've had a very mild heart attack. Now stop asking questions and get some rest." Eunice replied softly.

Reg noticed that Eunice still had the same clothes on from the Miss Bolton Night. "Have you not been home yet Eunice?

What will your husband think of you staying all night in the hospital at my bedside?"

"Never mind about what he thinks. He's not at home at the moment and anyway its nothing to do with him what I do." she replied.

Even in the condition he was in, Reg thought this was a strange response from a lady who, to all intents and purposes, was in a happy and seemingly consolidated relationship.

Very quickly Reg was coming round, and the pieces of the jigsaw were falling into place. "What happened to the contest? Did everything go well? Who won? Was it a good night on the bar? Did Jock and his cronies behave?"

"Easy Tiger!" said Eunice, "Things took care of themselves. Dicky's coming down later and I'm sure he'll give you a more accurate breakdown. You stop worrying about the club. In my opinion that's the main reason you have ended up in here. Now stop worrying about that dammed place and get some rest."

While Eunice was delivering her instructions to Reg, she was joined at the bedside by a young nurse who had a badge bearing the title of Staff Nurse Burrell.

"That's the best advice I've heard today, Mrs Birtles. Let's hope he takes it on board, or he'll be in here longer than any of us want," said Nurse Burrell.

"Oh, I'm not Mrs Birtles," said Eunice, "I'm just a close friend who was at the club when this happened. He had nobody else close to him at the club that evening." Eunice paused for a moment and looked closely at Staff Nurse Burrell, "Excuse me but aren't you the daughter of John Burrell from the cricket club. Is it Christine?"

"Yes, I'm John's daughter. I used to go in the club when I was very young but haven't been in for years. I actually thought it was the same Mr Birtles from the club when he came in last night. Last time I saw him about six years ago he had a full head of hair. Centre parting and huge sideburns underneath wafty long hair. No wonder it's all fell out with the stress of that place. My dad's on the committee there but from what I hear Mr Birtles is never away from the place.

Mum keeps dad on a tight leash when it comes to that place. He was there last night, wasn't he?"

Eunice replied "Yes, he was there last night. He was operating the spotlight and did a great job." Shifting the topic of conversation quickly, Eunice offered an apology, "I'm sorry. I never introduced myself. My name is Eunice Braithwaite. I'm also on the club committee. My husband and I are relatively new to the area. We moved here about eighteen months ago from north London as my husband had to re-locate. We love the area and the club. Everybody is much nicer up north." Offering her hand, Eunice concluded her introduction, "Pleased to meet you Christine."

"Pleased to meet you Mrs Braithwaite, and I'm sorry for the misunderstanding. I must say though my mum wouldn't agree with your opinions on the club. She reckons Dad spends way too much time there even though it's nothing like the time Mr Birtles spends there. She often says the arsonists who torched the place ten years ago were bungling amateurs. They mustn't have had enough petrol or matches. Says if she'd have known she'd have gone and bought an extra gallon and some more matches from the garage and paid for them herself! For a period after the arson attack Dad was sure Mum was the secret arsonist. She actually caught him smelling her gardening gloves for petrol. They never got anyone for it. Mum was quite friendly with Mr Birtles' wife Hillary. Says she didn't blame her for running off with Barry the Bin Man."

Christine continued, "Anyway, putting the club and our opinions and feelings away, I can tell you that he's had a mild heart attack. He needs some prolonged rest until Doctor Bobb comes to see him on his rounds later today about 3.30pm. Will you be coming back today? If you are it would be better after tea from six till eight. Is anybody else planning on coming?"

"From my recollection he has no close family nearby and I can't really see Hillary pitching up and making an appearance. The last time they were in the same building was in Hagsfords Kitchen showroom when she went for him with a bathroom towel rail. Threw it at him and ended up bending it. Mr Birtles had to pay for it though."

"You're right Christine. He has nobody else apart from his friends at the club. It's a real shame he's all on his own as deep down he's a lovely guy. I'll speak to his friends at the club and see who's coming. I'll definitely be coming though. You did say between six and eight, didn't you?" asked Eunice.

"Yes, that's correct. I'm finishing my shift in half an hour and won't be here when you come back. That is unless my next shift relief nurse doesn't pitch up. I tell you the staff shortages we have to put up with are shocking. Anyway, he's in good hands and everything is under control. I'll have to go as it looks like they're having a dispute over the channel selection on the ward telly. I'll see you around in the next few days no doubt?"

Eunice smiled. "Yes, and thank you for all you have done in making him comfortable." Nurse Burrell made her way up the ward and began to resolve the TV channel dispute.

All the time this conversation between staff nurse Burrell and Eunice was taking place Reg lay motionless on the bed. Although he had his eyes shut, he was far from being asleep. Listening and digesting all the comments being made by staff nurse Burrell and Eunice.

He turned his thoughts over and over in his head. It sounded like Eunice actually cared for him, but he couldn't actually decide whether this was out of sympathy or genuine affection. It was long-time since Reg had felt the affection of a woman.

He thought about the years of effort he had channelled into the club. He reflected on the hundreds if not thousands of hours of unpaid dedication as both a player and committee man. And what did it bring? A heart attack, a divorce, and a future which at this moment was leading down a lost, lonely, and unhealthy road to a single bed in a soulless house with no company except a faded scrapbook of yesteryears and a few tins of Lion Bitter to console him through the lonely nights. All this commitment to the club also brought a messy and confrontational divorce which, by taking his eye off the ball during exchange of correspondence, had nearly left him bankrupt.

Here he was, fifty-five years old and all alone lying in a hospital bed with a heart attack to recover from. He thought to himself, who knows and quite frankly who cares what impact this heart attack would have on the rest of his life on this mortal coil? Reg felt lonely, vulnerable, and angry at himself. If the club was a person, then he would at this moment gladly punch it straight in the face.

Yes, for sure, when he was playing, he enjoyed himself thoroughly, but those days were gone and now seemed like a lifetime away. And even then, he'd suffered injuries which had cost him time off work without pay. A fact that his long-suffering wife Hillary would constantly remind him of over the years.

He opened his eyes and Eunice was stood at the bottom of his bed reading the doctors clipboard. "You awake now Reggie?" she asked. "I'm still a bit groggy but I guess I'm better off than a lot of folks in here" Reg replied.

"As I said before its just a mild attack and everything is under control. I'm not sure how long they're keeping you in mind. Doctor Bobb will be doing his rounds later on and Nurse Burrell said they were planning on conducting some tests as soon as is possible. I'm going home now but I'll be back later. I think Dicky Hampton is calling later along with Charlie Mather. Try and get some rest. I'll see you later when I've had some tea, had a shower, and got into some clean clothes. I feel dirty in these clothes Reggie."

This last statement was accompanied with a kiss on Reg's forehead and a cheeky smile as Eunice turned and headed for the exit.

Reg was confused. Why had Eunice devoted herself for the last 24 hours to his welfare? He once again thought about the strange relationship that Eunice and Roger were engaged in. If Reg was indeed Roger Braithwaite, he would be asking some very pointed questions about his wife's behaviour. Thinking of Eunice, he nodded off into a much-needed nap.

Two hours later Reg heard words from his bedside. "Is he awake or not? Reg, are you still with us?" The enquiry came from Harry Flatley who was stood at the bedside with Dicky Hampton and Mo Mather.

"He's coming round now. You alright Reg?" Reg had indeed woken up and opened his eyes.

"Am I alright? Am I alright?" Reg repeated. "I'm in hospital after passing out with a near fatal heart attack. Other than that Harry, I'm bloody marvellous!"

"Crikey Reg there's no need to get funny with me!" Harry retorted, deeply offended, "I've come to give you some support and comfort as a mate who's known you for years. I can soon go home you know. There's a good war film on ITV at seven." Harry was clearly upset at Reg's response and sought support from Dicky and Mo. "I'm right aren't I lads? We don't have to be here. I mean it's times like this when family rally round. You'd do well to remember we're the closest thing you've got to family, so think on. We're here because we care about you!"

Reg didn't think too long before replying to Harry. "I'm sorry Harry. I'm just a bit touchy at the moment. It's all been a big shock." Reg knew that everything Harry had said was absolutely right. Here he was with no blood relatives of any sort in attendance and a sure-fire bet that none would be attending apart from members and friends from the club.

Even though Reg was hospitalised and nowhere near the club, he couldn't resist making enquiries about what had transpired during the Miss Bolton Night. Turning to Dicky Hampton he asked, "How did the rest of the evening go Dicky? Did you manage to get things back on track and was there a winner?"

Dicky Hampton took on the responsibility of putting the picture together for the rest of the Miss Bolton Evening.

"Well after they carted you off in the ambulance the remaining judges took control of the evening. We worked on the principal of *the show must go on* and Iain Redwood took over as compere and did a great job. The winner was Mavis Tickle who was Miss Heaton although it was a close-run thing.".

Reg was pleased to hear this news but wanted to have a much bigger account of events. "What about Jock Tuck and his cronies. Did they behave themselves? I seem to remember they were getting a bit rowdy. You didn't have to bring Archie and Degsy in to sort things out, did you?

Dicky shook his head, "I have to say that for the large part of the evening they were a little bit boisterous. Especially during the contestants' catwalks and interviews, but that was all in good fun. The only person who got a bit touchy was the mayor Arthur Weatherby when the lads from the battery plant were winding him up over the dog lead incident at Alf Tyson's Rubbers Health and Fitness Club. You were there and saw all that though. After they took you to the hospital there was a bit of do between Jock Tuck and Brains. That was after the contest had finished though. Jock and his pals wanted a bit of afters drinking-wise, but Brains shut the bar about half twelve. Brains said he'd had a tip-off from PC Gordon about *Operation Panda Pint Purge* which is a secret police operation to clamp down on after-hours drinking. Jock got a bit confrontational but he's from Scotland so what do you expect. It soon passed. I think Brains had his eyes on Miss Breightmet rather than serving Jock and his mob. You remember? She was called Karen Hilton?"

"Miss Breightmet?" said Reg. "She was a bit rough if I remember rightly. Brains won't want to be going back to her place on the Withins Estate in his new Lada. They'll have it up on bricks before he gets into her flat never mind her knickers..." The four of them broke into laughter, drawing looks from the other visitors.

It was at this point Harry Flatley rejoined the conversation. "Speaking of cars Dicky, don't you think you'd better give Reg the bad news about his?"

Reg sat up in his bed. "Bad news? bad news? What bad news? Bad news is the last thing I want to hear when I'm reaching for the grapes in hospital. What's happened?"

"Well, it's like this," began Dicky, "The morning after the contest I was just going out to do some shopping when PC Gordon turned up at my house. He asked me if you owned a blue/white Austin Cambridge and told me the registration number. I told him that it was indeed your car and asked him why he wanted to know. He wouldn't tell me why, but he asked me where you were. So, I told him you were in the hospital suffering from a mild heart attack..."

Dicky continued, "PC Gordon said your car had been involved in a ram-raid on the *Rumbelows* shop on the precinct. Apparently the blaggers had nicked your car off the drive at your house by hot-wiring it and drove it down the pedestrian walkway on the precinct and rammed it right through the shop windows. PC Gordon reckons they got away with 20 of them new video type things plus about a dozen tellies, thieving scumbags. I called at the scene of the crime on the way in. The recovery truck was just towing your car down to Rayners scrap yard. It's a write off Reg. I'm assuming your insured?"

Reg rolled his eyes, "I'm insured with Swinton Insurance but its going through all the hassle of claiming and sorting out a new motor. I've no doubt I'll have to pay the excess on the insurance. It's all wrong. Why should I have to pay when I'm the affected one?"

Reg paused for a minute and raised another question. "Hey Dicky, PC Gordon didn't think that I was part of the criminal gang that carried out this crime, did he? Jesus, he's known me over thirty years. He knows I'm no criminal. And another thing, I'm the victim here. Where was PC Gordon and his gang of Keystone Cops when my car was being nicked and used for criminal gains? Probably trying to catch a few people having a quiet after-time gurgle rather than be out there bagging the blaggers! I wouldn't mind PC Bob Gordon isn't averse to a bit of after-time gurgling himself. When he's not on the beat he's usually knocking them back in the Brittania way after closing time."

"You'll probably have to call in at the station with your car documents when you come out of hospital Reg," said Dicky. "Have they said how long you're likely to be in for? You're going to have to take it easy when you come out. You'll have to give the ale a rest and cut down on the chippy teas!"

"I'll be alright," said Reg, "I know my own body limitations and I've managed to survive the last few years on my own."

The conversation was interrupted by the appearance of Eunice. Looking radiant in a pair of denim jeans, white Nike tee-shirt and black Harrington coat, she looked every inch a sixties female mod. "Hi everyone. How's our Reggie feeling? Have you had some rest? Has the Doctor done his rounds yet?"

Reg focused on the woman of his frequent erotic dreams and spoke in a tone that was totally different to the way he'd been talking for his male visitors. It was a tone that reached out for sympathy. "I'm feeling OK Eunice and yes, I have had a little bit of rest but still feel tired. More than anything I'm worried about my future when I get out of here." He was almost whining.

Both Dicky and Harry looked at each other with puzzled faces. This wasn't the resilient, boisterous, and master of independence Reg was portraying and promoting five minutes ago. Now he sounded hapless and almost homeless. Reg certainly wasn't fooling Dicky and Harry in his wounded animal approach. Dicky was certain that Eunice wasn't fooled either and was merely playing along with Reg's search for sympathy.

"Anyway Reg," said Eunice, "when the nurse comes round, she can get that sweaty string vest and whatever you've got on underneath that blanket off. I've bought you some new pyjamas from the Co-op. Nice cotton ones, not your cheap rubbish from Ali's stall on the market.

Reg's tale of woe was interrupted as Dr Bobb appeared with Nurse Burrell. Dr Bobb and Nurse Burrell attached some electrical leads to Reg's chest leading to a selection of electrical monitoring devices at the side of the bed.

"Bloody hell Reg!" said Mo Mather who until that moment had said nothing during the visit, preferring to watch Top of the Pops on the ward television. "You look like Frankenstein. Is he plugged in Christine?"

"Before we start these tests, we'll have to ask you to leave," said Nurse Burrell, "However, Dr Bobb will be another five minutes. So, it might be best you say your goodbyes in a minute or so."

Eunice looked at Dicky Hampton, "Look Dicky, if you, Mo and Harry go now, I'll ring and catch up with you after the tests. I'm sure Christine won't mind if I stay outside in the corridor while the tests take place. What do you think?"

"Sounds good to me Eunice," said Dicky. Turning to Reg the visitors each said their goodbyes and left.

Eunice and Reg were now alone, it wasn't the first time they'd been alone together that summer. However, the situations, times and places were never ideal for Reg to really open up to Eunice about how he felt about her. He wondered once again about the night when Eunice had told him that "there's a lot you don't know about me and Roger..." Reg desperately wanted to know what she meant, but the situations were never ideal for him to pose the question.

Many times, during his musings on the situation, he wrestled with his conscience about Eunice's husband Roger. If, and it was a big if, something did happen between Reg and Eunice then would he be no better than Barry the Bin Man who did the dirty on him?

"Reg, I want to help you get better," said Eunice. "I need to speak to you alone. That's why I've stayed and sent the rest of the lads home. We haven't got much time as Dr Bobb will be here in a minute. I need your house keys. Don't ask why. All I'm saying is when you come out, you'll need a lot of support. And there's the issue of the car insurance. Don't ask any questions. I have the right intentions and your best interests at heart. Trust me. Now, where's your keys?"

Reg didn't need to debate this offer and replied. "The car and house keys are in my jacket pocket. The alarm code is my birthday which is 2004 or 20th April. I'm guessing PC Gordon will need the car keys as proof that I'm not a teenage ram-raider."

Eunice got the keys from Reg's pocket, leaned over, kissed him on the forehead and left him wondering what the future held.

He was sure that Eunice would be part of this picture...

16
Coming Home

After two weeks of tests and observations, Dr Bobb decided that Reg was in no further danger and was indeed fit to be discharged. Before leaving for home, Dr Bobb gave Reg a thorough de-hospitalisation briefing on the dos and don'ts of post-hospital home life.

This included warnings on the dangers of unhealthy diet and too much beer which unfortunately were the two mainstays of Reg's life. After several years of living as a single man Reg hadn't mastered the intricacies of a healthy diet. Not because he couldn't, but because he hadn't even tried.

Dr Bobb finished his chat with Reg with a warning "You're lucky Mr Birtles. It could have been much worse. Now do as I say and with a bit of luck that's the last we'll see of you for a long time. It looks like you've got the love and support of a lot of friends. Especially your wife who as you know has been here every visiting slot."

Dr Bobb had made the same mistake as Nurse Burrell in assuming Eunice was Reg's wife. As pleasing on the ear as that was, Reg felt obliged to correct Dr Bobb.

"She's not my wife Doctor. She's just a very close friend from the cricket club."

"Oh right. I apologise for being so presumptive. I was under the impression she was your wife," said Dr Bobb.

"No such luck Doctor. But you'll be the first to know should things change!" Reg laughed.

Doctor Bobb left Reg waiting for his lift home. Eunice had said she would pick him up around 4pm. It was now ten to four and the time was dragging. Whilst Reg had been in hospital Eunice had been and bought him a few clothes to come home in. Included in this undiscussed clothes shop were two black thong type pairs of underpants. This was something of a shock when Reg saw them and were a complete opposite to his normal bog-standard white Y fronts in his undie drawer next to his bed. All of which had seen much better days.

Within five minutes Eunice arrived wearing a sky-blue track suit and Adidas trainers. "Well, how's my little soldier? Are you ready for the trip home?" she asked. "Ready as I'll ever be," said Reg. "Have you come on your own or is someone with you?"

"Nobody else Reggie." she replied. "They're all busy at the club. It's a big game tomorrow against Barnworth. Harry said the wicket will be like a concrete road. Whatever that means."

"I know, it's the biggest game in the club's recent history. A title decider in fact. We really need to improve after our recent form." replied Reg. In the period of Reg being laid up in hospital the team had lost two league games, been knocked out of the Brunton Cup at Morley, and been completely washed out without a ball being bowled at Northrop.

Eunice drove her Hillman Avenger out of the hospital car park and set off for Reg's house. This involved driving past the club. As Eunice turned into Potter Road, they were confronted on either side of the road with full size hardboard cut outs of young girls in bikinis holding signs. One sign had the invitation "Do you want a hand job? The other one saying, "Topless car wash tomorrow."

Reg wasn't pleased. He remembered Alf Tyson mentioning this at the recent party for the Blower sisters. As much as he despised Alf, he really hadn't the energy to make a fuss. He asked Eunice: "What's the weather forecast tomorrow Eunice?" Glancing across briefly at Reg, she replied, "Well, it's down to be a very warm weekend. I'm sure that Alf Tyson will make a killing. I'm guessing there'll be cars backed up all the way on Potter Road. Where's he actually having his car wash place Reg? Surely, he's not doing it on an open road?"

"No" said Reg "There's a spot where an old garage used to be. It's all falling into place now. Alf has got his hands on some of those full-size modesty screens with wheels from when they knocked the old hospital down. Remember, I was going to use them for the Miss Bolton Evening, but Archie changed my mind. Harry Flatley was storing them in the garage. Just wait 'til I see Harry..."

The Hillman Avenger made its way past the club which was a hive of activity in preparation for the big game the next day. Pulling up outside Reg's house, Eunice got out of the car first and straight away went for the boot to get his case of belongings. Reg tried to take ownership of his belongings but was quickly pushed away. "There's no heavy lifting for you now Reg, you need rest". She inserted the key and opened the door and led the way in. Following her, Reg couldn't believe his eyes and nose. For a man not easily impressed he was immediately amazed.

Reg wasn't an unhygienic type of guy and did his best to keep his house clean and tidy. However, he was like most men in his situation of living alone whereby the general tidiness wasn't top of the priority list and would leave something to be desired. Indeed, when Eunice first entered Reg's home in the aftermath of his heart attack the kitchen certainly needed a woman's touch. A half empty bottle of milk, a breadboard heavily populated with breadcrumbs and a frying pan that was crisp with the remnants of at least a dozen fried eggs since it had last seen the soapy Brillo pad. Add to that a nearly overflowing pedal bin and a sink full of unwashed pots sitting in murky water. A veritable breeding ground for all sorts of bacteria.

The living room was a testimony to what Reg was doing exactly before the taxi came to take him to the Miss Bolton Night. The ironing board still standing erect with a coat hanger left in the middle of the chair. This chair being a well-used member of a worn three-piece suite.

A half empty mug of cold coffee stood alone on a table which had clearly not been an item on Reg's spring, summer, (or any other season for that matter) cleaning list, given the number of ringed stains from previous drinks.

Whilst Reg had been in hospital, Eunice had certainly gone to town on Reg's home. Each and every room felt the force of a housekeeping hurricane as she hoovered in the spots generally ignored by Reg's token methods and wiped all the window boards which seldom if ever felt the force of Reg's wet flannel. No place was sacred as Eunice and her hurricane entered the ultimate challenge of Reg's bathroom.

Hung on the radiator was a bathroom towel which had been subject to at least four weeks of unbroken after shower service with a bathroom shelf which was home to a tube of SR toothpaste, a discarded toothbrush with no obvious resting place and a bottle of Hai Karate after shave.

All of these items had one thing in common. They were left in the 'as last used' position usually favoured by most men. Including the lack of tops/lids/caps.

The bath didn't need the deducing skills of Sherlock Holmes to ascertain that it hadn't been properly cleaned for a long time. The black sweat rim around the bath being a target for Eunice's industrial strength grime remover.

The toilet was no better. Separate to the bathroom in location, only it too carried all the traits of a single man's occupancy. Three toilet roll empty cardboard tubes rested on the windowsill along with two half used rolls waiting to be located on the empty toilet roll holder. An overused toilet brush lurked next door to the toilet pan. Eunice didn't need to think twice about putting this over-used item straight in the bin without an inspection. The toilet carpet had been victim to many of Reg's poor aim in nighttime visits after several pints of Lion Bitter and needed a rigorous scrub plus the installation of an air freshener for Reg's post late-night curry visits.

"Eunice," said Reg "I can't believe the work you've put in in such a short time. You truly have done a marvellous job. I could put it up for sale under the pre-text of sold as seen."

"Let's see if you can keep it as tidy," replied Eunice. "I know you're going to be pretty restricted when it comes to the more physical tasks, but basic stuff like the bin overflowing need to be kept on top of."

"I promise I'll do all I can in respect of all your efforts Eunice." Reg replied assuredly. Suddenly Reg felt a surge of self-confidence that he'd never experienced whilst in the company of Eunice. The question was how much he should chance his arm.

He weighed his options up. He could offer up a friendly peck on the cheek and during this move develop it into a full-blown kiss. He could give her a hug of appreciation which, with suggestive squeezes in the right areas could also lead to a prolonged kiss. The third option was to ask Eunice out for a meal where he could gradually explain and hopefully develop and demonstrate his feelings for her.

Reg decided to take the less risky option. He didn't want all the good feeling that Eunice had been demonstrating towards him ruined by a rushed schoolboy type grope leaving his hopes, aspirations and most importantly desires in ruins.

"Eunice," said Reg, "I'd like to show you my appreciation of your terrific efforts and take you out for a nice meal tonight. I don't mean Joey Banglas but somewhere special. Maybe Smithills Coaching House where I believe the Falstaff Room has been renovated?"

Reg realised in a split-second that he was asking a married woman out, but he didn't care. However, he did care though that he could be putting Eunice in a tricky position. Still, it was too late now. The deed was done.

Eunice paused and looked wistfully at one of Reg's team photo's hanging on the wall. Fixing her eyes on the picture and deliberately with her back to him she replied, "That would be lovely Reg, but not tonight. I have some business on at home which cannot be avoided and delayed. But I have got a little surprise for you. I know you wouldn't want to be sat in at home on a Friday night, so I asked Dicky Hampton to come and pick you up and take you down the club for a couple of pints. Only a couple mind. We don't want a reoccurrence of the Miss Bolton Night do we? Dicky's coming to pick you up around half eight so don't keep him waiting. Also, I'll come to pick you up and take you to the cricket tomorrow. I know its going to be difficult while you've got no car. That's another thing. We need to sort the insurance out so you can claim and fund another car. Don't worry, I'll be back later to make you some sandwiches for tomorrow. Oh, and I forgot to tell you there's a bowl of hot pot in the oven for your tea."

Despite his medical condition Reg couldn't be happier. Here was the woman of his dreams virtually being his unpaid maid.

"I'm off now Reg. Give me a call in the morning. Enjoy your drinks with Dicky and take it easy!"

Eunice moved towards Reg and gave him a peck on the cheek which Reg treated with respect and resisted the notion to exploit the situation.

Reg looked out of the window and waved as the red Hillman Avenger left the driveway. He wondered how long it would be before their date would take place and he would be in the passenger seat with Eunice at his side.

17
Placards, Pandemonium and Photos

After a quiet couple of pints the night before in the club, Reg slept well and got up at around half past nine. After cooking himself a hearty if not healthy breakfast he made sure all the plates and associated cookware were washed and put away. Rather this than risk the wrath of Eunice and crushing the seeds of a possible growing relationship.

He looked at his watch and decided he had plenty of time to go down to the paper shop for his usual Saturday reads. This being the *Daily Mirror* and the local *Journal*.

He entered the shop and spoke to the proprietor Frank Harland. Frank was a well-known member of the community and had been the local newsagent for many years. In fact, apart from selling the news in a wide range of broadsheets and red top newspapers, Frank was a fountain of knowledge with regard to up-to-date gossip and scandal around the town. A virtual live news feed courtesy of two sources. First of all, his paper boys who unwittingly would disclose information such as whose car was at whose house when questioned at the end of each paper round. The other source was his wife Hilda who managed Frank's laundrette based right in the middle of the estate. Hilda was nicknamed Himmler after her unashamedly interrogation methods in the search for tasty gossip.

"Morning Reg!" said Frank cheerfully, "How's it going? I hear you've had a funny turn at the Miss Bolton Night. How you feeling?"

"Morning Frank. I'm feeling a lot better thanks. Could have been a lot worse I suppose." Reg replied.

Frank was clearly working himself up to either asking a leading question or spilling the beans on some local gossip.

Reg had known Frank for many years and knew all the tell-tale signs. This included winking with his right eye in time with tapping his nose excitedly, accompanied with an 'I know something that you don't know' grin.

As Reg expected, it was only a matter of seconds before Frank released his news. What was unexpected though was the topic of Frank's beansplling.

With no holding back Frank let loose, backing his oral delivery with a waving of the week's local *Journal*. "Looks like you've made the news for something other than cricket Reg. Big picture as well!"

Reg immediately grabbed the morning edition of *The Journal*. There on the front page was the headline: *Local Ram Raid Gang On Loose*. Under that the subhead read: *Police suspect local Mr Big behind raids!* Under which there was a picture of Reg's beloved Austin Cambridge wedged firmly in the local *Rumbelows* shop window.

Reg was clearly shocked and reached inside his coat for his reading glasses. Sadly, his search was in vain and out of pure desperation, and to Frank's obvious delight, Reg asked him to relay the story, word for word.

Frank could barely hide his excitement as he read beyond the headlines.

"Well Re,g it goes like this," said Frank, "Police are warning local shopkeepers to review their existing security measures in the wake of yet another ram raid on a high street electrical retailer. The incident occurred last Friday night/Saturday morning when a gang of robbers drove an Austin Cambridge through the main shop window and made off with more than twenty top-of-the-range Sony cordless remote control video recorders. Police have named the thieves *The Austin Cambridge Gang* as in the last five raids across the area have all featured this model of car. Local policeman and spokesman PC Bob Gordon said: 'Its clear why these villains are using this type of vehicle. These older cars are made of strong stuff. If you can imagine the old Austin Cambridge being made of three-quarter inch boiler plate and some new-fangled Morris Marina being made of baked bean tin steel, then it's obvious why the Austin Cambridge is the car of choice' PC Gordon also said: 'We think there's a Mr Big behind this operation. Possibly giving instructions to the thieves themselves and selling the goods on the black market. But the local police have a message for these villains. We won't give up and we will catch you. We have a number of reliable snouts in the area and given our undoubtable crime-cracking methods it's only a matter of time before you're behind bars. Finally, we have already a couple of tips and are mounting secret surveillance operations across the county.'

Frank broke away from reading the article. "Blimey, look at your car Reg. It's a right old mess. Where were you when this all happened?"

Reg was clearly angry at the article and in particular PC Gordon's quotes. "PC Bob bloody Gordon! He couldn't catch a tortoise with a limp. Also, there should have been something saying that in no way was the owner of the vehicle in the picture anything to do with the crime!"

Frank rubbed his chin, tapped his nose and offered an opinion. "Well Reg, there could be a reason for that. Maybe they think you're involved. They can't print something that might not be true. Like I say, it's a touchy subject."

Reg was going red with anger, "Can't print anything that's not true? Jesus Christ, that's a pre-requisite for any story from that rag of a newspaper. I wouldn't believe the date on the front never mind the so-called stories. It's gone down the pan the last few years. And quoting PC Gordon is seriously scraping the barrel. I'm ringing the station as soon as I get back and I'll speak to chief Keystone Cop PC bloody Bob Gordon. You'll see next week, there'll be a quote saying the owner of the stolen car had nothing to do with the crime."

"I wouldn't hold your breath, Reg." said Frank, "By the way, it's Barnworth at home today, isn't it? Need a win to clinch the title. You going to be up there Reg after all your health issues? Although from what I'm hearing on the grapevine you've managed to recruit, shall we say, something of a Florence Nightingale If you know what I mean?"

Frank ended this statement with one of his bouts of intentional winking and nose tapping. He was of course referring to the help that Eunice had been giving to Reg during his period of recovery.

Reg wasn't for taking the obvious bait placed by Frank and gave no clues in his reply. "I'll see you up there Frank."

As Reg walked away from Frank Harland's paper shop, he kept thinking about the newspaper article. It was really chewing him up. He decided not to go home but to head to the local nick and have it all out with PC Gordon as to why there wasn't anything in the paper that cleared him of any involvement.

Reg walked up the steps to the police station. A building which was long past its sell-by date with its dirty brickwork and cracked unwashed blue-framed frosted glass windows. He stood at the tall lectern like reception desk and pressed the bell. As Reg waited, he looked around at its brick walls painted over with sky blue paint and contrasting royal blue brick pillars that emphasised the colours of authority.

The stone floor looked like it hadn't seen a mop since the days of Sir Robert Peel with enough discarded cigarette ends or 'dockers' to fill a large ash tray.

Despite the presence of a large cast iron radiator the room was damp, cold and had an unhealthy smell of cigarette smoke even though Reg wasn't smoking. The blue walls were weeping condensation in certain areas the blue paintwork occasionally broken up by signs with anti-crime or advisory messages such as *Look Out...There's a thief about,* or *Clunk Click...Every Trip*. The whole place looked and felt like something from the Victorian era...which of course it was.

Reg rang the bell once again and a member of staff appeared. A rather large matron-like female with glasses resting right on the end of her nose appeared and made her way to the lectern.

Standing behind the lectern she announced herself, "Good day to you. My name is WPC Ethel Rumble. How can the Police help you today?"

Reg replied politely, "Good day WPC Rumble. My name is Reg Birtles. Would it be possible to see PC Bob Gordon?"

"I'm afraid not Mr Birtles. He's out with PC Huggins at the

moment attending to a bit of a disturbance." WPC Rumble then diverted the focus of attention of the conversation and asked a question of Reg. "Excuse me for asking, but are you something to do with the cricket club on Potter Road? I live close by and have seen you coming and going."

Puzzled, Reg replied, "Yes I am…why do you ask?"

"Well, you see Mr Birtles that's where you'll find PC Gordon. He's supervising and co-ordinating *Operation Braless* down on Potter Road where your cricket club is."

Reg was more than surprised and questioned WPC Rumble further. "What in God's name is *Operation Braless* and what's going on?"

"Well…" WPC Rumble replied, "It appears there's a topless carwash opened that's actually adjacent to the cricket club entry on the club's land. Not only is the traffic backed up and queuing right down to the end of Potter Road waiting to have their cars washed, but there's a busload of women protesting about it with placards and signs and such. They're members of an association called BLASE".

"BLASE…what the hell is BLASE?" asked Reg.

"BLASE stands for Bolton Ladies Against Sexual Exploitation. There's a coach load of them stopping anyone who's going on the ground whether they're going for a car wash or going on the ground for cricket." said WPC Rumble, "One of the head ladies from BLASE is a committee lady at your club. Someone called Verity Tinkle."

Reg was reaching boiling point. His main objective of the visit had been diverted from hunting down PC Gordon to learning about a female picket line and an ongoing public disorder incident right on the club's land.

He decided to put his issues with the PC on the back boiler and see what he could do to rescue the situation back at the club.

His mind went into overdrive as he tried to picture the scene back on Potter Road. He wondered what the rest of the committee members were doing, pondering each one individually.

Where were Dicky Hampton and Charlie Mather? What would the Reverend Adrian Gawsworth be doing? Knowing the Reverend's moral standings and bible-thumping attitude it wouldn't be a surprise if The Reverend was out with BLASE on the picket line. What about the easy-going John Burrell? One committee member came to mind who hadn't been seen for several weeks. That being Eunice's husband Roger Braithwaite. Last of all, but most importantly, where was Eunice?

Reg had last seen her the previous evening but had heard nothing from her so far. She did promise to call him before lunch. Reg decided that he would call her at home and see what she was doing. His objective was to get Eunice round to the police station as soon as possible and get a lift down to the club.

Reg reached in his pocket for a 2p piece for the public phone. Before he had chance to make the call, WPC Rumble stopped him. "You won't be able to use the phone. The cord got ripped out at the back by some kids from some Punk Band called The Snots who we arrested last night. Not only did they break the phone, but they had some glue they were sniffing and left some on PC Gordon's chair in the charge room. That super glue is powerful stuff. Me and PC Huggins had to cut him out of his trousers. Not a pretty sight for the faint hearted. If you need a phone, you can use the station phone but leave your 2p on the desk to cover the call. You know how it is with the local authority public service cuts."

Reg followed WPC Rumble into the back office, put his two pence piece on the desk and dialled Eunice's number. After what seemed like a lifetime the phone was picked up at the other end.

"Good morning, Eunice. Its Reg here. Did you say that you were picking me up and taking me down to the cricket this lunch time?"

"Morning Reg," replied Eunice, "Yes, I did say I'd pick you up, but I have to tell you that I, like all the other committee members were called and told to report to the club by PC Gordon. I don't know if you're aware Reg, but there's a right kerfuffle going on. There's a busload of women's rights protesters turned up with placards and the like objecting to Alf Tyson's topless car wash."

"I know all about what's going on. Why didn't PC Gordon ring me?" enquired Reg, trying to hide his anger from Eunice.

"I asked him that and he said he was in the process of calling you in for questioning over the Rumbelows ram raid robbery, but he got diverted. He said he'd speak to you after the trouble at the car wash breaks up. Sounds like he's got you in the frame."

"Me in the frame? Is he mad?" Reg raged. "So, PC Gordon has got me down as a local criminal mastermind, has he? He'd be better off looking a bit closer to Alf Tyson and a few of his cronies if you ask me. Eunice, I'm down at the cop shop. Could you please come and pick me up as soon as possible? I'll explain when you get here why I'm at the nick."

"Okay. I'll be as quick as I can Reg." came the reply.

Reg left his 2p on the desk, thanked WPC Rumble and made his way out of the police station.

Within five minutes Reg spotted Eunice pulling up on the car park in her red Hillman Avenger. Reg noticed that the car was sparkling in the sunshine. He wondered if Eunice had indeed been an early visitor to Alf Tyson's Topless car wash.

Reg got into the car and fastened his seat belt. "Morning Eunice. You don't mind if we go straight up to the club, do you? I need to get things sorted out so we can return to some sort of normality if that's possible. We've got a big game this afternoon."

"That's no problem, Reg, although I must tell you that I've been down and had my car washed first thing. I wasn't planning to, but I was calling in at the club anyway taking some tablecloths back. Alf Tyson offered me a free wash. I could hardly refuse, could I? I thought of it as a way of seeing what exactly was on offer so to speak. None of the BLASE Women's group had turned up when I was there. By the way, guess who's washing the cars?"

"No idea," replied Reg, "go on, surprise me".

"Well Reg you may or may not remember her. She was the winner of the Miss Bolton night. Her name's Mavis Tickle and she was Miss Heaton. Apparently, she's a bit of a rum girl who's nickname amongst the men is *Tits Out Tickle*. She's very well-known in the area and in town. How's she's won a credible competition like Miss Bolton is beyond me."

"God help us!" Reg huffed, "As if I've not got enough on my plate."

Eunice turned the car into Potter Road and had to pull up sharply. In front of the Hillman Avenger was a queue at least 80 yards long. At the front of the queue was a police car belonging to PC Gordon. Parked on Potter Road, half on the pavement was a 52-seat Mills and Seddon coach on hire for the protestors. At the front of all this chaos, waving placards and chanting, stood around thirty to forty members of the BLASE ladies group.

Reg decided he couldn't sit in the car and wait. "Excuse me Eunice but I have to go and see what the hell's going on. It looks like chaos is the order of the day. We've got a title-deciding cricket match supposed to be starting soon."

With that parting remark Reg made his way up Potter Road. As he walked past a brown Austin Allegro, someone who was well known to Reg grabbed his attention. It was Lee Hutton. A member of the Barnworth team. Lee was well known on the cricket circuit and aside from being a more than useful off-spin bowler and middle order hitter, wasn't backward at coming forward with his opinions. These opinions were usually delivered in a dry, sarcastic context. In short Lee didn't suffer fools.

"Eh up Reg!" said Lee, "Are they going to let me park on the ground or have I go to pay a quid to get me car sponged down by *Tits Out Tickle*? I wouldn't mind, but nearly everyone in Bolton has seen Mavis' Jaffas at some time or other!"

Reg was flustered and quickly replied, "Hi Lee. It's nothing of the club's doing this, but don't worry I'm on my way to see PC Gordon and sort it out. You'll be on the ground shortly. Just be patient please Lee."

Making his way up the queue, Reg spotted who he considered to be the villain of the piece: Alf Tyson. Alf also spotted Reg and they came together at the front of the queue that had now become longer thanks to the slowing down of the traffic by the BLASE women.

Alf was blunt and to the point, directing his anger at Reg: "Now then Reg, if you don't get these dammed women from the gates of this club they'll all be getting a free less than topless fully clothed rinse off my car wash girls."

"These women are nothing to do with me!" replied Reg, "I had no idea they were coming. Let me speak to them to see if we can come to some agreement."

Alf wasn't happy and replied in a forceful manner "Agreement? Agreement? There's only one agreement in place here and that's the agreement I struck up with your secretary Charlie Mather whereby I donated £50 to charity for the rent or hire of this piece of land for any two weekends."

At this point PC Gordon appeared and walked over to Reg. He was looking very harassed and had been speaking into his two-way walkie-talkie radio.

"Look Reg, I don't know what you're going to do or how you're going to do it but we need to ease this traffic and quickly. If we're not careful we'll have the jam butty squad pitching up and sticking their noses in and making it a major crime scene."

"Jam butty squad?" said Reg, "Who and what are the jam butty squad?"

"The motor squad in the white three litre Capris with an orange stripe down each side of the motor," said PC Gordon "All flashing blue lights and screeching tyres. Flash gits all of them if you ask me. They chuck them cars around like they're auditioning for The Sweeney!"

At this point Reg's attention was diverted by someone else who he had a current issue with. Taking photos of everything that was taking place was Dave Buckley. Dave was the self-acclaimed head photographer from *The Journal*. The very same photographer who had photographed and printed Reg's Austin Cambridge in *Rumbelows* shop window.

Reg shouted over to Dave. "Hey Dave. Ease up on the photos, will you? Who gave you the heads up that this was going to happen? Someone must have been in the know and let you in on the secret, so who was it?"

"Well Reg I'll let you into a secret," said Dave, "one of our people at the Journal is also a member of your cricket club committee and is also the head woman of the BLASE group."

"I know Verity Tinkle is one of the head members of the BLASE group and on our club committee, However, I wasn't aware she also worked for the Journal. What does she do?" enquired a very curious Reg.

"Well," said Norman, "She's our resident Agony Aunt who goes under the title of Dear Jennifer on our problem page. She doesn't like anyone knowing especially as she's been stood down for a few weeks pending an investigation into some advice she gave which led to a bloke losing it and setting fire to his neighbour's coal shed. I bet you didn't know that did you Reg? PC Gordon is heading the investigation."

"Blimey. You never know do you. Mind you I'm not surprised. I wouldn't be surprised if her God-fearing bible bashing sidekick Reverend Adrian Gawsworth isn't in on the agony aunt act somewhere."

The sound of honking car horns from impatient drivers either waiting for the carwash or being fed up being in the queue was building. Reg knew he had to act quickly. He walked over to speak to Verity Tinkle who was stood at the front of the picket line. He thought he'd use his newfound information about her to his advantage.

"Verity," said Reg, "I understand the point you are making. Don't forget, despite the differences between me and you, I'm no friend of Alf Tyson. However, I'm asking you, in the interests of the club, to call off the protest and let the cricket take place. Its only 45 minutes to the start of play. If I have a word with Alf and ask him to shut the car wash down in a couple of hours, will you call it off? If you can't call it off, I might be writing to Dear Jennifer for some advice…if you know what I mean? After all we wouldn't want the coal shed to catch fire, would we?"

Verity was visually shocked about Reg's knowledge of her alter-ego. "Who told you about that? Don't believe everything you get told. I've got a top Manchester solicitor on the case and he says I've no case to answer!" she said. "Whoa, whoa Verity!" replied Reg, "Nobody but me knows about your problem page and, to be quite honest with you, I've no intention of exposing you to all and sundry. All I'm asking is to gather your ladies together, tell them they've made their point, and it would be in the long-term interests of the BLASE group if they created some goodwill by calling off the picket."

Verity looked round at her group of ladies, gestured for them to gather round and began to speak: "Fellow members of BLASE. May I thank you all for attending and participating in this historic event in our town. We have shown the sleazebags of Bolton that there is no place in a civilised society for exploitation of women. We have made our point, and our work is done. I have been given an assurance that the car wash will return to fully clothed sponge ladies at 2pm. Gather up your placards and banners and prepare for our next challenge. Well done ladies!"

As instructed by Verity, the ladies made their way back to the bus and the car queue on Potter Road began to ease. As the bus departed, Alf Tyson walked over to Reg. "I don't know what you've said or done Reg, but thanks anyway. Who the hell is that Verity woman? She's Bolton's equivalent to Mary Whitehouse. I was reading the other day they've erected a statue in her hometown of Nuneaton. I'll bet that's the only erection she's ever approved of!"

"Its OK Alf. Just make sure the girls' boobs aren't bouncing around after two o'clock or we'll likely get a thunderbolt from God, ordered of course by the Reverend Adrian Gawsworth. On a serious note, though Alf, you should make a killing today with the weather forecast being hot and sunny all day." Reg nudged Alf, almost smiling, He still detested the man, but was just relieved he had managed to salvage the big match.

"I can live with that Reg," said Alf. "I should have made a decent butty by then. I'll buy you a pint in the club when I'm in."

All of a sudden, a car and driver familiar to many of the club members appeared from behind the screens. The vehicle was a grey VW Beetle. Its driver, smiling like a cat who'd got the cream, was groundsman Harry Flatley. Winding the window down on the Beetle, Harry looked apologetically at Reg and offered an explanation which was weak at best, "Just a bit of market research Reg. I'm sure you understand."

PC Gordon was next on the scene. He drove onto the club and parked his Ford Anglia panda car at the side of the carwash and spoke to Reg.

"I need to see you down the station Reg. It's about your motor being involved in the Rumbelows ramraid the other night. We need to take your fingerprints and get the boys down at the lab on forensics on the job. This is the fourth job the Austin Cambridge Gang have done in the last six weeks. The Superintendent is doing his nut. We need to make some progress and identify the Mr Big who's masterminding the whole operation."

"Fingerprints?" said Reg, aghast, "My fingerprints are bound to be all over the car. I've had it for five years. Doesn't mean I'm the head kiddy of the Austin Cambridge Gang, does it?" Reg was understandably angry.

"No-one's saying your in on the action Reg," said PC Gordon, "it's just a process of elimination we use in our crime-busting methods. We have to compare them with other fingerprints on the car. Although there was an old tea towel in the car that might have been used by the villains to avoid any prints. We'll have to see. Can you come down the station this afternoon?"

"Can't we make it tomorrow? I've missed three weeks of cricket and want to see the lads get back on track." Reg pleaded. "This is the biggest local derby we've had for years. Win this and we're the champions and the title will be in our hands."

PC Gordon rubbed his chin and gave Reg's proposal some thought. "I don't suppose that another twelve hours is going to make any difference. Anyway, I'm on early 6-2 shift this week starting today and don't want to get stuck down the station after two this afternoon. I've joined the Bury Birdwatchers Club and we're at Stoneleigh Brew tonight observing the birds. As the police psychologists say, in these serious days of spiralling crime, every Bobby needs his hobby!"

"I'll pop down around eleven then?" said Reg, "That'll give you plenty time to nip out to the Blue Café for a Belly Buster."

"That's fine Reg. Can't crack crime on an empty belly!" replied PC Gordon as he rubbed his stomach vigorously. "Even Sherlock Holmes was partial to a bacon butty!" Reg wasn't in the mood to question the validity of PC Gordon's last statement.

As Bob made his way to the Ford Anglia Panda, Alf Tyson caught his attention. "PC Gordon, that Ford Anglia looks like it could do with a wash, rinse, and a go from the magic hands and sponges of Mavis and the girls. What do you think? A freebie of course all in the interest of creating good feelings and police/local business relationships. No strings attached you understand?"

PC Gordon was never one to miss out on a freebie. Especially if it involved a couple of topless women. However, he weighed up the pros and cons in his mind and decided a polite but reluctant refusal would be the best decision. The last thing he needed was an investigation into dodgy behaviour and coercion between himself and a murky character like Alf Tyson who allegedly operated on the fringes of the local criminal fraternity.

No, PC Bob Gordon wasn't going to put twenty-nine years of service and his huge pension pot at stake just for the sake of a titillating topless car wash.

"Thanks for the offer, Alf but I'm afraid I can't take you up on it. All the cars and vans have to use the car wash at Billy Street's car sales. We're under contract in a deal struck up between Billy and the Superintendent."

Alf laughed. "I wondered why the Super's missus car always looks clean and shiny. Not much chance of any business off her."

With the departure of the BLASE ladies and the easing of the traffic, PC Gordon squeezed his body into the Ford Anglia Panda and left.

Almost as soon as he left, Eunice drove up and spoke to Reg and Alf. "Everything all cooled down now lads. Will the cricket take place as planned?"

"Yes, everything's in order" said Reg." Alf's girls are on topless duty till 2pm then the agreement is the tee shirts go back on. Though to be honest I think most of the punters will have been, got a car wash, got an eyeful, and disappeared by then, leaving Alf with a huge profit. How much you took so far Alf?" asked Reg "Just short of a ton," replied Alf confidently.

"Well Reg," said Eunice, "While you've been sorting out this kerfuffle I've been home and made you some food for this afternoon's cricket. There's a couple of your favourite ham and tomato crusty rolls, a couple of Arthur Butterfields best pork pies with mustard, a bag of cheese and onion crisps and a few jammy dodgers. That should keep you going for the day, or do you need anything else?"

"No that's fine," said Reg "You didn't need to go to so much trouble Eunice. I would have got something when the cricketers have tea."

Eunice raised her eyebrows and shook her head. "You would have got something at tea? What you mean is you would have hung around until all the cricketers had eaten their teas and then swooped like a hungry vulture on the leftovers. These leftovers being curled up sandwiches, bits of salad and broken biscuits. All of which will have been manhandled and discarded by sweaty cricketers' hands. Not enough for somebody who is recovering from a heart attack. Really Reggie, you do need looking after. You must learn how to eat properly!"

Eunice then reached into the back of her Avenger and pulled out a Kwik Save shopping bag. She passed it on to Reg and delivered him instructions, "Make sure you put that bag in the kitchen fridge. There's plenty of room. And another thing, don't be filling your boots up on Lion Bitter this afternoon just because the sun is out. I'll be back around mid-afternoon so take it easy".

"I won't." replied Reg "Where are you going, and what are you doing this afternoon Eunice?"

"Well, if you must know I'm off doing what every girl loves doing best. I'm going shopping and I'll leave it to your imagination Reg Birtles which department I'll be spending most of my time in!" teased Eunice with her flickering eyelashes.

"I think its safe to say Reggie that it's the most exciting department in the whole store! Maybe if you're a good boy and don't drink too much Lion Bitter I'll show you what I've bought. It'll have to be later on though…much later on. Now you be a good boy and I'll see you."

With that Eunice gave Reg a cheeky wink and drove the red Avenger off the ground. Alf Tyson couldn't believe that after all the hard miles he'd put in behind Reg's back that Eunice was seemingly making a play for Reg.

"Blimey Reg. I've got to give it to you there. She's really got her teeth into you. I think you're in there by the sounds of it. All that teasing as well. It's obvious she's off buying something a bit saucy. If I were you Reg I wouldn't be touching a drop of Lion Bitter today!"

Reg thought for a minute. Alf Tyson wasn't the kind of person he'd normally take advice from but everything he said seemed to make sense. Reg had spent a large part if not all the summer in pursuit of Eunice and all of a sudden it was all falling into place. Or was it? Still the question was nagging at his conscience. Where was Eunice's husband Roger?

A freeze frame photo developed in his mind which flashed up all afternoon. This picture was Eunice looking through Marks and Spencer's finest frillies. He decided to stay off the beer.

Over the Boundary and Under the Covers

18
Derby Day - and Title Decider

Despite it only being midday, Reg actually felt like he'd been on the go for a lot longer. It had been a very eventful morning, what with the hassle on the club's land due to Alf Tyson pulling a fast one taking advantage of secretary Charlie Mather's intoxicated state a couple of weeks earlier.

It had been an unusually warm summer and it felt and looked like local cricket was back in fashion. The local *Journal* reported that crowds were up and the standard of cricket on offer was better than it had been for years. There were several professionals playing in the league who were indeed knocking on the door of regional cricket teams back home.

Local rivals Barnworth Cricket Club had strong connections in both the West Indies and Australia and over the years had been instrumental in bringing in some exciting young players, some of which had made their way to the full national test teams.

This season was no exception with two Australians supplementing the team in the shape of Rod Tower and Scott Ducker. Both of them had made significant contributions with them in second position at start of play, making the match a title decider.

Along with Worley, Barnworth were seen as the big boys of the league when it came to spending money on professionals and overseas amateurs. With local businessman and timber merchant Henry Hagsford being the principal backer financially.

To his eternal credit, Hagsford didn't restrict his financial support to his own club. Almost every club in the league felt the benefit of his support. He was the archetypal local philanthropist. There's no doubt that a lot of his donations ranging from cricket to support for local schools' sports facilities went under the radar. He was a modest and generous man.

Reg looked around the ground. With the sun shining and spectators taking up positions he couldn't help but feel self-satisfied.

He thought back to the night of the first committee meeting of the year when he drove onto a ground that in his own words, "looked like a cross between the council tip and a Belfast bomb site."

What a difference several months of strong leadership had made. Reg's master plan and methods of management were certainly reaping rewards both on and off the field. Add to that the seemingly upward trend in Reg's private life in the shape of the lovely Eunice and apart from the heart scare, things were indeed very much on the up.

There was just one thing that was consistently nagging at the back of Reg's mind. That being one Roger Braithwaite. The husband of the lovely Eunice who nobody had seen for at least six weeks. The more Reg thought about this the more confused he became. Since his spell in hospital, she was hardly the model of discretion in overseeing his recovery. Spending time at Reg's house and being his personal chauffeur plus some of the comments and conversation between the two of them was very risqué to say the least.

Reg's mind went into overdrive…maybe Roger had left her? Maybe he was off on business for a long spell abroad and Eunice was only after a fling and fulfilment, a bit of slap and tickle until he came back? Maybe she'd hit him over the head, killed him and buried him under the patio? Maybe the Braithwaites were involved in 'open relationships' the like of what most people assumed went on at Alf Tyson's Throbbers "Health" club and Reg was being slowly lured into a sordid, seedy, depraved secret world of which he had no control.

He decided he was going to confront Eunice about her absent husband. In a nice kind of way of course. He didn't want to rock the boat too much, upset her and possibly lose the chance of a relationship with Eunice. That he thought was the way forward.

All of a sudden, his concentration was interrupted by groundsman Harry Flatley. "Jesus Reg, what's the matter? You've got a face like a dropped pie. What's on your mind?"

Caught a little off-balance Reg didn't reply straight away. When he did it wasn't a true reflection of what was on his mind. "I'm just thinking how the wicket's going to play today, Harry. If we win the toss, I'm assuming we'll bat and try to set a score of 200 plus?"

Harry concurred with Reg, "Whoever bats first on that road of a track will be in the box seat. The track's perfect for batting first. Plus, later there could be a bit of turn in it for our Sultan of Spin from the Market Street curry house. It's a great toss to win. I reckon it's a track that would suit my squirter ball."

Reg left Harry dreaming about bowling his squirter ball and headed for the club kitchen where he placed the food Eunice had given him in the fridge. As he left the kitchen he bumped into Brains on the club car park. It was the first time Reg had seen Brains since his heart attack. "How you feeling Reg? I see you've had a busy morning with the BLASE women!"

Reg noticed that Brain's new Lada Estate was looking almost showroom shiny and couldn't resist a sly dig. "Looks like you've been lining Alf Tyson's pockets. Did you put the Lada through the car wash?" Reg enquired.

"I did!" replied Brains. "To be honest Reg, they actually do a great job. Not expensive and the bonus of a couple of bouncing boobs. That Mavis Tickle is a piece of work. She asked me if I wanted any 'extras'. I didn't know what she meant until Alf Tyson mentioned something about getting my gearstick polished at the end of the wash and polish. I didn't take her up on the offer though."

"Good job you didn't!" said Reg, "Anyway, as I remember it you had a date lined up with Miss Breightmet. The contestant you caught with her drawers down. Obviously, I ended up in hospital that night. What happened? Did you have a drink with her after the contest as planned?"

"I did Reg," replied Brains "She's not what you would call a delicate flower. She wasn't totally honest with you when she was interviewed on the Miss Bolton night. She told you she was in a relationship with some geezer called Dwayne. The truth is she binned him off ages ago when he got sent down for a three-year stretch. He's off the scene now and it looks like I'm in there. I know she swears like a trooper, and she's been round the block a bit but she's growing on me."

"I've heard that Withins Estate she lives on is that rough that the milk float has a rear gunner!" joked Reg, "Seriously though, I heard that during last year's heatwave there was a lot of looting and rioting on the estate. PC Gordon and PC Huggins had a close call when they had a popped tyre on their Panda Ford Anglia from some deliberately placed broken bottles. They had to drive off quickly on three tyres. PC Gordon was off sick with stress and trauma-related illness for six months."

"I heard that as well," said Brains. "The big test will be if I get lucky and stay the night whether my new Lada will still be there in the morning. We'll see."

Looking out of the window, Reg noticed Iain Redwood and the Barnworth captain Melvin Hagsford walking to the wicket to toss up. They both looked at the pitch closely, with Iain Redwood studying both ends of the wicket intensely.

"Looks like they're tossing up," said Reg. "We could do with winning the toss and batting."

Both Reg and Brains watched closely as the captains tossed a coin, shook hands, and began to walk from the wicket to the pavilion. With captain Ian Redwood carrying out a forward defensive stroke as he walked to the pavilion indicating his decision to bat first.

"Looks like we've won the toss Brains," said Reg. "You joining me Harry and Dicky for a while?"

"I'd love to Reg but its going to be a busy day. Look, its only quarter to two and almost all the benches are taken. Give it an hour and there'll be loads on the ground. We need to make sure they don't go thirsty!" Brains enthused.

Reg smiled, "Fair play to you Brains. I tell you what, if it does get busy, we can have a cash prize raffle. If Eunice gets back around teatime, I'll ask her. She sold a raft of tickets against Worley the other week."

Reg left Brains and made his way to where Dicky and Harry were already sat close to the sightscreen at the Potter Road End. As he walked across the ground past the Barnworth players who were warming up doing all sorts of warming up exercises, he became reflective.

This was the type of day that Reg as a player loved to be involved in. Charging in from the Potter Road End, terrifying batters with a combination of bounce, speed and a large amount of sometimes-hostile banter.

Sadly, for Reg, he knew Father Time waits for nobody and accepted that being a spectator sat on his beloved Potter Road End was as good as it gets.

In a nice gesture as the Barnworth players came out, wicketkeeper Micky Bunn made a special effort to come over and shake Reg's hand. Micky had been a junior at the club many years ago and was always grateful for the coaching he received from Reg. He was now, without doubt, the best wicketkeeper in the league.

"Afternoon Reg. I heard about your heart scare the other week. Listen, if you need anything whatsoever you know where me and Clare are. In fact, after the game today we'll have a pint and a catch up," said Micky.

"Sounds good to me Micky. And by the way, thanks for the offer of help. You're a good guy. If you do want to do something to help you can drop some catches if they come your way!" Reg joked.

"Sorry Reg, no can do! Let's hope it's a great game played in the right spirit."

With that parting remark Micky Bunn clapped his wicket keeping gloves, did a couple of star jumps and jogged up to take his position behind the wickets.

The two opening batters in the shape of club skipper Iain Redwood and David Hedge made their way from the pavilion to the wicket, completing various exercises involving waving their bats or doing imaginary cover drives.

With Dave Hedge completing his pre-first ball ritual of adjusting his cap to the optimum position of comfort and vision, and Ian Redwood jogging on the spot at the other end, the stage was set for the most keenly-contested derby game for many years. A game that would decide whether the title would move out of the Barnworth trophy cabinet where it had been proudly on display for the last two seasons.

Indeed, local cricket journalist Percy Stratford mentioned in his *Beyond the Boundary* weekly column in *The Journal* that umpires Fred Moulden and Benny Hopkins would have to make sure that the game be remembered for the players heroics rather than an umpiring mistake. Fred Moulden, better known as Lord Fred, sadly was no stranger to controversy both on and off the field and was currently banned from Worley Cricket Club pending the outcome of an enquiry into his actions involving a tea lady and some dropped buttered scones. It wasn't the first time Fred had been involved in scandal with a tea lady.

Opening the bowling from the scoreboard end was Rod Tower. With long blond hair that went way past his shirt collar, three buttons open on his shirt displaying a larger than usual St Christopher medallion and both his sleeves rolled up almost to the armpit. He was the very epitome of sun kissed Australian masculinity.

The first ten overs of the allotted fifty went without too much incident as was familiar in a cat-and-mouse type situation like this. Both batsmen putting a value on their wickets with no exuberant or rash strokes being offered as the bowlers kept a good line and length. With 60 on the board and no wickets down, Iain Redwood would have been slightly happier than the Barnworth captain Melvin Hagsford.

From their bench at the Potter Road End, Reg, Dicky and Harry discussed the state of play.

"Not a bad start," said Reg, "Just the sort of platform for the rest of the batsmen to build on. What you think Harry?"

"Not bad," replied Harry. "We need to be keeping up this run-rate though in my opinion. Don't forget they have a strong batting line up and they've got some big hitters. I know at six an over we're on for three hundred, but it never works out that way. I'm more interested in the damage Rod Tower's size 16 boots are doing to the track. His feet are bloody huge!

I once had a dalliance with a girl called Mildred Hammersly who had enormous feet. Couldn't dance to save her life! However, going back to the cricket, his footmarks could be manna from Heaven for our Market Street Magician, Jimmy just dropping the ball in the rough. Or is it manna from Allah or whoever?"

At that moment the whole Barnworth team went up in appeal for a catch from the edge of Iain Redwood's bat going into wicketkeeper Micky Bunn's gloves. With no hesitation Umpire 'Lord' Ted Moulden raised his finger to signify the end of skipper Iain Redwood's innings. It was a decision that the skipper didn't contest, and he made his way back to the pavilion.

Next in was young Stuart Hopwood. Stuart lived on Potter Road and had spent virtually all his life at the club. His parents being regular social members.

At this point the triumvirate of Reg, Dicky and Harry welcomed local businessman Henry Hagsford to their company. Henry was no stranger to expensive cigars and as soon as he made himself comfortable reached for his lighter and best Cuban.

"Crikey, Bob!" said Reg, "That's not a cigar you're smoking there Henry, it's a telegraph pole!"

Henry took a big puff and exhaled the smoke. "All the way from Havana these Reg. The best that money can buy. Not just some cheap sweepings from the floor. No. These are the best. I tell you what, old Fidel and me may be at opposite ends of the political spectrum but when it comes to cigars we're chugging on the same leaves."

Dicky Hampton, who also considered himself to be something of a tobacco connoisseur, was chugging on his pipe in his usual laid-back fashion. He looked at Henry and said, "I could never take to cigars Henry. I've always been a pipe man since my days in the RAF. I find the pipe more soothing."

Harry Flatley couldn't hold back with his thoughts and weighed in, "That's the RAF upbringing in you Dicky. All flash fur lined leather jackets, clean white Y fronts and posh pipe if you ask me. Us boys in the north African desert had to put up with whatever baccy we were given. It smelt like camel droppings - probably was if you ask me. But we weren't moaning minies and still managed to drive Rommel and the rest of the Huns all the way back to Tripoli." Harry then switched his focus from North Africa 1942 to the present day and posed a question to Henry Hagsford.

"What do you think today then Henry. Which way do you think is it going to go?"

"Well," said Henry, taking a long, thoughtful draw on his cigar before letting out a plume of white smoke, "I think it's going to be a battle of the professionals and their associated overseas amateurs. Your two lads have done well this year and the kid they call the Market Street Magician has been a real find. Our two Aussie lads are very experienced though and have won the league twice before."

Henry was indeed correct. With a network of contacts out in Australia, Barnworth had very rarely failed when it came to recruitment of professionals and amateurs and the league title had rested in their trophy cabinet without being re-located due to back-to-back title wins.

With 110 on the board, the game dramatically swung in Barnworth's favour as both incumbent batsmen lost their wickets. Rod Tower produced a yorker which took David Hedges' middle stump clean out of the ground. Two overs later, with no addition to the score, Stuart Hopwood got a thick edge to an outswinger from Rod Tower which, following a spectacular dive, came to rest in wicket keeper Micky Bunn's gloves.

110 for 3 with professional Harold Haltz and Rod Norris at the wicket and twenty overs bowled. The momentum was with Barnworth. Their grip on the game tightening with each passing over as the two new batsmen struggled, with runs at a premium.

This was indeed a key phase in the game. The ground was as full as it had been for a number of years. With it being suitable to cars being able to park comfortably virtually all round the ground, the spectators also took the opportunity to bring their young children to play in groups as the parents sat in sun recliners indulging in alcoholic refreshments and various picnic food.

At this key moment in play the relative silence was broken by an ice cream van driving on and announcing his presence via accompanying music. This being the *Match of The Day* theme tune.

This wasn't unusual on a match day, especially when the weather was particularly favourable. The driver of the ice cream van wasn't a stranger to the club. Mohammed Masood - or Mo as he was known - was a regular visitor to the club both socially and in a business role. He had recently bought the ice cream van from a mate of Alf Tyson with financial backing from his Uncle Joe who was also young Jimmy Bangla's uncle. Joey Bangla was indeed a man who believed in investing in his family.

After three back-to-back *Match of The Day* tunes, Reg had heard enough. "What's the matter with Mo? That bloody tune's non-stop. The kids all know he's here. What's he playing at. It's beginning to distract the players!"

Whilst delivering that statement, Reg began to make his way over to Mo's Bedford CF ice cream van.

Business was good with a large queue developing and a very busy Mo delivering 99s, Mivvis, Zoom and Kwench lollies plus Mambos and Jubblys.

Reg was in no mood for queuing and barged his way through the waiting kids as *Match of The Day* played on. "Mo!" shouted Reg, "Turn the bloody jingle off. We know you're here. It's drivin' everyone mad!"

Mo served a teenager then looked up at Reg, "But Mr Birtles, I cannot do as you wish. There is something wrong with the electrics on this vehicle. If I turn the tune off, then the fridges and freezer go off making all my ice creams and lollies melt. I'm sure you understand?"

Reg was less than impressed. "I couldn't give a hoot Mo. You're going to have to do something to stop it or you'll have to go."

At that moment help was offered from an unusual quarter in the shape of Jimmy Spangles Spanner the local DJ.

Sticking his head through the van window, Spangles made a suggestion: "Tell you what Mo, put me, the wife and kids on free ice cream for the rest of the season and I'll fix the music player in the van. What do you say?"

Mo wasn't impressed by this offer. Spangles and his entourage being on free ice cream would make a severe inroad into Mo's profits.

"I thank you for your offer of help Mr Spangles, but sadly I cannot agree to your terms and conditions." said Mo.

Reg had heard enough. With the *Match of the Day* tune still ringing out, he issued an ultimatum: "Terms and conditions! Its not the United Nations. Either get that bloody racket switched off or get the van off the ground right this minute. If we're not careful Lord Fred will be over and telling us that he's going to suspend play. What's it going to be, and make it quick!" Reg raged, his face getting redder by the minute.

Sure enough, and as predicted by Reg after seven renditions of the tune, the game was suspended and Lord Fred Moulden began to make his way over to the ice cream van. Everybody who knew Lord Fred wouldn't have been surprised or expected anything else. He loved being the centre of attention whether it be signalling decisions with over-elaborate gestures or holding court in the clubhouse explaining the reason for some controversial and contested decision he'd given during the day's play.

Obviously milking the moment and maximising his moments at the centre of attention, Lord Fred walked at a pallbearer's pace towards the offending vehicle.

Fred identified Reg as his point of contact, having known him for over thirty years. "Reg," he said, "We need to end this noise and do it quickly or I will have no alternative but to suspend play. Furthermore, for every four minutes lost your team will lose one over. Is that clear?"

Reg saw this as a veiled threat and responded: "For goodness' sake Fred, I'm doing my best. What do you think we're up to? Anybody would think I've got Jimmy Hill and

John Motson lined up as surprise guest ice cream men!"

"You've got three minutes Reg before the clock starts ticking. Don't forget it's your club that's going to suffer." concluded Fred unsympathetically.

Reg turned to Spangles and Mo. "Look you two, I'll cut you a deal. Mo, you supply all Spangles' family with free ice cream just for today and I'll make sure that he gets four free pints this afternoon. Are we all agreed? Let's just get rid of this racket and get the cricket back on."

Mo was first to respond, "I am most willing to partake in this agreement as long as long as Spangles' children do not, how do you say, take the piss?"

Spangles chuckled and replied, "Don't worry Mo...it's not the kids you want to worry about. Since the missus found out she was expecting our fourth she craves ice cream!"

Spangles walked round to the door of the ice cream van and started fiddling with some decidedly dodgy looking wiring behind the driver's seat as Reg and Lord Fred squeezed their heads through the serving hatch eagerly monitoring what was happening.

After a couple of minutes silence descended and the crowd responded with ironic cheers.

"Mr Spangles," said Mo, "I am hoping that your repair will not affect my stock in the freezer?" Spangles replied with confidence: "You've no worries on that matter Mo. I can safely say that's the last you'll hear from *Match of the Day* and all your stock will stay cold until sold. Although if I were you, I'd get that wiring looked at. Looks like it's been hot-wired by Billy Fizz Bang. Billy was a well-known 'electrician' who had developed and acquired his electrical skills and qualifications whilst in prison for circulating fake five-pound notes. Safe to say Mo had indeed given the job of wiring the sound system to Billy.

Mo took his place up back in the van as Reg, Spangles and Lord Fred walked away in their different directions to where they were pre-*Match of the Day* crisis.

With the jingle drama over, the only noise was the sound of clinking glasses, children playing in groups and low-level chatter. However, just as Lord Fred was approaching the crease at the Potter Road End the silence was broken as the theme tune from TV show *The Sweeney* blasted out for Mo's ice cream van.

Reg stood up sharply and marched towards the van. Likewise, Spangles ran around the boundary and arrived at the van before Reg.

"I thought you'd fixed it?" shouted Reg, "For God's sake get it sorted Spangles. All we need is those overpaid and underworked custodians of the peace PC Gordon and PC Huggins to pull up sharply on the ground all handbrake turns, sirens blowing and flashing lights and start asking why we're breaking the peace with this racket!"

Before Reg finished his sentence the jingle stopped. "That's it now," said Spangles, "You won't be hearing any more racket from Mo's van." He then turned his attention to Mo. "The bad news is Mo that your jingle/music type thing is now out of action. The good news is that none of your ice lollies are going to melt. You need a complete rewire and I'd seriously advise you to steer clear of Billy Fizz Bang. At the moment you're driving an electrical tinder box."

Spangles then addressed Reg, "That's it for sure Reg. No more 'spot the TV theme tune' interruptions. I've completely disabled the jingle player. Let's go get a pint and enjoy the cricket. The weather's lovely."

Reg was mindful of overindulging on the beer. Especially bearing in mind what Eunice had (in his opinion) teased him with in the morning. Nevertheless, he decided one pint wouldn't impinge on whatever physical demands that may hopefully develop later in the day.

Reg spent an interesting hour with Spangles in the club. Spangles was in the know on a whole range of topics ranging from the Lady Mayoress Mrs Wetherby's recent fact-finding trip to the Paris Grand Prix courtesy of the ratepayers, to the ins and outs of the local criminal fraternity. Spangles was indeed a man who operated on the edge. He hinted at some 'top electrical gear' soon coming on the market. With no further information, except planting the seed in Reg's mind that "every home should have one".

Reg walked back towards his usual bench and re-joined Harry, Dicky and Henry Hagsford at the Potter Road End. With professional Harold Haltz and Rod Norris still at the wicket. A lot was riding on the H's contribution, and during the last 15 or so overs he had played a textbook innings, accumulating 60 plus runs taking no risks and picking out the odd bad ball for exploitation.

Rod Norris at the other end had rather ridden his luck. A big hit to the boundary being dropped and surviving a very strong LBW appeal trying to sweep a boundary off Lee Hutton. It was indeed a strange decision as it looked plum. Hutton was less than amused and entered into a heated debate with Lord Fred. This resulted in captain Melvin Hagsford being told to calm his bowler down.

Norris's luck ran out though when, on 170 for three, he was caught at mid-on after mis-timing an on-drive into skipper Hagsford's safe hands.

With Harold Haltz now being joined by his brother and six wickets left in the tent, the stage was set for an explosive last ten overs. Much was expected of the younger of the two brothers. As Trevor approached the wicket there was some sledging coming his way from Lee Hutton.

Trevor didn't respond, preferring to carry on walking to the crease waving his arms round in a circular fashion.

Coming into bowl was an old foe from down under in the shape of Scott Ducker. The two had clashed several times in district cricket back home and were well versed in the art of sledging. Ducker charged in from the scoreboard end and Trevor played a wild shot. The ball going straight through to keeper Micky Bunn's gloves. The next ball was the same with Trevor offering a wild 'agricultural' shot.

At this point bowler Ducker followed through on his run up coming almost face to face with Trevor, offering some not-so-welcome advice:

"It's red, round and weighs about five ounces, in case you were wondering what the ball looks like!" said Ducker to the batter rather loudly and much to his teammates' amusement.

Ducker steamed in for his third ball at Trevor who this time bludgeoned it straight over the bowler's head and out of the ground for six runs. With umpire Lord Fred still having his hands over his head signalling six runs Trevor walked down the wicket and taunted Ducker. "Well, you obviously know what it looks like. Now you go and find it!"

Sensing growing tension and the chance to be centre stage in all this drama, Lord Fred decided it was time for this nonsense to stop. Bringing both the players together at the bowler's end along with fellow umpire Benny Wadkins, Lord Fred took the lead.

"Look lads, we've got a lovely day, a full house, and the potential for a great game of cricket. Let's not ruin it over some feud that started thousands of miles away on another continent. After all its village cricket not the Ashes!"

However, Ducker couldn't resist the chance for another dig at Trevor: "Can't be playing for the Ashes if he's on the field. I mean what would he be doing anywhere near a cricket field if we were playing for the Ashes?".

Fortunately, Trevor didn't rise to the bait and walked back to his crease and prepared to face the last ball of the over. A still-angry Ducker bowled a long hop which Trevor gleefully dispatched for four more runs.

Unfortunately for Trevor it was a short stay at the wicket. In the next over he tried once again to hit the ball out of the ground but only succeeded in being bowled by an ecstatic Lee Hutton.

This wasn't ideal and Trevor's irresponsibility didn't go unnoticed by the panel of experts sat on the bench at the Potter Road end.

"Lost that psychological battle there," Harry mused, "That could cost us the game. There's only JB and young Barry Sandfield left who you would class as decent run-scorers."

Reg was a little less downbeat. "Sure, we could have done with Trevor hanging around a while longer, but all is not lost. JB can lay on if need be and Barry's no stranger to the odd six."

With Harold remaining unbeaten on 77 and both JB and Barry Sandfield making more than useful contributions, the innings ended with a total of 220 for seven.

It was a good day for the club. The sun was shining, the bar was busy, the barbecue was cooking and there was hopefully more exciting cricket to come. Chewing his jammy dodger, Reg's eyes lit up as he saw a red Hillman Avenger drive through the club gates.

For a few moments Reg completely forgot there was a local derby title-decider at stake. His mind went into complete overdrive as he wondered what Eunice may have purchased from Marks and Spencer's lingerie department.

Reg finished his biscuit, made his way across the ground and approached Eunice who was busy speaking to the club treasurer, Verity Tinkle. Eunice was clearly running out of patience with Verity who was less than happy with the topless car wash being a source of substantial reward for Alf Tyson. A man who according to Verity and the Reverend Adrian Gawsworth was the very personification of evil and the Devil incarnate. After almost five minutes of fire and brimstone from Verity and the Reverend, Eunice made an excuse and headed for the ladies' room.

Reg was waiting for Eunice as she appeared from the ladies and carefully ensured the Reverend and Verity were nowhere to be seen. "Hi Reg. How's the cricket going? You've not been drinking too much have you? We don't want you back in that hospital bed laid up. Not when I've got plans for you!"

Eunice made sure this wasn't a private conversation and all in the company heard her. Several raised their eyebrows including Brains the steward.

"Listen Reg," said Eunice, "There's a big crowd in here today. Do you want me to drop a blouse button, flicker my eyelashes and run a raffle? I reckon there's a couple of hundred spectators. Forget the name cards. We only make 50 percent profit on those. Offer a hefty cash prize of say £50 which should tempt them and we should sell 200 tickets at a pound apiece. That'll rake in £150 profit. What do you think Reggie?"

Reg was indeed impressed. Eunice was clearly more than a pretty face. "Well," said Reg, "If you strike while the iron's hot just after tea then I'm sure you'll clean up. The Barnworth supporters may be a bit boisterous and rowdy but they're certainly not frightened of putting their hand in their pockets. What you need to do is a couple of laps so you don't miss anyone. When you think you've done everyone I'll come and help you do the draw. Is that OK?"

"That's fine by me," said Eunice "I'll go put some more lippy on and sort my lashes and we'll make a start."

With the Barnworth innings due to start, Reg walked the long way around the busy ground. This was to pass on thanks to Susie and Shirley Blower who had volunteered to run the barbecue for the afternoon. As he approached the them, he noticed that they were being given supplementary assistance by Maureen Pollitt and the one and only *Miss Butterfields Crumpet 1978,* Mavis Tickle who, only a couple of hours ago been a member of the topless car wash staff, such was her range of skills.

"Thanks for all your efforts this afternoon girls. It doesn't go unnoticed. When you've finished go see Brains and there's a few drinks on the club for your efforts."

However, as Reg walked away he couldn't help wondering if Mavis Tickle would behave herself. Indeed, despite being *Miss Butterfields Crumpet 1978,* she was certainly better known by her well-earned nickname of *Tits Out Tickle.*

Reg drew a little comfort from the thought that surely even a girl as brazen as Mavis wouldn't risk being burnt in a delicate area by spitting fat from a king-sized burger on the barbecue. In a counter-scenario, Maureen Pollitt wasn't exactly a shrinking violet when it came to antics of the flesh and would need little encouragement to partake in some topless mischief. Add to that a large contingent of leery Barnworth fans fuelled by copious amounts of Lion Bitter and cases of Snoggerburger Pils lager and there could be a recipe for disaster. Only time would tell. Reg tried desperately to think the best of people but found himself fearing the worst as he walked back to his bench.

Chasing 220 for a title win, Barnworth opened with captain Marvin Hagsford and the stylish and steady Rob Hutton, the son of spin bowler Lee Hutton.

From the bench at the Potter Road End the self-appointed experts all contributed an opinion, Harry first, "A lot will rest on whether young Jimmy Bangla can get the ball into those footmarks left by Rod Tower. If he can get it right, then Barnworth could be in trouble. If I was bowling, I'd be tempting them with my squirter ball right in the rough."

Henry Hagsford was confident that his club, and in particular his son Melvin were more than capable of chasing the runs down. "We bat right down to number ten. The only player in our team who struggles with the bat is Micky Bunn. Although his self-belief is to be admired it frequently colours his judgement of his actual batting ability. Why only the other week he told me that he shouldn't be batting eleven. I told him he was batting at eleven because we can't play with twelve!"

Sat in his white short-sleeved shirt and the club tie, chugging on his pipe, Dicky Hampton looked every inch the TV cricket pundit and offered a balanced view: "It really could go either way. Barnworth's two Aussies are key in my opinion. If we can get them cheaply its up for grabs."

However, Reg offered no opinion. His eyes and mind were occupied elsewhere on the ground. Over near the clubhouse he spotted the lovely Eunice carrying out her raffle duties with the assistance of fellow committee member Edna Pilling.

What bothered him was the sight of Mavis Tickle and Maureen Pollitt still working away on the barbecue but seemingly getting the worse for wear on bottles of Snoggerburger German imported lager which, unbeknown to Reg or the rest of the committee, Brains had bought from Alf Tyson in a special deal. With one bottle for 50p or two for 75p stock was moving fast. Alf reassured Brains that there was plenty more where that came from.

Brains didn't actually ask *where* it had come from, although soon after he'd made the deal, he saw Bob Greaves on the *Granada Reports Crimewatch* section appealing for witnesses to a stolen vanload of bottled beers that was hijacked en-route to the wholesalers. Brains was sure that Alf Tyson was involved but knew better than to ask questions.

On the field Barnworth made a more than steady start and with 15 overs gone were well in touch with the required run rate with 80 runs for the loss of just one wicket. That being Rob Hutton who was caught on the boundary following an attempt to hook Harold H.

Captain Melvin Hagsford, although maybe not the most flamboyant of opening batters, was a steady anchor. Even his father commenting from the Potter Road bench opined, "Our Melvin..more blocks than a box of Lego. But steady as a rock," as Barnworth approached the hundred mark with one wicket down and 23 overs left of the allotted 50.

It was at this point Eunice and Edna approached the four occupants of the bench at the Potter Road sightscreen asking if they wished to purchase raffle tickets.

"Come on gents. Support the club by purchasing a raffle ticket £1 each or 3 for £2. £50 first prize drawn later today." said Eunice in a well-rehearsed pitch.

As Edna collected the various amounts, Reg pulled Eunice to one side out of earshot of the rest. "What's with the special offer of 3 tickets for £2? I thought they were £1 each. What's the thinking Eunice?"

"Reggie my dear," replied Eunice, "The number of tickets is irrelevant. It's the number of nice green one-pound notes is what counts. Every ticket we sell over 50 is pure profit. Your only selling pieces of paper. We've sold over 90 tickets and are only halfway round the ground. Keep your eye on the clubhouse door and I'll give you a wave so you can conduct the draw."

Reg reflected on Eunice's financial acumen with the raffle and asked with a smile on his face: "You mentioned in your raffle sales pitch that £50 was first prize. Dare I ask what's second prize?"

Eunice smiled "My dear Reggie, you're getting to know me so well. The £50 first prize is a sprat to catch the mackerel and so far, today it's been a successful ploy. If anyone actually asks what second prize is, I'll tell them it's a mystery prize. Such a mystery we don't even know what it is!"

Reg laughed and began walking back to the bench to join the rest of the company who were engrossed in this title decider.

Just as Reg was getting comfortable he was accosted by a very attractive and polite lady dressed in a red cheesecloth shirt, blue denim loon pants and a silk headscarf.

"Excuse me," she said "Are you Reg Birtles? And are you something to do with the club?"

"Yes, I am Reg Birtles. What can I do for you?" said Reg.

"Well Mr Birtles my name is Tina Matthews and I have say, I'm none too impressed with the hygiene standards of one of your catering staff on the barbecue."

"Why, what's brought you to form this opinion? I know all the ladies on the barbecue. They are all volunteers," said Reg.

"Volunteers or not, it's no excuse for negligence of basic hygiene procedures. If you can spare me a minute, I'll enlighten you as to why I have formed this opinion. I have to say though it's not for the faint-hearted or anyone with a queasy disposition."

"Please enlighten me," said Reg, "and I'll take action where necessary."

"Well, about half an hour ago I was sat in one of the toilet cubicles. Without going into intimate details, I left the cubicle to wash my hands and brush my hair. As I stood over the sink it was quite obvious the person inside was smoking despite signs indicating this was not allowed. After the flush was pulled the person inside exited the cubicle and went straight out of the door without a spot of water being administered in the interests of personal hygiene. Now a person's personal hygiene is their own affair but when such negligence transcends into the public domain and could affect me then that's when I get a little twitchy."

Tina Matthews was not only eloquent in her delivery of her feelings but obviously an educated lady. Making her points and even distracting the wise men of cricket from the events on the field.

Reg intervened and chose his words carefully. "I'm sorry to hear about this Miss Matthews. Although I am sure you would agree that sadly I cannot be responsible for a person's individual hygiene."

"No, Mr Birtles," said Miss Matthews, "I understand that. It was what followed that worried me. After calling at the bar I walked back to my seat, and I passed the barbecue. Imagine my shock when I saw this lady serving out jumbo hot dogs and burgers. This very same lady who five minutes earlier had shown no regard for personal hygiene. Furthermore, I am led to believe that this lady is one Mavis Tickle who happens to be the current holder of the Miss Bolton trophy sponsored by Arthur Butterfields Bakery. I'm sure Arthur Butterfield would be less than happy if he was aware Miss Tickle was carrying out her titled duties in such an unhygienic manner."

"Miss Matthews," said Reg, "I can only offer my apologies in the hope that you will accept them in the spirit they are offered. I promise I will immediately remove Miss Tickle from catering duties without mentioning the origin of complaint. If I deliver this promise, can we bring closure on this matter?"

Tina Matthews considered Reg's proposal. "Yes Mr Birtles. That will be fine. Thank you very much." With that promise from Reg, Tina Matthews made her way away from the Potter Road End.

"Blimey Reg," said Harry, clearly impressed with Reg's unusual diplomacy, "Reg Birtles…. the new Henry Kissinger. You ought to be out sorting the Middle East crisis the way you handled that issue. That Tina Matthews has contacts at the council and could have made things difficult for us catering-wise. Now the tricky bit is delivering the bad news to Mavis Tickle. She won't be amused if I know Mavis."

"You leave Mavis Tickle to me. I'll sort her out. Watch this space and keep your ears open." said Reg as he rose from his bench and started to walk round to the barbecue area in a confident manner.

On the field of play the game took a dramatic swing away from Barnworth's control, going from one wicket down to losing three more in as many overs.

First was captain Melvin Hagsford, trapped LBW by young Jimmy Bangla who had steadily put a stranglehold on the run flow by bowling as Harry Flatley had indicated in the bowler's foot marks.

The big breakthrough though came with the dismissal of the two Australians Rod Tower and Scott Ducker. Once again Jimmy Bangla was the bowler. First of all a brilliant diving caught and bowled removing Tower and then another plum LBW which had Ducker on the back foot straight in front of the sticks.

Next batters in for Barnworth were local lads Lee Hutton and Billy Coates. Two well-respected players who had come through the Barnworth youth scheme. Billy Coates was probably the best gully fielder in the league whilst Lee Hutton was a more-than-useful bowler with hands the size of frying pans giving some really tricky off spin bowling. However, it was in the batting department that their skills were required to see Barnworth home from their current position of 170 for four with 12 overs left chasing 221 to win.

Reg was over near the barbecue which was without doubt the busiest and noisiest part of the ground. With every run being cheered on by the Barnworth members of the crowd fuelled by Snoggerburger.

Mavis Tickle was on onion duty stood at the back stirring a giant pan of onions. Reg approached her.

"Mavis. We need you to carry out one of your duties as the current Miss Bolton," said Reg, "I know its short notice, but we need you on the podium at the front of the club when the players take drinks to do the Grand Raffle draw. So, leave the onions alone now and go get scrubbed up. I think The Journal might be taking a picture of you…not a page three type though Mavis."

Mavis needed no encouragement and deserted her onion stirring post almost immediately, "What time do you want me there?"

"Go and see Eunice. She's in charge of the raffle schedule." said Reg, "Just make sure the camera's the only thing that's flashing when the big moment arrives."

Reg then sought out and informed Miss Tina Matthews and informed her of Mavis's 'departure' from the barbecue catering section.

He then decided that it might be best if he stayed around the front of the club house whilst the grand raffle draw was taking place. He spoke to Eunice away from listening ears. "Eunice, I've had to use some nifty footwork and remove Mavis from the Barbecue and on to raffle draw duties. I'll explain why later but just give her the big build-up and let her do the draw. I've managed to get Dave Buckley from The Journal to take a few pictures and then get her off the podium pronto before she lives up to her nickname and gets her jaffas out."

Sure enough, when the drinks were taken for the second time in the innings due to the heat, Eunice appeared with the club microphone and a bucket full of raffle tickets.

"Ladies and gentlemen," began Eunice, "Thank you for supporting the grand raffle on this lovely afternoon. Before we start, let me tell you that due to the generous support from our members and friends from Barnworth we have not only got two cash prizes but have increased the first prize to £75. Furthermore, we are indeed honoured as we have the recently crowned 1978 winner of the inaugural Miss Bolton competition Mavis Tickle here to complete the draw. So, without further ado Mavis, can you pull out the winning ticket for the first prize."

The crowd cheered as Mavis walked up to the ticket bucket and pulled the winning ticket out. "7 9 seventy-nine," said Mavis. "That's number 7 9, seventy-nine!" Eunice repeated into the microphone. "Has anybody got number seventy-nine?" Nobody stepped forward.

"Well, we can't hang about as we need to get back to cricket," said Eunice, "What we'll do is draw the second prize and if anybody has the winning ticket, please produce it straight away or bring it to me in the club house within the hour. So, Mavis could you please draw the second prize?"

Mavis stepped forward and reached for the second prize ticket. She looked at it, raised her arm up and shouted, "Second prize 1 2 5, one hundred and twenty-five."

"Over here!" came a voice from the back. This voice belonged to groundsman Harry Flatley who began a steady walk to collect his winnings.

Eunice gave further instructions, "Check your pockets and purses for that winning ticket. If you find it come and find me. I'll be in the club til late but if I've gone then see Brains the steward. Now that's enough from me, can we get back to cricket, but before we do that can we have a big hand for your very own Miss Bolton, Mavis Tickle."

Reg made his way back to his position on the bench with his friends at the Potter Road End. "This could be a real nail-biter" whispered Harry. "These two are both steady Eddie type batters who could grind a victory out. If Barnworth should win, then it would be with two proper club lads at the helm."

Lee Hutton was the more expansive of the two batters. After dispatching Trevor Haltz for two fours followed by a huge six which landed near the barbecue it was looking favourable for the visitors.

With the score on 200 for 4 with 5 overs left it seemed the Gods of cricket were smiling fairly and squarely in Barnworth's favour. However, the game took another twist as Lee Hutton went for a straight six only to be caught by Barry Sandfield on the boundary.

Billy Coates was next as Jimmy Bangla sent down a virtually unplayable ball which had him twisting and threshing and facing a successful LBW appeal.

At 203 for six Barnworth were on the ropes with skipper Iain Redwood applying the pressure by bringing the field in tight. The seventh wicket fell with another catastrophic runout following a mix-up between the two batters.

Next in at nine was one of Barnworth's younger players. Simon Worth who was the regular second team wicketkeeper and had been selected for this vital game more for his ability to hit anything bowled "in the arc" for six runs irrespective of the size of the ground than his developing wicketkeeping skills.

"Get young Worth out," said Harry, "and the games ours. After Worthy there's only Neil Fynd and Micky Bunn as last man. It's crucial we get Worthy out though. He sees the ball so well and clubs it miles."

"I agree," said Reg, "I think they've taken a liberty though by including a lad who's been a regular second teamer in the first team for the last game of the season."

"I know. It caused a right ruckus at selection on Tuesday," said Henry Hagsford. "I felt sorry for the young lad Steven Marsh who's played all season. We know he's only a ball wiper but to drop him for the glory game was a bit mean. His mum's said she's not doing the second team teas anymore and she's jacked in running the bingo nights on Mondays. Add to that his dad 'Pot Black Pete' has left the snooker team and gone playing for The Legion. Caused chaos throughout the club. I hope for our Melvin that the gamble pays off and he steers us home."

"Lot of pressure now though on the young lad," said Harry, "If I was bowling now at young Worth, I'd test him with my tempter ball. OK, it might go for runs but the next ball would be the squirter, pitching right in the rough, keeping low and hitting him right on the pads as he wafts his bat aimlessly nowhere near the ball. That's what I'd do. Net result positive LBW appeal." concluded Harry.

At 203 for 7 with Worth and Stuart Hawls at the wicket the stage was set for a dramatic finish. There was indeed a lot of pressure on young Worth with only four overs left.

Harold Haltz was recalled, replacing Jimmy Bangla at the Potter Road End as Simon Worth recognised the importance of playing an innings of maturity way beyond his youthful years. However, the guile and craft of professional Harold Haltz took the wickets of Stuart Hawls and the incoming Neil Fynd in his next over with the addition of four more runs.

At 207 for 9 chasing a winning total of 221 with three more overs left, the tension was tight. The clubhouse was virtually empty with each ball bowled and each shot played being analysed on its merits by a crowd engrossed in the early evening sunshine.

Trevor Haltz was recalled, bowling the first of three remaining overs from the clubhouse end. With skipper Ian Redwood virtually changing the field placings with each passing ball.

The young Australian turned, began his run up and sent a bouncer down the wicket. Worth sussed out Trevor's intentions and ducked early. The next ball was a replica in delivery but this time young Worth saw it even earlier and played a textbook hook shot for four runs down to 'Cow Corner'.

211 for 9 chasing 221. Ten more runs needed. The overs remaining were now irrelevant, as long as Worth could keep the strike. The remaining four balls of the over seeing a thick edge through the slips being rewarded with two more runs. The problem for Simon Worth was he hadn't managed to keep the strike leaving Micky Bunn exposed to professional Harold Haltz.

211 for 9 and skipper Iain Redwood brought the field right in. Harold bowled a good line ball which Micky Bunn to the amazement of anybody who was aware of his batting skills drove through the covers to the long side boundary. After completing two runs safely, young Simon Worth wanted another to grab the strike. Safely ensconced at the striker's end, Micky Bunn was having none of it and sent young Worth back. Fortunately for Worth the return throw was poor and he managed to scurry back safely without being run out. The rest of the over was safely navigated with no addition to the score and no loss of wicket.

The sun was slowly going down as the church of St James rang out the bells for 7pm. Mo's ice cream van drove off the ground having sold his last lolly and the Blower sisters served the last burger on the barbecue for the season.

Very soon the season would be over and before anyone would have time to think, the leaves would be falling on the ground as winter would take its grip. All that would remain would be a mind full of memories accompanied by a team picture on the club wall.

Stood at the Potter Road End, Reg spoke to his entourage of friends, "You know what lads, I can honestly say that today, cricket's the winner. We've had a lovely day weather-wise and witnessed some top quality competitive cricket played in the right spirit on a ground that's full to the brim." Moving towards Henry Hagsford, Reg shook his hand and proposed: "Win or lose we'll have a booze!"

Henry shook Reg's hand vigorously and smiled, "Absolutely Reg. I've had a wonderful day with all my old friends and one-time foes".

213 for 9 with one over to bowl and eight runs required. Simon Worth and Mickey Bunn at the wicket. Trevor Haltz to bowl the last over. It was anyone's game. The last two overs had taken almost 12 minutes to bowl but that was all irrelevant now as the match reached its peak.

Trevor turned and ran in to bowl one that lifted and went straight into wicket keeper JB's gloves. "Come on Trev!" came a shout of encouragement from Shirley Blower who was now officially Trevor Haltz's squeeze after *the night of the lost keys*.

The next ball was a little shorter in length and Simon Worth saw his opportunity to strike a beautiful on-drive which never went more than six inches above the ground apart from when it cleared the boundary for four precious runs. 217 for 9. Four runs required with four balls left to play. Following the successful shot for four the two batters met in the middle of the wicket. Presumably to discuss tactics for the final four balls.

Worth returned to the crease and, possibly savouring the moment and the crowd's attention, did a full range of pre-ball idiosyncrasies and exercises. This included adjusting his cap, squatting down on his haunches, swivelling his neck, and rotating his bat in a 360-degree arc.

Trevor turned, ran up and delivered an unplayable yorker which removed young Simon Worth's middle stump. The title was won. On the pitch the players hugged each other. Local lads and youth team graduates Stuart Hopwood, Barry Sandfield and skipper embraced. Professional Harold Haltz and is brother Trevor carried out a series of high fives with Rod 'The Cod' Norris and wicketkeeper JB rolling around on the ground in a very unmanly embrace.

In a subtle act of dignity, skipper Iain Redwood approached young Simon Worth and put his arm round him offering genuine condolences and support. It was obvious that Simon Worth was distraught.

Outside the clubhouse the members gathered to clap the players off the field. Iain Redwood led the team off and once again made a special effort to seek out one of his team.

Young Jimmy Bangla was clearly overcome by the moment and his emotions were getting the better of him. The skipper hugged him and told him: "Always remember the first trophy you win Jimmy because, irrespective of the opponents or circumstances, the first is always the best. You have been a vital part of our title win this season. We wouldn't have done it without you. Well done Jimmy!"

At the Potter Road End Reg, Harry, Dicky and Henry Hagsford began the crossfield walk towards the club where a table for presentation was being hastily assembled by Degsy and Archie.

As Reg made it to the clubhouse he was approached by skipper Iain Redwood. "Reg, when you said back in April that we had a chance to be champions this season I thought you were losing your marbles. But here we are five months later lifting the trophy. The whole club owes you a debt and I'll make sure that everyone knows how much you've put in. Not only this year but going back many years."

At that moment the league president and *Journal* cricket correspondent Percy Stratford made his way to the podium where Eunice stood holding the microphone. She began to speak in her still prominent home counties accent, "Ladies and gentlemen, boys and girls. First of all, I'd like to thank the players of both clubs for putting on a nail-biting spectacle which has kept us on tenterhooks right to the end. Thanks to all the club members as well who donated their time and efforts particularly on the barbecue. We have a guest of honour to present the league title today. A much-respected gentleman who has been a loyal unpaid servant to the league and cricketing correspondent from the Journal. Would you join me in welcoming the league president Percy Stratford."

After a polite round of applause Percy took his cigarette out of his mouth and squeezed it dead in a nearby Lion Bitter ashtray. Percy always tried to look dapper but never really cut the mustard when it came to choice and style of clothing. The collar of his shirt well-worn to threadbare supporting a tie with a knot the size of a half house brick. Add to that a pair of (once) light-coloured slacks which had rarely if ever seen the inside of a washing machine let alone the pressing force of an iron. These trousers carried the stains of cricket teas from every clubhouse in the league. He was however a fountain of knowledge and despite his shortcomings in the clothes and style department was much loved and respected throughout the league. Prior to his retirement Percy was head of the English Literature department at the local grammar school and frequently during match reports in the *Journal* would use descriptions and quotes more akin to a Shakespeare classic than a local once a week parochial parish pump journal.

"Here we go," chirped Harry, "Percy Stratford. Chief waffler of Waffleland. We could be here for half an hour whilst he waffles on instead of getting to the point. Using words nobody except a grammar schoolteacher could understand."

Receiving the microphone off Eunice, Percy began to speak: "Thank you for those kind words, Eunice. Well, I must say that today has indeed been a resplendent effort from both a cricketing and event aspect. Both teams have served up a menu of gratuitous beauty cricket and catering wise. Why I can't begin to express my gratification at the delectable beefburgers that were on offer. But I'd now like to request the presence of one Mr Iain Redwood. A player, member and committee member since he was knee high to his dad's butchers apron, Iain has played through some glory days but also some sad days where he has shown a high degree of loyalty and steadfastness beyond the call of duty. Please come forward and collect the league title trophy."

Accepting the invitation, Iain Redwood moved forward to the podium and shook Percy Stratford's hand to the cries of "Speech!"

Taking control of the microphone Iain began his acceptance speech. "Thanks to everyone for the applause. As Percy quite rightly pointed out I have seen good days and bad days. The funny thing is that really you should only remember the good times. The winning times. However, remembering the bad times helps you enjoy the good times even more. I think you all know what I mean. Not sure I do!" Iain laughed as he realised he'd become a little bit tongue tied.

"At the start of the season I thought we'd be competitive. Nothing more. Although not ideal it would have been an improvement on last year's wooden spoon debacle. Nowhere in my mind did I think we'd finish as champions. But we played as a team all season, playing for each other, supporting each other, winning and occasionally losing as a team. I'd like to mention a few players who have made major contributions. We've been lucky to have as professional Harold H. I seriously hope we can do a deal for next season before Harold and Trevor head back down under. Trevor, I hope will come back but I understand there are clubs from both our league and others who are interested in procuring his services. I'd like to give a mention to a player who was a last minute trialist who proved to be an essential and vital part of our bowling attack…I give you Jimmy Bangla…The Sultan of Spin!"

The crowd broke into a generous round of applause and Jimmy humbly tipped his cap in acknowledgement of the applause.

Iain Redwood continued, "However, there's one man who has been a constant source of support throughout the close season and summer months. A man whose leadership and love for the club is undeniable. His efforts are unquestionable, his loyalty non-negotiable and his integrity intact. A man who loves the club and always acts in the club's best interests and without his efforts and perseverance we wouldn't have ended up as the 1978 champions. I'd like to extend a huge thanks and an even bigger round of applause for the one and only Reg Birtles!"

This was the moment Reg had waited for since 1970. He was close to tears as he received a round of sustained applause from the crowd.

Both Iain Redwood and Reg acknowledged the applause as Iain lifted the trophy from the podium table and made his way to the dressing room where the rest of the team was waiting along with several vigorously shaken bottles of cheap champagne.

Eunice appeared from the clubhouse and sidled up to Reg. "Reg, I know you've been a busy little soldier, but I need to speak to you in private as soon as possible."

"What's the problem?" said Reg, "Can I see you in the kitchen? Say about five minutes?"

"That's fine," said Eunice and made her way back into the club.

Reg was curious as to the reason for the privacy of the meeting with Eunice and churned it over in his head. She had been to Marks and Spencer's underwear department by her own private admission. Was she asking for Reg's approval for a certain pair of frillies? Or did she have some bad news about her seldom-seen husband Roger?

Reg approached the kitchen where Eunice was talking to John Burrell who was busy counting a large amount of £1 notes.

Reg walked in, "You wanted to see me?" he said. Looking at John Burrell and Eunice. Reg added tentatively, "er, in private?"

"Oh no. It's a matter that John's involved in. You know the cash prize raffle we had this afternoon? Well, the first prize of £75 wasn't claimed. We were wondering if we should have a redraw. What do you think Reg?"

"There's only one solution. We don't re-draw. What if someone comes across the lucky ticket and comes to claim it and we've redrawn it? Said Reg "No. It's not ethically right. We'll keep schtum, play dumb and the club can keep the dosh. £75 could fund the new urinals in the gents which are well past their splash-by date."

Reg was looking forward to an evening of celebration and possible passion with Eunice. For now, though Eunice recognised that Reg wanted to celebrate with his team. Pulling him to one side she whispered in his ear, "Well done my Reggie. Now I'm going back home to get freshened up. I'll be back in an hour. Meantime you celebrate, but not too much beer now!"

Reg was in his element. This was the night he had dreamed about all season. The club was full to bursting point with members and lots of cricket-related people of all ages swapping stories and enjoying the evening. The club was indeed thriving, and it would be impertinent not to enjoy the moment and collective feeling of euphoria that the title win had brought.

Behind the bar Brains was rushed off his feet although he was reaping the benefit of training the Blower sisters for bar duties. The one and only Mavis Tickle had departed earlier in a taxi with one of Jock Tuck's buddies from the battery plant. Meanwhile Maureen Pollitt was demonstrating her generous nature and dedication to the club cause by collecting and washing the pint pots. She was keen to make a play for Brains who was still dating Miss Breightmet.

Brains was made aware of Maureen's feelings for him by the Blower sisters and all through the evening had managed, through nifty footwork, to keep a comfortable distance from her.

Unbeknown to most of the club members, Brains had actually spent a night of passion at Maureen's flat after his ex-wife decided she was gay and made off with the captain of the Red Lion's women's darts team.

Most of the club members were aware of Maureen's 'comforting' skills, especially with any male members who were enduring romantic trauma of some sorts. These 'comforting words and gestures' usually ended up with the usual result. That being a one night stay at Maureen's flat or as some members christened it, 'Maureen's Heartbreak Hotel.'

However, Maureen was after something more than a one-night stand with Brains. She wanted a full-on relationship and was prepared to do whatever it took to achieve that objective. Even to the point of running the risk of a confrontation with Miss Breightmet. Maureen Pollitt was indeed a woman on a mission.

All of a sudden Brains was summoned by Susie Blower shouting across the crowded busy bar, "Brains, the bitter's gone. You need to put a fresh barrel on and pretty quickly!"

Brains acknowledged this request, finished at the till and headed down the stairs to the cellar where all the beers were in place. Normally this operation would take no more than a couple of minutes. However, Maureen Pollitt had other ideas. Having heard Susie's request for the barrel change she decided that now was the time to make a re-claim on Brains and whisk him away from the vice-like grip of Miss Breightmet..

Watching him make the short journey down the stairs to the cellar she waited until he was out of sight then made her move. She tiptoed down the steps making sure Brains was indeed trapped and cornered with no escape route. As Brains bent over and began removing the pipework, Maureen seized her opportunity by grabbing him in the nether regions. Brains was clearly startled and fell forward lying over the empty barrel.

"Still no change there then Brains," said Maureen, "There's plenty of lunch in that box. I hope there's some meat and two veg for your good friend Maureen!"

Brains quickly re-composed himself and turned round to face a smiling, giggling Maureen. He was in no mood for Maureen's advances.

"Pack it in Maureen. You know I'm seeing someone," said Brains. Maureen was shocked by his response.

"What's your problem big boy?" she teased. "I don't remember you being so fussy after you got binned off by your missus. If I remember rightly during our pillow talk you said I'd kept you on the straight and narrow and restored your faith in your own masculinity. Now the boot's on the other foot you're keeping your lunch box firmly sealed?"

"Maureen," said Brains, "We've both moved on. I really like Karen and I've asked her to come to Skegness for a rock 'n' roll weekend in a couple of weeks. We've got a luxury double chalet with its own toilet. If we get on well, I'm going to ask her to move in with me. Please don't spoil it for me. I know you were a good friend, no, a *great* friend - with benefits in my hour of need - but as I said, we've both moved on. Let's forget what's happened these last two minutes and stay good friends. You know how much I think of you."

Maureen thought for a few seconds. She looked at Brains, and a smile spread across her face. "OK. I was only chancing my arm thinking you might fancy a break from Miss

Breightmet. No harm done except my broken ego!"

"Thanks Maureen," said Brains, "I really appreciate that. Now lets go serve the thirsty throng in the club."

After an hour of backslapping and congratulations, Reg was ready for the next phase of this glorious day in the club's history and maybe, just maybe, his romantic future.

Eunice arrived, as promised, a little earlier than expected. This bothered Reg not one bit and after half an hour she got his attention and whispered in his ear, "Time we were heading elsewhere Reggie. Hope you've not had too many pints of Lion bitter?"

"No," said Reg, "I've only had two pints. Should we leave separately. You don't want people talking, do you?"

Eunice's reply shocked Reg. "I really don't care because it doesn't really matter. All will be revealed to all those that matter at Tuesday night's Annual General Meeting. Now come on Reggie. The Avenger awaits."

Reg needed no second invitation and, with Eunice, said his goodbyes...

19
Consummation and Clarity

As they both left the busy clubhouse taking the short walk to the Eunice's car, to say Reg's head was in a spin was an understatement of biblical proportions.

Eunice demonstrated no discretion, grabbing Reg's hand as they left the building, virtually flaunting her and Reg as a couple and demonstrating what seemed like a determined desire to get all tongues wagging at maximum level.

However, despite Eunice's extravagant, excitable, and exuberant behaviour, Reg had doubts about the next few hours. Here he was with a known married woman heading for what to all intents and purposes was basically a night of promised passion with someone he had desired, lusted, and dreamt about all summer. The question once again regarding Eunice's husband was raised in Reg's mind. Where was Roger Braithwaite?

Reg decided to take the easy way and banished all thoughts of Roger from his mind. He would go with the flow of what had been a so far fantastic evening. So, what if Roger was back at the Braithwaites house…if that was indeed where the Red Hillman Avenger was going. Where was Eunice taking him anyway? Surely not a quick fumble down Crommy Lodges?

"Reggie," said Eunice, "I know this might sound a little corny but would you like to come back to mine for coffee?"

"I'd love to. Especially if you've got a tipple of brandy to ripen it up," said Reg.

"Oh Reg," purred Eunice, "I have some fruit-based brandy all the way from Majorca. I'm sure that'll have the desired effect."

With both Eunice and Reg now entering full tease mode the innuendo was getting saucier and cornier with each passing statement.

All of a sudden, the pre-bedroom banter and build-up was broken as Eunice looked in the rear mirror to see a blue flashing light on the top of a Ford Anglia police panda car. After a few seconds the blue light was supplemented by the flashing of the headlights. This being the instruction for the driver to pull over.

"Jesus Christ!" said Reg, "How many drinks have you had Eunice? Let's hope its PC Gordon. A few flickering eyelashes and a flash of your sussies should put him off the ale trail. If it's someone we don't know though we could be in trouble."

"Don't worry my Reggie. I'll have him eating out of my hand before I've finished with him. Nobody - not even PC Bob Gordon - is going to ruin our night of passion."

Sure enough the robust and portly figure of PC Gordon appeared at the driver's side of the Avenger, indicated to Eunice to wind the window down and began the discussion. "Good evening, madam. Are you the owner of this vehicle?"

"Officer Gordon, you know this is my car. You've seen me plenty of times coming out of the gym after I've done a workout down at Throbbers. You do seem to spend a lot of time there. One would think you were on some sort of routine stake-out. Particularly when PC Huggins brings out his binoculars."

The PC responded, "Can't be too careful these days. There are criminals everywhere. It's like an epidemic of lawlessness."

"I agree," said Eunice, "However, I hardly think that the ladies' changing room window is the focal point or epicentre of international crime, do you PC Gordon? I'm sure after a few years of training with you that his surveillance techniques would be MI5 standard."

"It's true Mrs Braithwaite that I am aware this is your car." said PC Gordon, "But I have to go with procedure and protocol I need to ask you a few questions, it's all about getting the numbers up for the force. I'm sure you understand? Now what is the model and registration of this car? Furthermore, who is the passenger?"

"It's a Red Hillman Avenger, registration number GFR 148S and you know who the passenger is as well. Isn't this a little trivial and more to the point time-wasting? Will that suffice or do you want some more information such as the colour of my underwear?" replied Eunice "Anyway I think I have my driving licence in the side compartment. Let me open the door and find it."

The thought of Eunice's underwear nearly had PC Gordon in a state of hyper-ventilation. As Eunice carefully and slowly opened the door she deliberately hitched up her skirt making sure PC Bob Gordon got an eyeful of her legs and suspenders.

"I'm sure it's down there somewhere officer. Are you looking in the right places?" teased Eunice. "Maybe you need to get a torch or flashlight for a better look?"

The tease and quick flash had an instant result. As a wheezing PC Gordon got back from his hunched position he stated, "I can tell you're not drunk at the wheel, so we'll skip the breathalyser. All I need you to do is produce your driver's licence, MOT and insurance documents down at the station desk within five days. I assume that shouldn't present any problems?" said PC Gordon.

"No problems whatsoever PC Gordon but you still haven't given me a reason for being pulled over?"

"Well, er..." stuttered PC Gordon, "You clipped the kerb as you turned left at the lights on Albert Road, and I thought it might be because you had some large boxes in the back."

"Large boxes in the back. What are you talking about" asked Eunice.

"Well," replied PC Gordon, "We've had it on good authority that a well-known local businessman is bringing in a van load of saucy magazines from Sweden. The word from our snout was the van was pulling up on the motorway services and the load was being broken down into smaller car size loads to avoid being caught. We can't patrol the motorway network and services, so we leave that to the jam butty brigade in their flash Ford Capris. Seems like they got their information wrong though. As they were staking out the northbound side of the services the mucky book truck was quickly unloaded and disappeared from the south bound services. Hence, we're on the lookout for carloads of mucky mags".

At this point in time PC Gordon wandered over to the passenger side of the Hillman Avenger indicating an instruction for the passenger to wind the window down.

"Well, well, well. If it isn't Reggie Birtles. What you up to and where are you heading? As if I didn't know!" said PC Gordon.

However, before Reg had time to speak Eunice interrupted the flow of the conversation, "We're off back to mine PC Gordon and feel free to make a note of that fact in your little black book if you so wish. After all you only deal in the currency of facts. And the facts are that Reggie is heading for a night of rest and recuperation following the strenuous events of the last few weeks. Not that our private lives are anything to do with the tongue twisting hoards of the local gossiping community."

It was at this moment that the chat was interrupted by a voice on the two-way radio clipped onto PC Gordon's tunic, "Come in Ford Anglia Panda One. Come in." PC Gordon reached for his walkie talkie button, "Ford Anglia Panda One receiving loud and clear..."

The voice on the end of the radio continued, "Ford Zephyr One here. With regard to Operation Razzle, we have a suspect car on the move down near to the motorway at junction four. Vehicle is a grey Volkswagen Beetle registration number E for echo F for Freddie E for echo numbers 1 5 5 D for Delta. Seeking senior advice from PC Gordon. Do we approach or keep our distance. Please advise?"

PC Gordon was in his pompous element. Keen to demonstrate his authority as head of *Operation Razzle*, any potential misdemeanours involving Reg and Eunice were quickly forgotten as he made his way back to his panda car, instructing PC Huggins to join him.

"Looks like we're moving in for the kill on Operation Razzle. I'm sure there's one shifty character we both know who'll be reaching for the panic button should it be a success. Without going into too much detail I think we both know who that is!"

Eunice was getting a little tired of PC Gordon and his sideshow and questioned his intentions. "PC Gordon, are we free to go home as you clearly have more important things on your schedule for the evening. Plus Reg needs to get home. Don't forget it's only a few weeks ago that he had a heart attack."

"That's fine," said PC Gordon as he climbed into the passenger's side of the Ford Anglia, "Don't forget to bring your documentation down to the station within five days."

With this final instruction the panda car moved off heading for the rendezvous with the Ford Zephyr.

Eunice got back into her car and started the engine. The journey was a relatively short one across town and despite *Operation Razzle* being in full swing there was no visible evidence or flashing blue lights in sight.

"You're very quiet Reggie?" said Eunice, "You're not getting nervous over the contents of my shopping bag from Marks and Sparks are you?"

"No, not at all," said Reg, "It's something I heard from fifteen minutes ago. Do you remember the model and registration of car that PC Bob Gordon was discussing on the radio?"

"No not especially," replied Eunice, "Why is it someone you know?"

"Well, if I heard it right and the registration is as I think then that car belongs to Harry Flatley the groundsman," said Reg.

"Well Reg," replied Eunice. "If Harry Flatley chooses to be part of a porno mag crime syndicate, then there's not a lot you can do about it. Now come on stop worrying about that dammed club."

The Avenger swung into the drive at Eunice's house. A smart sixties-built detached on Mayfair Drive in the corner of the cul-de-sac. As Eunice stopped the car on the drive in front of the large double garage, she activated the electric remote control on the roller shutter. As the shutter rose Reg held his breath and his thoughts. As soon as the shutter stopped the automatic interior garage light came on.

To Reg's delight there was no sign whatsoever of Roger Braithwaites brand new Morris Marina.

With the car parked safely in the garage the next few minutes were going to be very crucial. To make the wrong move or say the wrong thing could have disastrous results. Reg was prepared and composed himself as he stood in the kitchen.

"Now Reggie," said Eunice, "Are you going to prepare those drinks we talked about or are you just going to stand there like a dummy in Burton's window?"

Reg decided to take a chance and walked towards Eunice, "Let's see how wooden this dummy is shall we?" With that he wrapped his arms around Eunice and began kissing her. This gesture was met with encouragement rather than resistance as they clearly began to enjoy the moment.

Reg resisted the temptation and instinct to begin the normal male on female 'wandering hands' routine and kept his hands from exploring into what at this stage of the relationship would be considered no-go zones. He decided Eunice's bottom was as far as he would go as he caressed her firm cheeks.

"Now Reggie. I'm going to make my way upstairs and slip into something a little bit comfier and cosy. I'll give you a shout when I'm ready and you can bring the drinks up," Eunice purred teasingly.

Reg decided that as soon as he'd poured the drinks he'd wait at the bottom of the stairs. Years of working next to heavy industrial machinery at the Royal Ordnance Factory had taken its effect on Reg's hearing. The last thing he wanted was to miss the call of invitation from his new love bird.

He didn't have to wait very long, "Reggie. Oh Reggie…are you bringing the drinks up?"

Reg replied, "Are you decent Eunice?"

"I used to be a decent lady but I'm completely indecent for you Reggie. Now are we going to get those drinks or not? By the way, turn off all the downstairs lights before you come up. You won't be going anywhere else but my room for the next few hours."

Reg quickly scuttled around downstairs switching all the downstairs lights off before making his way upstairs. He entered the bedroom where Eunice was sat on the end of the bed in a basque, stockings and suspenders.

He needed no second invitation and immediately lay next to Eunice and they embraced in a passionate kiss writhing on top of the silk bed sheets as Eunice stripped Reg down to his recently purchased black silk thong.

Suddenly Reg pulled away and stopped.

"What's the matter Reggie. You feeling OK?"

Reg didn't reply right away and an uncomfortable silence held for what seemed like a lifetime, before drawing breath. He *had* to ask the question.

"Eunice. I think you have known for quite some time now how I feel about you. And I don't want to sound like I'm being presumptuous, but I think your feelings are reciprocated. We wouldn't be in this bedroom if that wasn't the case, would we?".

Reg smiled, looked at Eunice and continued. "Eunice, I need to know what your position is. Where is Roger? Here I am in his bedroom cavorting with his wife when he could very well walk in at any time and, based on what he sees, go for divorce with you and I being fairly and squarely the guilty parties."

"Just let me know if what we have is serious or just a bit of slap and tickle while Roger's away on business".

Eunice sat up on the bed and took a sip of her drink. She began to speak softly, slowly but concise and to the point.

"Reggie my love. Roger has gone, never to come back. We never were man and wife. It's a long, difficult situation for me to explain but trust me, both you and I are doing nothing wrong. I will explain everything in detail tomorrow before we go looking for a new car at Billy Street's car lot. Please, please trust me on this matter. Like you, I've waited all summer for this moment to develop and enjoy. Now come over here, climb into bed and make me feel special...

Reg didn't need any more convincing. Yes, tomorrow was a bag full of unknowns. But it was a bag that Reg was prepared to face up to. He climbed across the bed and took Eunice in his arms...his moment had arrived.

20
The Final Chapter

As arranged, the Annual General Meeting for 1978 took place on the Tuesday following the title-winning weekend. It was a full turnout committee-wise except for one conspicuous absence. That person being Roger Braithwaite, husband of Eunice. There was a healthy number of social members as well which usually wasn't the case. A sure sign in Reg's opinion that the club was indeed on the up in all aspects.

Reg looked around the room and his memory flashed back to the meeting last winter when, according to his view, the committee was littered with doubters to his vision, philosophy, and the direction of travel he wanted to take the club in. How wrong they were on all fronts…in his opinion anyway.

The team were champions, the bar takings were up, a deal had already been done with both Harold and Trevor Haltz for next season and the junior section was growing, thereby creating local talent. The function room was busy with very few available nights free for bookings in the next six months. Also, in a throwback to years gone by there were a number of members actually putting their names forward to challenge any incumbent members who were due for re-election.

Reg was indeed happy with his lot. Indeed, events and revelations in the last couple of days had made his world a much happier place to be. Especially a two-hour heart to heart in Eunice's kitchen about their future together which was the icing on his cake. This heart to heart was so important that it had made the Annual General Meeting agenda under the *any other business heading*. Furthermore, he was also unconcerned about a challenge for power from Alf Tyson and a couple of his 'friends' as Reg was in his second year of a three year residency as Chairman and as such was immovable.

However, there was business to attend to in the shape of today's meeting. Reg sat at the top of the table. Part of the power triumvirate which had been in place for many years. Indeed, Reg was well aware that despite the club's healthy position there were still committee and social members who thought Reg and his cronies had held power in a vice like grip for far too long. Some of whom were sat around the table at that very meeting.

The God Squad whose unofficial membership featured The Reverend Adrian Gawsworth and Treasurer Verity Tinkle had recently been augmented by additional convert Edna Pilling. As Reg was keen to point out, Edna's switch to the church was possibly a conversion to Christianity born out of necessity to avoid a custodial sentence for prolific shoplifting from Kwik Save. Edna asking for 33 other known offences to be taken into consideration when being sentenced.

Reg stood up and opened the meeting, "On behalf of all the club members I'd like to thank you all not just for your attendance this evening but to thank those of you who have helped and contributed throughout the last twelve months. This comes not just from members but from me personally. I am well aware this has been successful year, but the club is only as good as its members. You have all been outstanding. Thank you."

Reg ruffled his notes as the members gave a polite round of applause. He stood up and acknowledged the applause. "Members of the club, welcome to the 96th Annual General Meeting of our beloved club. In line with the rules and traditions of the club, the AGM is going to be treated as an open type committee meeting. I have an agenda which everyone is welcome to question or comment on, but please wait till I have finished and then raise your hand and you will have your chance to speak. Please refrain from being rude, impersonal and the use of foul language is not permitted. Anybody not following these rules will be asked to leave the room. Finally at the end of the meeting there will be a free pastie and peas supper kindly supplied by Butterfields Bakery."

Another polite but not excitable round of applause followed as Reg began the agenda for the meeting.

"First item on the agenda is cricket. The first team as we are all aware recently crowned league champions. Good news all round on this front members as both the professional and his brother have signed already for next year. Also, our newly crowned King of Spin Jimmy Bangla has refused an offer from one of our competitors and agreed to stay. The second team had a good season finishing third and reaching the semi-final of the Trimble Trophy. Some of the younger 13 and 14-year-olds have made the huge step up from junior cricket to second team very comfortably. The junior section continues to thrive under the stewardship of John Havington and Abigail Worthing who have re-opened links with all the local schools which had sadly been left by his predecessor. Yes, all in all a great last season and a healthy future. Any questions before on cricket before we move on?"

However, Reg's flow was stopped as Ronnie Blower lifted his arm as per protocol outlined by Reg.

"Yes Ronnie. What would you like to say?" said Reg.

"What I want to know," he began, "Is how much is the pro's brother getting money wise. We know he had offers from not only other clubs but from other leagues. Let's be honest with ourselves, between these four club walls he's not coming back because he likes the teas. What's he getting? I don't see why we should allocate the club's money on some randy Australian when we need a new telly in the vault with a remote control that's compatible and doesn't play havoc with my hearing aid."

Ronnie's indifference towards the Australian was clearly influenced by the night of the lost keys when both of his daughters were involved with the pro and his brother. The lasting memory in Ronnie's mind of that night being Trevor Haltz stood in his front room dressed in just a pair of purple Y Fronts.

Reg replied very quickly: "Ronnie, You ask a valid question and I have an answer for you. Trevor Haltz is coming back because of several reasons. First of all he loves playing at the club. Secondly, yes, he is receiving money but before anybody starts ranting and raving its not coming out of the club's coffers. Local businessman Alf Tyson is moving into the pest control business and has offered Trevor a summer job for next year. A lot of members won't know this, but Trevor is working towards a degree in Insect and Reptile Study which is available as a short study course at Manchester University. This is a very rare course and Trevor rang me this morning to let me know he's been accepted for the 1979 enrolment. Also, Ronnie you'll know better than everyone that Trevor and your daughter Susie are quite an item these days - more than a cricket season romance I'd say? Finally, I agree we need a new telly in the vault. One that doesn't cause you so much pain from the remote control. I will be proposing a new telly installation later in the meeting. Does that answer suffice Ronnie?"

"Reg," replied Ronnie, "I have to give it to you. You're the master of the politician's answer. You really should be in Parliament. As long as there's a new telly in soon then I'm happy."

"Any more for any more whilst we're on cricket?" as Reg looked to close the topic of cricket. "Before we do close on cricket, I'd like to offer congratulations and a thank you to our captain Iain Redwood, A man who as seen the club through thick and thin and could have departed many times. His loyalty isn't something we see very often these days where players will move clubs for a free tea - if you know what I mean. Thanks Iain as well for agreeing to captain the team for next year. Now, next topic on the agenda is finance. I'd like to invite our honourable and much respected treasurer Verity Tinkle to give us a breakdown of the club's financial position."

Although Reg was no fan of the recently widowed Verity, he actually thought she was a very good treasurer who did a good job even when it came to reining in some of Reg's excesses. Nevertheless, Reg still viewed her as on the 'other side' of the committee. One of the Reverend Adrian Gawsworth's disciples.

"Ladies and gentlemen," she began, "You will see on the tables in front of you a balance sheet replicating the club's financial position as we conduct the AGM for 1978.

I understand that to the untrained financial eye that this may be a little difficult to follow. With that in mind I have compiled a brief description of the position in layman's terms. Is everybody happy with that? Do I have a proposer and seconder as per AGM protocol?"

Verity looked across the room and as expected the Reverend Adrian Gawsworth raised his hand followed by Edna Pilling.

"Thank you, Adrian and Edna," said Reg. "There being no objections from the floor then please continue Verity".

"Thank you, Reg. The balance sheet tells us the following. The club at the moment has £12432 in the bank. We have invoices to pay that total £3275 which include the brewery bill for next month, the professional's final payment, the club's annual grounds and buildings insurance and the return air fares to Australia for the pro and his brother. On the plus side we also have a payment due from the insurance company for losses incurred due to the break in. This represents another £2000 approximately. However, we have yet to agree a final settlement. Notwithstanding it's clear even to the untrained eye that the club is in a healthy position financially."

"Thank you, Verity, for that easy-to-follow summary of the accounts. Has anybody got any questions regarding finance?"

In the corner of the room sat Jock Tuck and several of his pals from the battery plant. Jock raised his arm to pose a question.

"Yes Jock," said Reg, "The floor is yours. What would you like to ask Verity?"

"I thought that Terry Fiddler from Battersby's Travel was going to fund the cost of the air fares for the pro and his brother. That's what was agreed in the spring. What's changed there then? Don't forget Terry Fiddler has a bit of a reputation for promising and not delivering. Remember when me and the lads got wrongfully arrested in Magaluf for allegedly streaking down the main street. Took him three weeks to post the bail money after a whole heap of undelivered promises. I wouldn't book a day trip to Morecambe with him. So how come he's not standing the bill?"

"With Verity's consent," said Reg, "I'll answer Jock's question."

Verity gave Reg a nod and he stood up and once again took the floor. "Battersby's Travel are having financial difficulties at the moment. Apparently, they are being sued by a party of holidaymakers who booked a fortnight all-inclusive at the Hotel Splendido in Torremolinos. Everyone on the trip developed a dreadful dose of the runs. Until compensation has been sorted out Battersby's are, in simple terms, struggling for cash. Terry Fiddler assures me that should we fund the return flights then we will be re-compensated as soon as the funds are released."

Jock was unimpressed but understood there was little he could do. He had a more pressing matter on the meeting agenda to attend to.

Reg once again took control of the meeting.

"Moving on we come to a topic that covers many areas and aspects of the club and Its members. That being 'Any other business'. I'd like to start with our present position with the brewery. As you know we have been with Twigleys Brewery for at least five years now and to be fair they have been very accommodating when it comes to prices and products. The cellar service they provide has been fine and as far as I'm concerned, I'm happy to continue the contract which is now up for renewal. Of course during renewal talks with Eddie Lumpitt, the brewery rep, the committee will be looking for a better deal as we have gone way beyond our projected sales for the period August 1977 to August 1978. With the members consent do we carry on with Twigleys or should we talk to others? I know that Calders Brewery are very interested in becoming our brewery should we choose to part company with Twigleys. What do the members think?"

Once again Jock Tuck stood up and raised his hand "Yes Jock," said Reg, "What do you think?"

Jock stood upright and spoke clearly and despite his strong native Glasgow dialect was easy to understand. Combining his speech delivery with bodily gesticulations it was clear that Jock was not unfamiliar with public speaking. His oratorical techniques being finely honed speaking on the stump on picket lines from the Glasgow shipyards to the local battery plant.

Launching himself into what his workmates and close friends called 'Arthur Scargill mode' Jock began.

"You see Reg and members of the club, it's like this. Stand still and be ruled by the fear of change will bring complacency. I say if Eddie Lumpitt wants to keep his business here then we nail him to the floor. The existing deal has been part and parcel of Eddie Lumpitt being awarded Twigleys North-Western rep of the year. That my fellow members is in no small part due to the amount of ale we sold this summer. I say there's nothing to lose in speaking to Calders. Looking at their product range its got much more of a wider appeal. Two different lagers and Kiltmans best bitter. Anything has to be better than that Shepherds Staff lager that Twigleys have. That Lion Bitter tastes like Hamster piss if you ask me."

Dicky Hampton, who until then had sat quietly, offered an opinion, "I think Jock's right. Not that I drink or know what Hamster piss takes like of course." This remark brought a sound of restrained laughter. "No, I think Twigleys have had the better part of the existing deal for quite some time now. Maybe its time we reformed the bar committee again. We could ask Jock to chair that committee. Eddie Lumpitt will certainly know he won't be in for an easy ride with Jock at the helm. What's that the management say about you Jock down at the battery plant? 'What's the difference between Jock and a terrorist? You can negotiate with a terrorist'. What do you think Jock?"

"Let me think it over Dicky," replied Jock, "I've got a lot on at the factory at the moment. We're due a new round of pay talks starting next month for the 1979 pay rise. But I'll certainly give it some thought."

"OK then," said Reg, "The feeling I'm getting from the floor is that we need to bring both breweries to the negotiating table and see what they can come up with. Anybody else got anything to say regarding the brewery?"

Nobody replied. Reg saw and took the opportunity to move the meeting on to the next topic on the agenda.

"Moving on but still under the topic of Any Other Business we've been approached by the Bolton Little Theatre with an enquiry regarding putting on the nativity play for this Christmas. I know it's a long way off but following the unfortunate fire recently they are looking at procuring a venue to promote this year's production. They are willing to pay room rental fees up front and prepared to give us 33% of all takings. Personally, I think it's a good deal and will bring people in the club for the festive season. What do the members think?"

The Reverend Adrian Gawsworth was quick to raise his hand. "Yes Reverend," said Reg, "I'm sure you've something of value to add on what could be your Mastermind specialist subject!"

The Reverend however was quick to respond to Reg's sarcasm, "The Lord only knows what your specialist subject is Mr Birtles. One thing is for sure though, the Lord's forgiveness will be severely tested and stretched when you reach the pearly gates."

"I'm sure Jesus will look at my body of work and maybe squeeze me through them Reverend," said Reg "Anyway what is it you have to say?"

The Reverend stood up and looked across the room and began to speak. "I'm sure it's still in the minds of many of the more Christian-minded members of the club of the debacle when the independent 'Alternative Theatre Productions' hired the stage and room out for their 'alternative' Nativity Production a couple of years back. This was blasphemy at its worst and has no place in our club. The new Bishop of Bolton Father O'Farty was my personal guest of honour. What we expected to see and what we actually saw was nothing like the story of Baby Jesus. Totally out of step with the nativity story we all know and love. Why, some of the younger children could have been mentally scarred for life..."

Reg chuckled and added his own comments, "Yes, for those who weren't here or haven't heard, it was quite funny really. The three Kings were actually three Queens mincing around the stage all gay like. Baby Jesus' dad wasn't sure if he was

Joseph or Josephine and Mary was looser than a bag of bolts in and out of the Shepherd's tents like I don't know what!"

"Added to that on the first night they borrowed a real-life donkey from Jubb's farm for authenticity. Trouble was once the donkey got a whiff of the pastie and peas it was out of control and bolted to the kitchen."

"I spoke to the producer/writer, and he reckoned that the 'Alternative Theatre Nativity' was a better reflection of events than the bible version. It certainly was different. Only lasted one night instead of the week." concluded Reg.

"Are you sure this is a bona fide nativity production?" said The Reverend, "I'll invite the good Father again but don't want him to go through the trauma he went through last year. He had a month off pulpit and confessional duties. Some say he's not the same man."

"I'm sure the Bolton Little Theatre's production will stick solely to the story and the stage won't be inhabited by an assortment of farmyard animals," said Reg, "Why we can pop in and take a sneak preview and put everybody's mind at rest." However, the Reverend still looked worried as he sat back down in his chair.

"Now ladies and gentlemen we have a special guest," said Reg, "Taking some time out from liberating our streets from what seems like an onslaught of petty and major crime would you please give a warm and genuine welcome for our local Bobby PC Bob Gordon. PC Gordon has come to give a short speech on some easy steps you can take to help you stop becoming a victim of crime. Ladies and gentlemen, PC Bob Gordon."

Following the welcome came a light round of applause as PC Gordon assumed his position stood at the front of the stage. Dressed in full uniform, PC Gordon hardly looked like a fully fit crime busting machine. His pot belly only just being kept in check with the assistance of a belt on the last hole link and a severely stressed pair of police issue braces. With huge feet filling a pair of size 14 boots and his armpits now issuing some considerable sweat, PC Gordon began to speak.

"Ladies and gentlemen, I stand in front of you today in what seems to be a virtual crimewave. Recent crimes have seen the repeated use of Austin Cambridge vehicles for what have been christened ramraids on local electrical retailers. Other crimes include the theft of the new must-have electrical device, the video recorder, from our own front rooms. This type of theft is still rife despite the simple way of avoiding theft. This by placing a dark coloured tea towel in front of the digital clock."

"Plus, the fight to keep the streets clean and free from a plethora of pornography is vital to establish a decent society. We as crime-busting officers of the law need your help though. The police force, just like any other public service, is suffering from cuts in funding and needs the public's help. However, its not all bad news. Thanks to our high-tech evidence-gathering and surveillance techniques we have managed to arrest, charge and convict well-known criminal John Tate. I personally carried out the arrest on the Co-op building roof where he was moving very suspiciously with a cloth sack full of lead. When I accosted him, he said he was looking for his lad's rugby ball. I told him if his son could kick the ball so high it lands on the Co-op roof he should be having trials with Wigan. He then changed his story to one about pricing a roofing job up for the Co-op. I wasn't having none of it and last week he got a six-month sentence."

Turning to Reg, PC Bob Gordon thanked him for the platform and returned to his seat.

"Right, everyone" said Reg "If nobody's got anything else to add, then barring one topic the meeting is over. Thank you for your interest, attention, and contributions. However, I have an announcement to make which I'm sure will be of interest."

This announcement delayed the emptying of the function room. "What's the big deal Reg?" asked Jock Tuck, "Not got back with the ex-misses, have you? Or is the daughter up the duff? No don't tell me you've gone and bought a new Ford Capri to pull the birds? Come on Reg, spill the beans..."

Reg looked deadly serious and began speaking: "Members of the club. Over twelve months ago our club welcomed two new members who immediately embraced the ethos and values of our club despite not coming from the area. These two members as you know are Roger and Eunice Braithwaite. Within a month these two members joined the committee and began making more-than-useful contributions. Especially Eunice. As time went by Roger became more distant and we all assumed it was through work. As the months went by it's no secret that, in particular after my heart attack, I became quite attached to Eunice. I didn't realise that those feelings were being reciprocated until recently."

Reg wasn't expecting an easy ride, and it was Jock Tuck who broke up Reg's narrative, "Get on with it Reg! Skip to the juicy bits man!"

Reg offered a smile to Jock and was surprised as Eunice broke away from the members area and joined him in front of the stage linking his arm as Reg once again began to speak. "Like everyone else I was curious as to Roger's whereabouts. I wondered if I was walking head-on into another divorce case. Having had the dirty done on me by Barry the Bin Man I didn't want to be the propagator of a divorce involving two dammed nice people. Well, I have to tell you fellow members I had nothing to worry about. Nothing at all. You see Roger and Eunice weren't even married! Better still, from my point of view, they weren't even a couple! Prepare to be shocked people. Listen hard and listen good. There's a lot to take in."

"Eunice moved up here with Roger as part of a witness protection programme. Roger is in fact a policeman from Special Branch who was delegated the task of protecting Eunice who gave vital evidence in a major crime trial down in London. After the trial Eunice was deemed to be at risk in the aftermath of the judgement which of course she still cannot talk about."

"However, after nine months she was offered a return home to Surrey and lifetime protection from Special Branch or a chance to make a new life up in Lancashire. I'd like to think that I had some bearing on her decision to stay up here. And here's the best news of all. After learning all this only 24 hours ago myself I took the plunge, asked and Eunice has consented to become my wife…the new Mrs Birtles!"

The whole room broke into spontaneous clapping and whooping. Kisses and handshakes were the order of the day as all Reg and Eunice's friends offered thanks. Dicky Hampton and Harry Flatly were first up followed by John Burrell. Brains, seizing the moment, cracked opened a bottle of champagne and PC Gordon stepped forward, doffed his cap, and shook Reg's hand.

Even Reg's usual opponents The Reverend Adrian Gawsworth, Verity Tinkle and Edna Pilling offered congratulations. "Well done Reg and sincere congratulations. I know you're not of a Christian or faith disposition, but may God bless you and Eunice for the future."

"Thank you Reverend," Reg replied, "It genuinely means a lot to me for those sincere good wishes to come from a member of the church. Who knows, we may require you to tie the knot for us!"

An hour and several drinks later, Reg called *Mortax* and booked a taxi home. For Reg it had indeed been a year that had spectacularly changed the landscape and the future of his whole life. A dream come true. Now he had Eunice to share the rest of his life.

But what would the future hold?

Also by Victor Publishing...

Printed in Dunstable, United Kingdom